"The sex scenes were gorgeous; hot, magical whirlwinds of intensity that were exactly right for the characters and the story, and were also deeply romantic. I loved these aspects of the story, and would name the sex in this book some of the best sex scenes I've read in a romance involving a trans main character."

—Xan West (Author of *Show Yourself to Me*)

"...a lovely-written paranormal romance!"

—Anna Zabo (Author of *Syncopation*)

"It's a dark little fantasy that touches on all the tropes I love about witches and paranormal romance with enough new stuff to keep it fascinating."

—E.M Hamill (Author of *Nectar and Ambrosia*)

"Darkling is queer witchy magic guaranteed to make your toes curl."

—Michelle Osgood (Author of *The Better to Kiss You With*)

THE PORT LEWIS

WITCHES

Volume One

Brooklyn Ray

A NineStar Press Publication

Published by NineStar Press
P.O. Box 91792,
Albuquerque, New Mexico, 87199 USA.
www.ninestarpress.com

The Port Lewis Witches, Volume One

Printed in the USA
First Edition
November, 2018

Print ISBN: 978-1-949909-21-0

Warning: This book contains sexually explicit content, which may only be suitable for mature readers, scenes of bloodletting and death (and resurrection) of an MC.

Table of Contents

Reborn   1
Darkling   35
Undertow   167
Honey   283

REBORN

NIGHT SKIES BLEED. She'd known that all her life, from the time she was a girl, climbing onto the roof to look at the stars, to now, walking on cold misty streets in a town she'd never considered coming back to. Thalia's chin tipped up, dark skin highlighted by streetlamps and the glow of cracked movie theater signs. She studied the November sky, tracing the blurred pinpricks where stars peeked through fog and deep navy collided seamlessly with pitch-black. Everything dripped—moonlight into the nether, starlight into the horizon.

Look, Thalia, watch time cut it open. The sun would sink and Thalia would wait. *The night bleeds and we're reborn.* Once the sun was behind the distant mountain range, Thalia and her family would set off into the woods. The stars and moon would bleed white and gold, and the witches of Port Lewis would mirror the act above by spilling blood below.

Thalia's hands had been clean for three years. She didn't intend to dirty them again.

A buzz vibrated the front pocket of her black jacket. She stopped to lean against the brick wall of a familiar pizza parlor and pulled out her phone. "Christ," she bit, wincing when the bright screen flashed in her eyes. Her gaze fell over one message after the next, the first from her brother, the second from her aunt, and the third from her father.

Every message said the same thing in varying tones.

Your mother is dead, Thalia. You're the next matriarch. Come home.

Thalia had been reading the same texts for a week now. The Darbonne Witches were without a leader, and a clan without a leader would fall apart within a year. But Thalia Darbonne wasn't any witch—she was a deserter, a stain on the reputable name her family had carried for generations.

Nights like these, when the sky bled and the fog was thick, Thalia remembered magic.

She felt it echo in her veins, a whisper of heat, a weighty soreness that felt brittle under her skin.

Nights like these reminded her that magic was a terrifying, savage thing.

Her thumbs hovered over the screen. She typed a message to her brother, backspaced it, tried again, line after line after line, and backspaced everything she'd written for the second time.

She settled on two words. *I'm here.*

Thalia hit send. As soon as she saw Luther had read the text, she slid her phone back into her jacket pocket and looked back up at the sky. Magic stirred within her, jostled awake by her hometown, her mother's untimely death, and by something else. A familiarity. A distinct shift in the air, odd and transparent, like a switch had been flipped and the lights dimmed, water ran the wrong way, things were unmade.

Somehow, the night recognized the collision of energies before she did. The natural magic in the air shuddered and retreated, urging her to do the same.

But Thalia knew this darkness. She'd had it etched into her skin. She'd worn it under her clothes. She'd let it slither down her throat.

"I felt you a mile away." Her voice hadn't changed any. It carried the same rasp, the same quiet wisp. "What's a Darbonne runaway like you doing in a soggy town like this?"

Thalia remembered the shape of Jordan's lips, too full on the bottom, too bowed on the top. She remembered her small chin, the cliff of her cheekbones, the prominent angles of her face. They hadn't softened over time, but her brows were thinner now, higher, and there was a ring through her left nostril. Her hair was still shoulder-length and ashy, the blonde people paid to get rid of at a salon, with loose waves created by coastal air.

"My mom died," Thalia said because small talk was for people who didn't kill to appease their lineage, or steal magic to raise the dead. "They want me back."

"They could've asked me," Jordan purred. The uncomfortable truth of her practice made Thalia's guts twist. "All I need is a body and an invocation."

Thalia's head listed to the side; her arms crossed over her chest. The knot low in her abdomen worked in tandem with the heat rising into her cheeks. Nervousness battled with disregard. Desire fractured the eaves in her mind where Jordan's low voice dusted old memories.

"Why'd you come find me?" Thalia shifted. The click of her ankle boots ricocheted off the alley walls behind the pizza parlor. She felt Jordan's sharp gaze on her face, the rake of it down her neck, past the silver chain between her collarbones, to her torso. "You know what happened, Jordan. This town's too small to get something like a Darbonne death past you."

"Death never gets past me." Jordan's dark, slate eyes caught Thalia's flighty gaze. "You know that."

Each word stretched open, filled with purpose and warmth. No matter how many years had gone by, Thalia couldn't shake the soft brush of Jordan's magic against her own. Unnatural meeting natural, a drop of blood in a clear lake, a clawed hand wrapped around the stem of a flower.

Thalia found herself looking back at Jordan, searching through days and weeks, months and years. *Why didn't you come looking for me sooner?*

The quiet between them broke around car tires on wet asphalt, and the beat of wings cutting through the air.

Jordan straightened her back as two black feet landed on her shoulder. She hummed, regarding the crow with a tilt of her head before her gaze slid back to Thalia. "Yeah, you remember who this is," Jordan cooed. "Don't you?"

For the first time since Thalia had crossed the county line, she smiled. "Hello, River."

River cawed at her. The feathers on his throat ruffled as he tucked himself against Jordan's ear. Her shoulder sagged under his weight, the jut of her clavicle poking through her white T-shirt.

"Have you gone to the woods yet? I'm sure your familiar would love to see you." Jordan arched a fair brow. Her mouth twisted into a peculiar, knowing smile.

"What makes you think King hasn't come to see me?" Thalia hadn't meant to snap, but her teeth clacked anyway. She scrubbed her palm over her head, her buzz cut a reassuring scratch against her hand.

"Has he?"

Thalia huffed. "Yes, actually. I see him every few months."

Jordan's smile deepened. She dipped her head, impressed. A lingering smile later, and the pass of their gazes prompted Jordan's lips apart. She said, "Meet me in the woods tomorrow."

"No," Thalia said quickly. She averted her gaze to her hands, clasped together in front of her waist. She fiddled with a chunky moonstone ring. "No," she repeated, softer this time, more to herself than to Jordan.

Jordan eyed her carefully. Thalia felt her gaze like spider's feet, darting here and there, settling somewhere Thalia would mentally swat at only to feel them elsewhere a moment later. Old wounds stung when they began to peel open. Memories seemed surreal when they resurfaced in situations like this one—on nights when the sky bled, in places where witches and necromancers stalked the streets.

River cawed again. Jordan inhaled a deep breath and sighed.

"Meet me in the woods," she said again.

Thalia looked at the ground until she couldn't possibly look any longer. When her gaze flicked forward, Jordan was walking backward, eyes lidded and smile lazy as if she'd seen this play out in a dream and knew the outcome.

Thalia watched Jordan's lips mouth the words silently once more.

Meet me in the woods.

PORT LEWIS WAS a rainy little town pressed against the cliffs on the West Coast, nestled in the tall, mossy Washington trees. Thalia hadn't realized she'd missed it until now, as she looked over the balcony in her family's old house. A cup of tea warmed her hands. The pitter-patter of morning showers danced across the roof.

The sliding glass door opened. Thalia tilted her head, acknowledging heavy footsteps. Luther and she had been born on the same day, two years apart. Luther was the eldest, but at twenty-two and twenty-four, there wasn't much wisdom he'd acquired that she hadn't. Witches far and wide called them constellation twins, siblings sharing space like stars shared patterns.

He appeared beside her, broad shouldered and square jawed, tall opposed to her petite. He glanced at the slender spoon sitting in the mug. The air vibrated, and the spoon turned in circles on its own. "Your honey will get stuck to the bottom if you don't stir it," Luther said.

A soft smile crossed Thalia's face. She wanted to cook up an explanation, find a way to make the last three years seem secondary, but she didn't know how to. It'd be a long time, and this unknown was her consequence.

"Did it happen naturally?" Thalia lifted the mug to her mouth and set it against her bottom lip. "Or was it retaliation?"

Luther draped his forearms over the banister. She watched his jaw flex, a shadow turning his dark skin darker in the hollow under his cheekbone. "Natural. It took us six months to get her to see the doctor. Once we dragged her there, they ran the tests, and—" He paused to shrug. "— nothing much we could do at stage four."

"Stubborn," Thalia hissed. She focused on the tree line behind their fence. A greenhouse loomed next to a dainty metal table, its bottom covered with long grass and gray-capped mushrooms. She remembered spending afternoons there, listening to her mother's voice, practicing spell after spell. *Like that, Thalia.* Her mother's long fingers curled under her chin. *Focus. Ask the trees for assistance, call to Isis.*

Despite being a Darbonne girl, Thalia never had been as receptive to their magic as Cher. It hid inside her, buried under the weight of her mother's success, and her grandmother's wisdom, and every matriarch who had come before her. Instead of reaching for light and balance,

Thalia's magic lunged for passing shadows and twisted power.

Darbonne's weren't black magicians. They were sacrificial—ancient in their rites and craft. But somehow, someway, Thalia had found herself wandering into the shadows, toward a den of alchemists who used outlawed magic to bend nature to their will. There, she'd found herself wrapped up in one of them, bleeding with one of them, loving one of them.

"She was," Luther said. His voice shook the memories away. "You must've gotten it from her."

"Must've," Thalia agreed.

Silence fell over them again, broken up by the rain and a whistling kettle on the stove inside. The kettle died down. Thalia caught the sound of her father hushing it.

"I can sense her on you," Luther said under his breath.

Thalia's eyelids curtained closed.

"She leaves a trail. Impossible not to," he chirped, waving a hand dismissively down Thalia's body. "Her energy latches on to people like us. It wants to syphon from us, take and take and take."

"I didn't mean to run into her." She adjusted the cuff of her long-sleeved shirt, fidgeted with the self-stirring spoon in her mug. "And I don't need you pulling on my collar like I'm a leashed dog. I know what she is, and what she does."

"Didn't stop you before." Luther eyed her down the slope of his wide nose. The two gold studs in each of his nostrils glinted in the whitewashed morning light. "Mom warned you—"

"Mom cut me off," Thalia interjected. Heat rose into her cheeks. She felt the crackle of magic spark in her wrists. "She gave me an ultimatum, and it wasn't fair—no." She flashed her palm when Luther opened his mouth to speak. "You don't get to chastise me. I left Jordan."

"You left everyone," Luther snorted.

Thalia's teeth gnashed. "I'm here now, aren't I?"

"Oh, good," Luther mocked, "Thalia came home for her mother's funeral. Everyone please, a round of applause."

She jabbed him in the chest with her index finger. Her eyes narrowed, mouth pinched in a tight line. "You know this isn't just about burying her."

He rolled his eyes.

"If I could give this shit to you, I would." Thalia scoffed. "I wish we could trade places, trust me. You're older; it should be you anyway."

"But it's not," Luther said gently.

Thalia snarled and turned to look at the greenhouse. She caught the shape of pale horns between the trees behind it, the twitch of a brown nose. "No, it's not."

"Celene's coming over for dinner. She wants to talk to you."

"Wonderful." Thalia loved her aunt, but she wasn't ready to deal with Celene. She could hear it already. *Stay away from the Wolfe clan, Thalia. They're dangerous. Their brand of magic is seductive; it'll pull you in. You won't know it has you until it's too late.*

"Dad will be there," Luther added.

"I know."

"And you'll be gone tonight, right?"

Thalia's gaze shifted sideways, darting curiously around his face.

He lifted his chin and arched a thick brow, head cocked to the side, expression loose and pliant. You're my sister, he said with his eyes, I know you. "I won't tell, but be careful."

Thalia didn't indulge him or his caution. She looked at the greenhouse and the old table, replaying images of her mother in flowing dresses and wide-brimmed hats, flowers tucked into her wiry curls. Three years ago, Thalia would've been fighting with Cher about the sigils carved into her skin, about the marks on her neck and the mingling of Wolfe and Darbonne magic.

It isn't safe, Cher would've said. *This magic comes at a price.*

Magic was like driving too fast or snorting a line of cocaine or walking across hot coals. It made people believe it wouldn't betray them. But cars crashed and hearts stopped beating and people got burned.

Thalia inhaled a deep, sharp breath. The ghost of Jordan's lips dusted her jaw from a faraway memory, her whispered voice loud in the stillness, *Do you feel that?*

Her phone buzzed in her pocket. A pang of guilt spiked through her, followed by warm, effervescent desire. She read the text once, twice, three times.

Jordan Wolfe: *Need a ride?*

Thalia didn't answer.

LUTHER: *CELENE IS a lot, but she's just trying to help.*

Thalia: *I must've missed the part where she helped.*

Luther: *What time will you be back?*

Thalia: *Don't know.*

Luther: *Are you coming back at least?*

Thalia: *Yes.*

Yes happened to be the truth, despite Thalia wanting to book a ticket on the first bus back to Los Angeles. She pulled her jacket tightly around her, boots thudding against the concrete as she walked through downtown.

Port Lewis was small but lively. People stood in front of the movie theater and shared greasy food at the pizza parlor, looked through boutiques, and sipped hot drinks from the coffee carts and cafes. Thalia weaved through them, arms crossed over her chest, taking in certain places and fitting them to memories.

The fire escape on the apartment building across from the pizza place was where Thalia met Jordan for the first time. Jordan's legs had been dangling off the side of the red platform, a cigarette pressed between her lips. She'd said, *Hey, white witch,* and despite knowing better, Thalia had stopped and said, *Hey, necromancer.*

It was an odd meeting, seeing as they'd known *of* each other, but didn't *know* each other. They'd run in opposing circles, kept the peace between spell-casters by only ever eyeing each other carefully over tables at restaurants, or across halls at school. Back then, they'd been two sixteen-year-old girls who wanted to know what they could do—to the world, and to each other.

That day, wonder turned into fascination.

All the days that followed knotted that fascination into something deeper and stranger and far more brutal than they'd ever imagined.

As if on cue, Thalia felt her. Jordan's long strides and musky, cinnamon perfume. Her achingly dark energy and warped, inside-out magic. "Hey, white witch," she said, falling into pace next to Thalia. Her lips were dusty rose against her olive skin, curving into a heartfelt smile.

Thalia looked at the fan of Jordan's lashes against her cheek, the curl of fresh wounds peeking above her collar where she'd drawn a new sigil. Thalia remembered carving those spells into Jordan's flesh, the taste of her blood, wet and warm on her lips, the glow of Jordan's dark eyes and the whispers from other planes, from ghosts and demons and deities. *Look at these two,* they said. *Their magic is deadly.*

"Hey, necromancer," Thalia dared. The words felt heavy in her mouth, but once she said them, elation bloomed where guilt used to be.

Jordan grinned. War itself would tremble in the wake of that smile.

"I'm guessing you've already had dinner," Jordan tested.

Thalia nodded. "This isn't a date."

"'Course it isn't. My car's around the corner next to the gelato place. I'll drive us out if you wanna go." Jordan looked straight ahead. Her long coat swung behind her, thumbs pushed through the belt loops of her ripped blue jeans.

"Yeah, let's go," Thalia said. She swallowed hard. Her mother's warnings and Luther's *Be careful* played again and again in the back of her mind. Celene's string of duties and rules, her grating voice from hours ago, so much like Cher's. *Your mother is gone. You have a responsibility now, and it's not to some Wolfe woman. You have to take this seriously.*

But Jordan wasn't just some Wolfe woman.

Thalia tried to steel her nerves.

Three years was a long time to go without having what they'd had.

Jordan nudged Thalia with her elbow and shrugged toward the parking lot. They walked silently to the silver truck, the same one Jordan had been driving since she was sixteen. River perched on the side of the truck bed. He waved a foot at them as they approached, cawing softly and ruffling his wings.

"Meet us there," Jordan said. River took off into the night.

Thalia slid into the passenger's seat. A strand of crystal beads hung from the rearview mirror. A bundle of half-burnt sage was crammed in one of the cup holders next to an old Starbucks cup, and a few clusters of amethyst were strewn across the dashboard. She tried to keep her eyes on the road, but her gaze kept drifting to Jordan's long fingers tapping idly against the steering wheel. Her mouth parted around lyrics to a song playing on the radio, shirt half untucked and slouching over one shoulder.

"Why'd you leave?" Jordan said suddenly. She kept looking at the road, illuminated by two bright headlights. Soon, the town was behind them, and trees stretched in every direction.

Now that Jordan's jacket was gone, Thalia saw the intricate design of the sigil low on her neck. It extended over her shoulder, angry red cuts in varying shapes where a knife had sliced her open. Several runes decorated the piece. She recognized some—power, manifestation, clarity.

"You know why," Thalia said slowly.

Jordan huffed a laugh. "Because Cher said you had to choose?"

"Yes."

"And?"

Thalia chewed on her lip. "And it would've been you, so I left instead of choosing."

"Is martyrdom a Darbonne trait, or is it just you?" Jordan's tone edged on playful, but bitterness hung heavy over each word.

"It's not like you came looking for me, Jordan."

"Didn't know you wanted me to." The road grew bumpy and dark. Trees darted by close to the windows. "Answering my calls or texts might have helped. Or leaving a note. Fuck, giving King something to bring me to let me know where you were, I don't know. Something to tell me you hadn't just—" Her hands floundered on the steering wheel. "—left me here."

"I didn't come out here to do this with you," Thalia snapped.

Jordan shoved the truck in park. She glared across the center console and clicked her tongue. "What exactly did you come out here for then?" Her voice was even and heated, anger building between her teeth.

Something large knocked against Thalia's window. A deep, wet breath fogged the glass, and a wide, brown nose pressed against it.

Thalia jumped. Jordan's sour expression faded. It hadn't been long since Thalia had seen her familiar. They'd met in San Francisco and Portland from time to time, and she'd caught him pacing the tree line behind the greenhouse that morning.

But for some reason, this meeting seemed more exciting than the others. Maybe it was because these woods had given birth to King the same day, hour, minute that Thalia had been born. Maybe it was because this was the place where Thalia had practiced her magic on her own, where she'd sat with King in open meadows and doodled in her grimoire. Maybe it was as simple as being back in the place that defined so much of her youth. Here she was again in this old truck, looking out the window at King, with Jordan sitting beside her.

Something about it felt surreal, like time had fractured where memories overlapped with potential.

"You scared me!" Thalia slapped her palm over her chest. A wide grin pulled her lips upright. "Well, back up so I can get out," Thalia said through a laugh. King's antlers scraped the door as he stepped back, dark hooves sinking into soft grass, his oak hide a stark contrast to the pale, cream-colored horns jutting from behind his ears.

She slid out of the car and paid close attention to Jordan's footsteps around the front of the truck. King's wide brown eyes blinked down at her, his height a testament to how large elk truly were.

"You don't like LA much, do you?" Thalia teased. He blew a puff of air at her and leaned forward. His face pressed along her forehead and nose. She scratched under his chin and felt along the ridges of his white horns, the sharp points and curved edges. Moss draped over the hollows were bone twisted with bone, making King appear mystical and unreal. "No, I don't blame you. Too many people, huh?"

"That's where you've been?" Jordan's voice came from behind her. "Southern California?"

"You never did a locator spell?"

Thalia listened to Jordan sigh, heard the shift of her hips against the side of the truck.

"I didn't know if it was right or not," Jordan said softly.

"Yes, you did." Thalia threw the words over her shoulder. "You just didn't follow it."

Jordan's energy thickened, her concealed nervousness made itself known in shifting breezes and rustling leaves. Around them, the forest came alive. Moonlight lit a thin layer of fog. Branches craned over them, covered in copper leaves. Maroon leaves shaded the canopy, twined with green vines and gold-stemmed flowers. Moss climbed tree trunks. Ferns hid mice and salamanders who watched them from their burrows.

The night sky darkened from navy to dense black, bleeding red where Mars twinkled and white where the moon hung high.

"I was scared," Jordan admitted. She stepped next to Thalia. One hand came to rest on King's antlers. "I didn't know what would happen if I found you. I was nineteen. I thought you leaving meant we were done."

Thalia wanted to believe they'd been done, too.

River swooped down and landed on King's back. The elk huffed again and whipped around to look at the crow, almost gouging Jordan with his horns in the process.

"Easy!" Thalia scolded. King made a dismissive noise and ignored her, paying attention to River instead and then to the juicy grass at his feet. She swallowed and glanced at Jordan, catching vulnerability cross her face before her expression hardened. "Don't do that," Thalia said. "I'm not a stranger. You don't need to act like I'm out to get you."

"You come back after three years and ask me not to be guarded?" Jordan's nostrils flared. Her brows flicked, followed by a snarl that shouldn't have been pretty, but was. "What do you want, Thalia? What are we doing here?"

"You asked me to come out here with you." Thalia stepped over a cluster of mushrooms and headed farther into the woods. The trees whispered in a language she couldn't understand. She imagined they were spreading rumors. *They're back. The white witch is back. The bone bender is back.* "I'm here. You're here. The end."

Jordan's hand snatched her wrist. Thalia's head spun. She exhaled a pained breath, enduring the fast, cruel stitching of energy over energy. *There you are*, it said. Thalia's magic leapt out of her. The indistinguishable whispering grew frantic. Jordan's breathing turned labored and winded. Magic knew magic, and after so much time apart, their magic didn't hesitate to reacquaint themselves.

Power wracked Thalia's nervous system. Her blood rushed against itself, speeding in the wrong direction. Her fingertips went numb. Everything she'd been raised to avoid gathered in her elbows and kneecaps, seductive, dark, blistering magic. It purred at her, wrapped around her, soft like snake scales, hot like sun-warmed metal.

"You're stronger," Thalia whispered. She tugged her hand away, but the deed was done. She knew it. So did Jordan. Their unavoidable limits had been breached, and now all Thalia could do was stand there, wading between dazed and the clearest she'd ever been. Her pupils dilated. Adrenaline pushed her senses out of comfort and into primordial urgency.

"Surprise," Jordan rasped. Her hand hovered in the air, knobby fingers twitching as if they still clutched Thalia's wrist. "I didn't think that would happen. Sorry."

"It's just..." Thalia closed her eyes and waved her hand at the surrounding trees and toward the sky. "It's this place and what we did when we were young and..." She trailed off, unable to explain it in a way that didn't lead back to *them*.

"We're still young," Jordan said matter-of-factly. Her chestnut eyes flashed to Thalia.

"Our magic isn't," Thalia shot back.

"Is that why it's like this?"

Thalia's teeth sank into her bottom lip. They both knew why it was out of control. Magic like theirs—magic that'd once coexisted in closeness and intimacy—didn't fade. Somewhere under three years of silence and distance, Thalia and Jordan were still linked. But Jordan had been practicing, and Thalia hadn't. The imbalance between them showed in Thalia's trembling hands, and Jordan's steamed breath. Thalia's body tried to make room for it, to stretch open around years and years of buried invocations. Jordan's magic was wound tightly enough to snap.

The scars on Thalia's hips and ribcage stung. Everything that had fallen asleep, the raw, thick, unrelenting magic she'd run from woke up and writhed under her skin.

Jordan's wild, sharp gaze flicked restlessly over Thalia's face, darting from her lips, her full brows, to her round cheeks and rich eyes. Her jaw slackened. Thalia watched her top lip pull away from the bottom, glimpsed the tip of her tongue dart across her bottom lip.

The woods went silent.

Thalia's face flushed.

"Do you still..." Jordan trailed off. Her confidence splintered.

"Do you think I'd be out here if I didn't?" Thalia snapped. Her eagerness was embarrassing. The way the trees seemed to lean toward them, the way the mist had dissipated, and their familiars watched from a few feet away—it felt staged as if Port Lewis had been anticipating this moment for long enough to go quiet in its presence.

Jordan was graceful in ways people weren't meant to be graceful. Her hands landed firmly on Thalia's waist. She pushed Thalia backward, the tip of her nose bumping against Thalia's cheek in the process. Steam trickled over Jordan's lips. The black of her pupils fanned over the rest of her eyes, an unveiling of her Wolfe lineage. Her hand was uncomfortably hot on Thalia's jaw, thumb set hard against her chin.

This, Jordan pressing Thalia against a mossy tree in the middle of the woods, her black eyes fixed on Thalia's mouth, was a dangerous reminder of their wickedness.

The trees chattered again. The wind kicked up.

"This is not something to play with," Jordan seethed. A thousand voices spoke under hers, low and haunting, the voice of every life she'd taken and every life she'd brought back. "My heart won't pay the price for your martyrdom again, Thalia Darbonne."

Magic squirmed and thrashed in Thalia, pushing out from her fingertips when she gripped Jordan's ribs. Strands of blonde hair tickled Thalia's face. "I'm matriarch now," Thalia bit. "I decide who I get to have."

"I'm not something to be had." Jordan's hot breath gusted Thalia's mouth, wet with steam and tinged by the smell of blood.

Thalia had missed that smell—blood before it soured, the essence of life contained behind Jordan's teeth. She remembered the way it tasted years ago, like burnt coffee and pennies. "Are you done yet?" Thalia's voice split, manifesting into different versions of itself as if she'd whispered and screamed and howled at once. The gold flecked through her eyes sparked like cinders.

Jordan sucked in a deep breath. Her hold on Thalia's waist tightened, sending heat through her clothes, into the scars settled there. Thalia glanced at the fresh sigil on Jordan's shoulder, pronounced and glowing mahogany against her fawn skin. She reached up and pressed her fingertips against it, watching Jordan wince when she dug her nails in and broke it back open.

Blood coated Thalia's fingertips. She brought them to her mouth, but Jordan snatched her wrist.

"Blood magic is powerful," Jordan said. It was a warning every elder and every witch in Washington had given them, but it wasn't new. They'd spent years together, setting blades against thighs and chests and throats, followed by teeth and lips. Despite the constant warnings, Thalia and Jordan had never listened.

Thalia's gaze traced Jordan's lashes, the waterline on the inside of her eyelids clashing with opaque, inky black. She pulled until her bloodied fingertips pressed against her lips, opening her mouth to set them against her tongue.

Jordan made a wounded sound. A punched-out whimper, a gravely hum.

Magic poured between them. The woods were still, as if the trees held their breath, and the animals had stopped scurrying. Thalia's magic surged. Her head spun. Every invocation they'd done, every deity they'd contacted, every blood rite, ritual, and spell came back to her like a lightning strike. The sigils under her clothes burned. Her breath shook. She relished the taste of life and death.

She heard Jordan unsheathe the knife from her belt. Felt the cold edge of it press below her chin.

"That's the boline, right?" Thalia asked.

"Yes," Jordan said weakly. "Tell me to do it."

Thalia tipped her head back against the tree. Jordan's fingers tugged at her bottom lip, dragged over her chin and down her throat. She opened her eyes. Everything was brighter and sharper. Jordan's black eyes, her bloody neck, the white of the boline against Thalia's umber skin.

"Since when have you needed my permission?" Thalia asked. She licked smeared blood off her lip.

Jordan leaned forward. Her mouth hovered dangerously close to Thalia's. "You know why, matriarch."

Thalia grinned. Her power whipped and bucked. She craned up, pressing her throat against the blade. "Go on," she said through a sigh, "take it."

The tip of the crescent-shaped knife sank into the flesh below Thalia's jaw. A half-inch line pooled with blood. Jordan's fingers twitched in the air. The steam she exhaled dampened Thalia's skin, hot and winded. Thalia watched Jordan's index finger bend, her thumb jutting awkwardly from her hand, girlish and flexed. A string of beaded blood floated from the cut on Thalia's neck. Perfect red spheres spun in the air, wobbling when Jordan's concentration slipped.

The world slowed down.

The trees whispered *usurper, usurper, blood queen, bone bender.*

This part always made Thalia consider the concept of time. Her blood in the air, Jordan's open mouth, their power mingling.

The forest whispered *thief.*

"I'm no thief," Jordan said. A thousand haunted voices rippled under her own.

Necromancers took—it was their gift. They stole what they needed, ripped it from the earth, shredded and syphoned energy to redistribute it. A white witch giving her life force freely to a necromancer was sacrilegious. But Thalia ran her hands along Jordan's sides. Her hips canted, and she pressed her thigh snugly between Jordan's legs.

Magic was ferocious.

The moment Thalia's blood touched Jordan's lips, every break and fissure between them slid into place. Thalia felt Jordan's past confusion, her heartbreak like a brand on her chest. They swam in and out of each other's thoughts, memories, emotions. Tears sprang behind Thalia's lashes. A short, clipped sob built in her throat, but she choked it down.

King's hooves pounded the ground. River cawed and screeched.

As quickly as it came, it went. The lakes of black in Jordan's eyes pulled to the center, crawling backward like an inverted paint spill. Jordan's warm palms gripped Thalia's cheeks.

"You never should've left," Jordan snapped.

Thalia didn't bother talking. She grabbed Jordan's hand, fingertips playing along the ridge of her knuckles, and breached the short distance between them. They kissed clumsily at first. Their teeth clicked. The steam in Jordan's mouth was breath-stealing. But after the collision, Jordan tilted her head and Thalia relaxed. It softened into a rush of mouth on mouth, Thalia's hand in Jordan's hair, Jordan's hips pressed hard against Thalia's pelvis.

They'd changed and they hadn't.

Jordan tasted heady, like nutmeg and blackened sugar. She wasn't as quick to bite Thalia's lip or shove her hands up Thalia's shirt. Instead, she exhaled hotly between their lips, tongue soothing across Thalia's eye teeth. Her palms drifted from Thalia's cheeks to her thighs, where she wrapped them around and tugged until the air between their bodies was eaten up.

Three years ago, Thalia would've been fumbling with the button on Jordan's jeans. But tonight, she took her time. The magic pulsed and ached, riding their breathing, the brush of their hands and fit of their legs. It was kissing like drowning—all encompassing.

A rasped moan rumbled deep in Jordan's throat. Her hands gripped Thalia's thighs harder.

Somewhere lurking under the adrenaline and the car crash of energies, Thalia wondered how long this would last, if it would last at all.

River cawed at them again.

Jordan's lips slid away. Thalia chased them.

"Hush," Jordan said to the crow. Her gaze fixed on Thalia as she heaved in breath after breath. "Do you smell that?"

Thalia's nostrils flared. She relaxed against the tree, one hand settled on the nape of Jordan's neck, the other on her shoulder. "Rain."

Jordan's cheek brushed against Thalia's. She mouthed along her jaw, down her throat. "It's only a matter of time," she said.

The first raindrop hit Thalia's brow, cool and sudden. Raindrops the size of quarters came after. Water soaked through their clothes and battered the forest floor, chimed off the roof of the truck, and distorted the black, bleeding sky above.

King bounded off into the woods, and River flew after him.

"I can take you home," Jordan said.

Thalia turned until her nose bumped against Jordan's. Until she could see water gather in her brows and on her lashes, watch it drip steadily off the swell of her bottom lip.

The Grim Reaper would look at Jordan Wolfe and see his undoing.

Thalia looked at Jordan and saw something more. Something akin to future, but broader, wider, longer.

"You still live in the loft?" Thalia untangled herself from Jordan and stepped away, adjusting her jacket as she went.

"Yes," Jordan said. A sly smile twitched on her mouth. "At St. Maria's."

Thalia nodded. She looked at the sky as she walked. Rain splattered on her cheeks and forehead. The trees whispered. The closer she got to the truck, the louder their hushed voices became.

Heart render. Fire starter. Earth worshipper. Stained.

THALIA REMEMBERED THE smell of St. Maria's. Wax and ash, dusty ceiling beams, and polished wood. She remembered the rows of pews and Jordan's knees on the soft green pads as she knelt for prayer. The way her lips moved quickly over every memorized passage, how solid the priest's wrinkled, white hand looked on the back of Jordan's head during a blessing.

Tonight, the candles burned low in their candelabras. The cross on the wall was blackened by shadows. Faces of saints and martyrs looked down at them from the stained-glass windows, obscured by flickering flames and midnight silence.

A nun dipped her fingers in the marble bowl of holy water across the room from them. She caught Thalia's eye as she set her wet fingers against her forehead. Her delicate features hardened. *Blasphemy*, the nun said with her stare. But there was nothing the nuns could do about it.

Not after Jordan had brought the priest's sister back from the dead five years ago.

"C'mon," Jordan said. "You're getting water on the floor."

They crept up the creaky wooden staircase to a simple door. Jordan unlocked it and walked inside. Thalia followed, pausing to take off her jacket as she looked around the room. Baskets of plants hung from the exposed beams, their tendrils curling and swaying. Candles littered the desk against the wall, across from an unmade bed. Books stood in stacks beside the nightstand. Under a window on the far end, looking out into the night, a circle was drawn on the floor in chalk, riddled with runes.

Jordan's magic kept the plants alive, turning their vibrant green to muted blue and violet. Three candles sparked to life as the door closed.

Thalia draped her jacket over the open closet door and kicked off her shoes. Jordan's lingering gaze brought pinpricks to the top of Thalia's arms. She turned toward the door, giving Jordan her back to stare at, while she played with the hem of her shirt.

They weren't in the woods. The magic between them had settled, buzzing contentedly under their skin. The trees weren't there to whisper or encourage.

Jordan's bare feet padded on the floorboards. Her breath warmed the back of Thalia's neck, hands slid under the bottom of her shirt to rest on the sigils carved over her hipbones. She thumbed at a scarred rune. Her index finger dragged along the point of a star.

"I can't believe they still let you live here," Thalia said. She closed her eyes, enjoying the familiar press of Jordan's chest against her back, the barely-there dust of her hand across the top of her jeans.

"St. Maria is the patron saint of purity, remember?" Jordan's lips hovered over the throbbing cut on Thalia's neck.

"I remember," Thalia said. "That's exactly my point."

"I'm pure," Jordan purred. She tugged on Thalia's hips. "Ask the priest's sister."

Thalia rolled her eyes. "Is that who's been keeping you company up here?"

"Don't ask questions you don't want answers to." The tip of Jordan's nose touched her jaw. She opened her mouth over the cut on Thalia's neck, the wet press of her tongue slow and heavy. "She said something to me once, though. It made me think of you."

Thalia tilted her head, listening.

"She asked me if it was possible for a necromancer to die. I said, yes, of course. I died to become one."

Thalia's eyes cracked open.

Jordan continued. "She asked, 'and if someone loves a necromancer, what then?'"

Thalia had heard this before, whispered against her neck, low on her belly, between her legs.

"What then?" Jordan hissed against her ear.

"Then they never die," Thalia said softly.

Jordan's grin widened against Thalia's shoulder. Another candle sparked to life. The plants hummed gently from their baskets, and at the snap of Jordan's fingers, music thrummed from the small speaker attached to her phone on the nightstand.

"Mood music, really?" Thalia laughed over the words, but her stomach flipped and tightened.

Jordan's breath turned to steam again. She felt along the grooves and fissures of Thalia's scarred hips, up her soft stomach to the curve of her bottom two ribs. "I want to kill you, just so I can bring you back." She turned Thalia around, gusting hot, haunting words against her mouth. "I want to rip the life from your body and stitch it back together inside you."

Thalia grabbed Jordan's face and pulled until their lips met. Her heart thundered in her chest. She nudged Jordan with her foot, sending them stumbling backward toward the disheveled bed.

Jordan stopped to pull her shirt over her head. Thalia watched, catching the flex of Jordan's slim waist, the concave of her collarbones as her shoulders rolled back. Thalia swallowed hard and tugged her own shirt away, tossing it to the floor. They'd done this before—stripped, crawled into bed, cast spells with their bodies, but this waded above the others, hovering in the surreal place where past met present.

Thalia watched Jordan watching her. The quick flick of Jordan's dark eyes, steam steadily leaking over her bottom lip. They'd grown in the last three years. Jordan's powers floated around her like lightening bugs, flickering on and off as the night went on. Thalia's leaked from her as if she'd collided with Jordan and been cracked open.

Jordan's eyes darted over Thalia's scars. They were deep, ruddy pink against her dark skin.

The sigil of Saturn was carved on Thalia's sternum, filled with the intricacies of their past. Runes decorated her ribcage, magical sigils were etched over her hipbones—the Sigil of Sol, the invocation of Leviathan, the call of Anubis.

One other person had seen Thalia's body since she left Port Lewis three years ago—a man she'd met at a coffee shop. He took her to a show, they went to a little diner, and after, she was brave enough to take him home. When he ran his hands along her body, he said, *Who did this to you?* Thalia turned on the lights, got dressed, and made him a drink spiked with belladonna. A glamour spell later, the man left after pressing a sweet kiss against her cheek, and Thalia kept away from strangers, their touches and questions.

"I remember doing this to you." Jordan sat on the edge of the bed. Her palm smoothed up Thalia's sternum, over the sigil of Saturn.

Thalia looked at the petal-pink scars on Jordan's abdomen. The fresh sigil on her neck. Every mark from Thalia's athame, or Jordan's boline.

"What else do you remember?" Thalia touched the top of Jordan's hand.

Jordan's fingers curled under the bottom of Thalia's bra. "I'll show you."

Going to bed with a stranger was one thing. There was an ease to it, an unknown that made touches less, and time speed up. But this wasn't any bed, and Jordan Wolfe wasn't a stranger.

The plants hummed in their baskets. The candles flickered, sending shadows across their skin. Thalia hooked her teeth over Jordan's collarbone. She pawed at her jeans until they were gone, dipped her palm over the lace front of Jordan's panties, and listened to her breath hitch.

Magic twisted and turned through the space between their limbs. It hid in the place where Jordan's arm was looped over Thalia's shoulder. It sparked under rasped moans and quiet gasps, came to life in the arch of Jordan's back and the cant of Thalia's hips.

Jordan stopped to slide a silver cuff over her finger, clawed at the tip like a talon. Her thighs hugged Thalia's bare waist and she loomed above her, wavy hair a mess of gold and bronze. Her lips were slick and red, cheeks flushed and chest littered with half-moon bruises left behind from Thalia's teeth.

"You're different," Jordan whispered.

Thalia blinked. The back of her hand was pressed against her mouth, knuckles worn where she'd gnawed on them. She traced Jordan's body. Her ribcage and bony sternum, the soft swell of her hips and small breasts. Thalia sat up, running her hands up the keys of Jordan's spine to the wings of her shoulder blades and nape of her neck. Their torsos pressed, magic stirring excitedly at the slide of their skin.

"So are you," Thalia said. "Does it bother you?"

Jordan shook her head. She pressed the sharp end of her cuffed finger against Thalia's pulse. "I'll hunt you down," she said against Thalia's lips. "If you leave again, I'll find you. I'll wrap a string around your soul. I'll dig my hands under your rib cage and rip out your heart. Keep it in a jar, put it on the nightstand, and watch it beat while I'm touching you." She slithered her hand between Thalia's legs. "Do you understand?"

"I expect nothing less," Thalia said. The words made Thalia keen. Her body quivered, a testament to how much she'd missed this—Jordan's lips and hands, her ruthless devotion and murderous love. She leaned forward and captured Jordan's mouth with her own, teeth edging along Jordan's bottom lip.

Jordan's silver claw dug into her neck.

Thalia's head spun. She held on to Jordan, one hand latched on the nape of her neck, the other pressed snugly beneath her belly button, between her trembling thighs.

Jordan pulled the claw back, wet with Thalia's blood, and broke their kiss to drag it obscenely across her tongue.

"How could I ever be with someone else after loving you, Jordan Wolfe?" Thalia threaded her fingers through Jordan's hair. "You make death look like a cheap trick."

Jordan grinned. The inside of her lips shone red, red, red.

LUTHER DIDN'T ASK questions. Neither did her aunt or her father. They fought through silence. Her family sensed Wolfe magic slithering across Thalia, but there was nothing they could do to stop it. For three days, Thalia kept to herself, nodding to her brother when she felt his gaze on her, apologizing to her father with a sad tilt of her head when he refused to look at her.

Jordan: *You're sure you want us there?*

Thalia: *Yes, I'm sure.*

Jordan: *This will change everything.*

Thalia: *Good. We need change.*

After three long, lonely days, the ascension ceremony began.

The extended branches of the Darbonne Witches met them in the woods before the sun went down. Thalia's nervousness buzzed inside her. She still felt Jordan under her velvet gown, beneath the soft cotton of her bra, the invisible imprint of her hand under the thin white choker around her neck. The crimson dress was her mother's and her grandmother's. It draped low over her shoulders and was cut close to her tailbone, exposing scarred runes carved over each of her vertebrae.

She wondered if it was fair for her to wear it, when it hid bruises from Jordan's clever mouth.

Other clans appeared through the trees. The Thistle Clan, the ancient Lewellyns.

The sun sank below the horizon and the night turned over on itself. Stars appeared slowly, blinking to life above them, and dripped into one another. The moon glowed high in the sky, bleeding into black and navy, obscured by starlight, passing comets, and distant planets. Thalia felt her mother's spirit hovering somewhere beside her.

Celene, whose wild curls reminded Thalia so much of Cher, whose pointed nose and full cheeks were mirrored features of the Darbonne women, brought Thalia the red-handled consecration blade.

"Are you ready?" Celene asked.

Thalia glanced at the faces in the darkness. "We're waiting for one more group."

Celene's jaw tightened. "How do you think this will translate, Thalia?"

"It will translate without pause," Thalia growled. "Without interruptions or uninvited opinions."

"You're making a mistake."

Thalia's eyes glowed. Her voice deepened into a hundred versions of itself. "You're speaking to your matriarch. Remember that."

Celene dipped her head, but Thalia caught the sting of disregard in her eyes. The trees chattered and rustled. *Bone benders. Night witches. Necromancers. Darklings.* They seemed to stretch away, making room for barely audible footsteps.

The Wolfe Clan brought black smoke with them. It whipped around their feet, dusting the forest floor with their particular brand of upside-down magic. Black cloaks covered them, large hoods pulled over their heads, obscuring their faces. They stopped at the edge of the circle, a meadow surrounded by ferns and trees that curved together, open in the center where moonlight bathed the ground.

Jordan swiped her hood back. Her black eyes fluttered around the tree line, gazing from one clan to the next, daring them to protest. None did. River landed on her shoulder. The rest of the necromancers stood behind her, lurking in their onyx mist.

The night stilled. The trees quieted.

Celene took her place next to Luther, hidden in the shadows where moonlight didn't touch.

Thalia watched the night sky bleed. She listened for her mother's spirit, and soon enough, the sound of large paws padded the forest floor. A wolf—Astor, Cher's familiar—walked into the circle. His white pelt was flecked gray and black, paws muddy, tail swaying gently behind him. King appeared from the other side of the circle, his antlers glowing in the darkness.

When they met Thalia in the middle, the trees whispered again.

White witch, they said. *Take it.*

Thalia stroked Astor's head. She memorized the shape of his eyes, the feel of his cold nose against her palm. "Are you ready?"

Astor huffed and sat on his haunches.

Thalia's throat burned. Her eyes stung. But she lifted the red-handled blade, waited for Astor to close his eyes, and sank it into his chest. The wolf went limp.

The last remaining essence of her mother was gone. It dipped through the trees, lifted into the air, whistled through bushes and flowers. The forest sang and howled. Creatures far and wide climbed onto branches to watch, scurried from their hiding holes to get a glimpse of the ascension.

Thalia refused to cry. Despite Cher being gone. Despite the last of her dancing among the bleeding night sky. She closed her eyes and readied herself.

Cher's energy was a cloud of white smoke. It spread out, undulating against copper leaves and maroon petals, until it surged into the circle, into King's nostrils and Thalia's mouth.

Thalia, darling.

Thalia sobbed quietly, listening to her mother's voice fade. Her power threaded through Thalia's, knotting itself in her joints, squirming beside her bone marrow. Thalia assumed it would be violent. She thought their energy would clash, fight, bite each other inside her body. But, no. This was Cher's laughter by the greenhouse, her playful spells to attract butterflies, and her voice on every full moon. *Look, Thalia, watch time cut it open.*

King bellowed and shook his head. He galloped in circles around the tree line, keeping the other witches from encroaching.

Thalia's knees hit the damp grass.

A moment later, she felt a hand on her shoulder, heard the rustle of someone kneeling in front of her. When she lifted her gaze, Jordan's black eyes blinked patiently. Steam leaked from her smile.

"You okay, white witch?" Jordan set her palm on Thalia's cheek.

The trees whispered.

Bone Bender.
Matriarch.
Blood Queen.
High Magician.

"Yeah, necromancer." Thalia laid her hand over Jordan's. "I'm fine."

A voice shouted from the Lewellyn Clan, "The Darbonne Matriarch has ascended!"

Cheers and laughter and whistles followed.

Thalia was filled with light. Her heart stampeded. She felt powerful and visceral and alive. Her mouth remembered Jordan's, so she leaned forward and kissed her.

Jordan smiled through it. "What now?"

Thalia stood up and pulled Jordan with her. She tilted her head back to look at the moon. River flew across it, cawing excitedly.

"The night sky bleeds," Thalia said. She rested her arms over Jordan's shoulders. The clans clapped. The trees sang. She kissed Jordan again, and again, and again before she pulled back just enough to whisper, "And we're reborn."

DARKLING

Chapter One

RYDER FLIPPED OVER the first card.

The Magician.

He flipped over the second card.

The Tower.

Liam watched him carefully. His hands were folded together, chin perched atop them like he might be praying. He tipped his head toward the cards on the table, gaze resting on the vibrant curved arcs of The Magician, a shadowy figure holding a scepter, his shape accented by a billowing red cloak. The card was faded and the edges torn, a testament to how often it'd been drawn.

How often Ryder had drawn it.

"So?" Liam prompted. His clear brown eyes flicked to Ryder.

"Nothing new," Ryder said. It was the truth and it wasn't. Ryder had pulled The Magician many, many times, but he'd never pulled it alongside The Tower.

Liam tilted his head and strands of chestnut hair fell over his brow. He sat back and pushed it out of his face, scrubbing a hand on the freshly shaved side of his head. They'd been friends for too long for Ryder not to know that gesture. It was frustration, the quiet, mellow kind that Liam had mastered over the last twenty-two years.

"That—" Liam pointed to The Tower "—is new."

Ryder rolled his eyes. "C'mon then, Princess. It's your deck, what does it mean?"

"Don't call me that," Liam snapped. He narrowed his eyes. Ryder heard the click-clack of his tongue ring bounce across his teeth, another Liam mannerism he'd become accustomed to since he joined the circle two years before. This one was a louder kind of frustration, a haughtier, angrier kind. "The Magician is a card of intellect. Yours is inverted, meaning you'll be making an illogical decision soon. A..." He sighed through his nose and struggled to find the word. "A partnership, maybe, through magic. The Magician channels through his own body, meaning ownership of oneself. But it's inverted, so you'll be giving something away soon."

Ryder licked his lips. Ownership of his body had been a struggle since he was a child, and he wasn't looking forward to giving any part of it away.

Liam glanced at him. "The Tower is a card of sudden change. Chaos, even. This—" He tapped The Tower. "—with that—" He tapped The Magician. "—is a witch's worst nightmare."

"It doesn't sound that bad," Ryder said. "I'll be having a sudden magical change soon. What's wrong with that?"

"Nothing," Liam said. He lifted his brows and slid the two cards off the table to shuffle them back into his deck. "If that's how you want to look at it, that's how it'll be."

"Let's see what the cards have in store for you, Liam Montgomery," Ryder said.

Liam's eyes settled on him for a moment too long. Ryder's gaze darted away, over the sharp edge of Liam's cheekbone, the line of his jaw and slope of his nose. Sometimes Ryder wondered if Liam did it on purpose, if he tilted his head the way he did to catch Ryder's attention, if he breathed the way he did, or smelled the way he did, or walked the way he did to distract Ryder from everything and everyone else.

"Where's your deck?" Liam's tongue clicked against the back of his teeth again.

Ryder huffed an annoyed sigh, embarrassed he'd been caught looking. "In my jacket behind you."

Liam handed Ryder his jacket. The deck was in a maroon felt bag, tied shut with delicate matching strings. Ryder pulled the cards out, their black backs a stark contrast to his pale skin, and shuffled them. Magic stirred and hummed. It looped through his knuckles, invisible, thrumming heat, and Ryder imagined it sinking into every card. He thought of Liam, who sat across from him, watching intently. He imagined Liam's mouth and the line of his broad shoulders, how his jeans hung low on his waist—*stop*. Ryder closed his eyes and redirected his thoughts to Liam's magic, the strong course of Water inside him, waves breaking and the sound of a river flowing over rocks.

There. Ryder swallowed hard and handed Liam the deck. "Shuffle then draw two cards."

Liam drew his cards and laid them on the table.

Something wicked lingered in the space between them. The air pulled away from whatever it was, as if the elements knew something the two boys didn't. It crept under Ryder's skin, nibbling at the darkness he'd kept at bay for years. It was getting harder and harder to control, and whatever this was, it wanted Ryder's twisted, unnatural magic to make an appearance.

Ryder focused on the Fire inside him instead and nodded to Liam. "Go ahead."

Liam flipped over the first card.

The Devil.

He flipped over the second card.

The Lovers.

Liam's breath hitched. He stared at the table, arms flexed and trembling beneath a tight-fitted black sweater. Heat darkened his cheeks and turned his tan skin the same color as Ryder's maroon deck-pouch.

"Fatality," Liam whispered.

"To ravage," Ryder corrected gently. "To undergo extraordinary efforts. Don't immediately jump to the cards worst meaning, Liam."

"And—" Liam flicked his wrist toward The Lovers. "— I'm about to make a fool of myself, apparently. Right?"

"It's not inverted, so no. You're going to go through something dark and difficult." Ryder tapped The Devil. "And it will either push you toward a new love, or it will be because of a new love. The Lovers can mean anything, you know that. It could be a partnership, a romance, a fucking..." Ryder shrugged and sighed. "A meaningless hookup."

"You know it never means that."

"Okay, but it could," Ryder hissed.

"I'm about to do something terrible with someone," Liam said. He looked at Ryder and shook his head. "Keep this between us?"

Ryder cocked his head. Liam never wanted to keep things from the others.

"Tyler will worry, so will Christy and Donovan." Liam sighed. His bottom lip was white under the weight of his teeth. "Please?"

"You've never been one to break circle pacts," Ryder said.

Liam's lips thinned. "I haven't, but you have."

Ryder narrowed his eyes.

"Ryder." Liam breathed his name, pleading in a way Ryder hadn't heard before. Apologetic, almost.

He tilted his head and dragged his gaze from Liam's pinched mouth to his feet. "Begging looks good on you."

"Are you done?" Liam's cheeks flushed darker. "Yes or no?"

"Fine," Ryder said. His lips curved into a sly smile. "I'll keep your dirty secret."

Liam didn't thank him. He shifted his gaze toward the candles on the other end of the coffee table and they went out, fizzling as if they'd been drowned. He sighed and pushed the two cards toward Ryder.

"Put them away. We're meeting everyone in a half hour." Liam's bare feet on the worn wood floors in Ryder's lackluster apartment was a familiar sound. He brushed past one of the many plants Ryder had littered throughout the living room, in baskets on top of the bookshelf on the far wall, in planters beside the entertainment stand, lined up in small pots on the kitchen counter. "Can I get a light?"

Liam plucked a bundle of sage out of a mason jar next to the sink. He walked back over and stood in front of Ryder, still seated on an ottoman in front of the coffee table. Liam held the charred end of the sage in front of Ryder's mouth.

"Can you?" Ryder teased.

Liam rolled his eyes. "May I, English major."

Ryder reached for the Fire buried deep in his veins, opened his mouth, and blew gently across the sage.

It lit.

"Whatever showed up to watch my reading, I want it gone," Liam said. Smoke drifted into the corners, over the table, all around. The window next to the front door was closed and the blinds were cinched shut, causing the tangy smell of it to fill the air. "Something about it wasn't right."

Ryder nodded. No, something about it wasn't right. But he couldn't say that, because Ryder shouldn't have been able to sense it. That was Liam's reading. Those were Liam's cards.

Only people affected by the reading should've been able to feel what Liam felt.

But Ryder had sensed the wickedness. He'd felt its eyes on them, lurking above and around them, like a wraith with a crystal ball looking at their future before they'd lived it. Their future. He stood, turning from Liam to conceal the surprise on his face. Understanding slithered restlessly in his chest. He wrenched the blinds up and opened the window, shooing whatever strange entity hovered in the apartment out with the smoke.

Whatever it was, it had tethered them. Chills scaled Ryder's arms.

The Magician. The Tower. The Devil. The Lovers.

A magical catastrophe brought about by a dark, vicious partnership.

Liam was probably right. They shouldn't tell the others.

THEY ARRIVED AT Crescent Coffee before the rest of the circle. The little café on the south side of Port Lewis was homey and warm. It reeked of Darbonne magic, the essence of it coppery on Ryder's tongue. It was ancient in a way only Darbonne's, Thistle's, and Lewellyn's could be. The old clans. The ones who kept order over all the rest.

But orderly wasn't his preferred practice, so he never mentioned his last name. He was always just Ryder, because being Ryder Lewellyn was a daunting half truth.

The counter at the front of the small café was next to a glass case filled with colorful pastel pastries. Banana muffins, carrot cakes, and macarons were lined up and labeled with neatly folded tags in front of them. A chalkboard above the case displayed the prices of coffees, sandwiches, and teas in swirling cursive. Tables were scattered throughout the rest of the café, wood-topped and surrounded by mismatched chairs.

"Boys," Thalia said. She was a stunning woman with umber skin and a warm smile. Her voice was always smooth and pleasant, opposite her newly acquired power, which rolled off her in waves. She nodded to Liam, then to Ryder. "Caramel latte and rooibos?"

Liam nodded. Ryder said, "With honey, please."

"Do you want a muffin?" Liam dug his wallet out of the back pocket of his jeans as he stood in front of the counter.

Ryder shook his head. He avoided Thalia's gaze, but her magic dug into him like talons. There was no sneaking past the Darbonne matriarch, no keeping his thoughts to himself, no weaseling out of a confrontation. He walked to the empty table in the back of the café and sat down in the corner chair closest to the wall.

Before Liam joined him, Thalia appeared. She lifted a brow at Ryder in accusation and tilted her head, eyeing him down her nose like a hawk would a mouse. Her palms settled on the tabletop and she leaned forward, the loose scoop of her white blouse obscured by a deep purple pendant.

"Ryder," she purred, gentle, soothing, the same way his mother used to say his name when he covered his chest after she walked into his room unannounced. As if she was sorry for something she had no reason to be sorry for.

His top lip curled back in a snarl and he rolled his eyes.

"You should tell him," Thalia whispered.

"You ascended last week and you're already everyone's therapist?"

Thalia shook her head, which was shaved to the skin. "I can feel your secrets. All three of them."

Ryder's gaze sharpened. His magic lunged at her, a warning bite. "You know my secrets. Don't."

Thalia's magic was strong and unshakable. It barely flinched. She ran her hand over the top of Ryder's buzzed head and pushed him playfully. "Or wait for the inevitable. Your choice."

"It *is* my choice," Ryder said. He looked away, uncomfortable with Thalia's knowing eyes staring back at him. A sigil peeked out above the collar of her blouse, angry red against her dark skin. He caught sight of Liam walking over with their drinks. The bell above the door rang and Christy's laugh followed. He glanced back at Thalia and quietly said, "I'm not hurting anyone."

"Not yet," Thalia whispered. She left the conversation there and turned to greet Liam with a smile as he placed their drinks on the table.

Christy twirled in, hands above her head, decorated in an assortment of chunky crystal rings. Her knuckles were blackened by stick-and-poke runes. Her long, wind-whipped hair was streaked pink and blue and black. Ryder had forgotten what color it originally was; he didn't even know if he'd ever really seen it.

Tyler and Donovan followed. Tyler talked with his hands as he spoke, engaged in a conversation that Ryder would guess was only half as interesting as it looked from afar.

"Thalia!" Christy swung her arms over Thalia's neck. "Congratulations! I was there, you know. It was a beautiful ceremony."

"Thank you, Christy. I saw you standing with the Thistles. And you guys too." She nodded as Tyler and Donovan approached. "Were they accommodating?"

"Yes, the Thistles always are." Christy batted her hand in dismissive fashion.

"Most of the outside families joined them for the ascension. I even saw Ryder with them, between the Lewellyns and the Wolfes, right?"

Ryder straightened his back. His magic flared, hot and furious.

Liam kicked his shin under the table.

"Yeah, we were all together for it. Figured it'd be best to stick with our circle." Christy grinned cheerily, her heart shaped face light and true. She didn't notice Ryder's murderous heat, which wasn't uncommon. Christy was as white a witch as they came. Her focus never drifted from light-working, so it never drifted to Ryder. He'd waited for her to notice it—for any of them to notice it, but somehow, they hadn't.

Ryder couldn't keep it contained forever, though. Flare-ups like that would lead to questions he couldn't answer.

Thalia hummed in agreement. She didn't bother looking at Ryder before she walked away, but he felt her magic shift. It stung him like a transparent blade pressed against his throat: *Don't test me.* The fluttering in his stomach calmed and his magic retreated.

"What the fuck was that?" Liam seethed.

Ryder chewed on his lip and shook his head. Two fingers pinched Ryder's jaw and tugged. Liam's thumb and index finger sent a jolt through him, and it deepened when he saw the recognition slide into place on Liam's face. Their magic collided, tangling and untangling, stretching to make room for one another. Ryder almost gasped, but he clenched his jaw to keep the sound at bay. They were sitting next to each other in a café, and their friends were sitting around them. Christy's singsong voice. Tyler's rambling. Donovan's quiet laugh. But all Ryder could focus on was how Liam's fingers loosened, and how their magic pulsed suddenly; a warning, a prelude.

Their magic danced between them. Water and Fire and something else, something darker.

Liam dropped his hand. It brushed Ryder's arm, and he shifted away, putting space between them.

"How'd the reading go?" Tyler had the voice of a charismatic spokesperson. He was eloquent and commanding, the kind of person who took the lead in everything he did. Especially their circle.

Ryder waited, but Liam said nothing.

"We skipped it and smudged instead," Ryder said. The lie came easily. "Are we doing anything for the full tomorrow?"

Thankfully, Christy ran with the subject change. Her silver bangles clattered around her wrist as she wiggled her hands excitedly. "Drum circle and fire pit at Tyler's. We invited everyone."

"Yeah?" Ryder nodded to Tyler.

Tyler nodded back. His black hair was slicked back, making the roundness of his copper cheeks stand out and the multiple silver hoops through both his ears glint in the light. His eyes were upturned and clever—fox eyes as Christy would say.

"It's in Pisces," Donovan piped up. His light eyes were as open and pure as Christy's, blue like the aquamarine pendant that hung around his neck. "You should set some intention, Liam."

"I will," Liam said. If he was shaken, he didn't show it. His face was as set and serene as ever; cheekbones that could cut glass, a jawline Ryder envied, sharp, smart eyes that flicked once to Ryder. They didn't linger. His gaze shifted back to Tyler and Donovan, but not before Ryder caught the distinct wave of his pupils, expanding out and in again, a flare of magic he'd snuffed out. Liam cleared his throat. "Did you figure out the communication spell, Ty?"

"We were just talking about that," Tyler said and gestured to Donovan with a wave. "I found a few things, but most of the instructions are in Latin, which none of us speak."

All eyes turned to Ryder. He knew what Tyler wanted, but none of them had the courage to mention it. So, they stared, urging Ryder with pointed gazes. Christy looked away first, then Donovan. Liam looked at his steaming mug.

"What?" Ryder spat.

Tyler shot him a knowing look, trying to get his point across without words.

Christy made a weak noise. "I don't think that's a good idea," she said to Tyler.

Instead of waiting for an explanation, Ryder cut them off and said, "Ask Thalia." He sipped his tea and averted his gaze to the table. "She's closer to her than I am."

"Didn't she used to tutor you, though?" Tyler asked. "It would be a short conversation, Ryder. You know I wouldn't usually recommend going to...them, but we need it."

"You don't need to talk to trees, Tyler." Ryder snorted a laugh. He replayed the way Tyler said *them* again and again, disgust under anger under fear.

"Yeah, we can work on something else," Christy said softly.

"It's not about me," Tyler said sternly. "Donovan hasn't been able to focus his energy. He's Earth; he needs the guidance. The forest is filled with spirits, ancients, nymphs." He tapped his finger on the table. "Answers. We can't not try."

"At least be brave enough to say her name then," Ryder said under his breath.

The table went quiet. Liam's eyes were all over him, pinpricks like spider feet.

"Ask Jordan..." Tyler stood up from the table. "Anyone want anything? I'm getting coffee."

Ryder noticed the space where Jordan's last name lingered, unsaid but there all the same. It was one thing for a matriarch to mention it, but discussing a dark clan was taboo for a small circle of beginner witches.

"Hey..." Christy rested her palm over top of Ryder's hand. He expected her to pull away when she felt the blistering heat rising from his skin, but she didn't. "If you don't want to—"

"It's fine," Ryder said.

Liam's foot brushed against his under the table. Another spike of energy shot through him. Christy flinched away, as if he'd shocked her. Liam swung his foot back and tucked it under the chair, far from Ryder.

Christy's pale eyes flicked between Ryder and Liam. She was psychic, but her gifts rarely manifested within the circle, which was a common practice. Psychic or not, circle-mates shouldn't have access to everything. Information dealing with emotions had the potential to be dangerous, and Christy was almost always respectful of their boundaries as a group. This time was no different. Instead of prying, her magic hovered around her as a shield, an instant response to Ryder's spark.

"I'm just nervous," Ryder explained. He offered her a smile, but it was heavy and faraway. "Sorry."

Christy nodded. She tucked a blue strand of hair behind her ear. "It's probably just the full moon. It gets everyone worked up." A white mouse crept out of the breast pocket on her slouchy black T-shirt. Willow's long whiskers trembled as she wiggled her nose. Christy scratched the mouse's head with the tip of her finger. "It's all right, Willow. He didn't mean it."

"Sorry, Willow." Ryder offered Christy's familiar another withered smile.

"Say it's okay, Ry," Christy cooed at Willow in a baby voice.

Tyler and Donovan appeared with their coffees. But Ryder's energy was too volatile for him to sit through a circle meeting. The magic he'd worked for years to keep at bay hummed deep in his belly. It made everything sharper, closer, more defined. He heard Liam inhale, listened to the sound of air sucked past his lips, the constant click of his tongue ring against his teeth. Liam shifted and Ryder's heart sped up. Liam moved his hands in his lap and Ryder's stomach clenched.

Being in proximity with each other after recently tethering was a bad idea. Especially after Liam had just put two and two together, and Christy had witnessed a collision of their energies, and Ryder was biting at the bit for a release.

"I'll go deal with this Latin bullshit," Ryder said.

"Ryder, really, it's fine. We can find another way," Donovan said. Orange freckles dusted the tops of his cheeks and across the bridge of his nose. He was the youngest of them, barely nineteen and barely a witch.

Ryder didn't blame him for wanting to harness his gifts. It was natural for most witches.

The notion turned Ryder's stomach, though.

"I don't mind. She was my tutor after all." He aimed the sarcasm at Tyler as he stood, adjusting the buttons on his peacoat. "See you guys tomorrow."

"Tonight," Liam corrected. "I'll see you tonight."

Christy's lashes fluttered, the way they always did when she caught a whiff of something supernatural. She glanced at Liam, then up at Ryder. Her lips rounded in a surprised O, but she stayed quiet.

Ryder didn't have the patience to ask her what she'd seen, and he wasn't sure he wanted to know. His eyes flashed to Liam's, and he was met with caution or confusion, both at once. Liam's lips parted, but Ryder walked away before he could say anything.

"Be careful," Tyler called.

Ryder flicked two fingers over his shoulder in a lazy wave. Thalia Darbonne watched him from behind the counter, her gaze knowing and strong. She nodded to him, and her magic gave a gentle push to the center of his back as he walked out the door.

Chapter Two

THE LOFT ABOVE St. Maria's Catholic Church was inhabited by a necromancer. Some people thought it was riddled with bones and corpses. Other witches thought they'd find skulls and black candles and cobwebs if they ventured inside. Most counted on the irony of the situation to mask the urban legend. A few dismissed it, thankful they'd never needed to knock on a necromancer's door in search of assistance to begin with.

White witches who weren't versed in dark magic thought it would swallow them whole if they even looked in its direction. But that wasn't quite the case.

Ryder stood at the top of the steep, narrow staircase in front of a thick wooden door. His fist hovered inches from its surface, but before he mustered enough courage to knock, the door opened.

Jordan Wolfe shared Ryder's sharp, fine features. Her cheekbones were prominent and her chin pointed. Her dark, sultry eyes were the same shape as his, tear-dropped and sad; sexy in a way that shouldn't be, but still was. Except Jordan had Wolfe eyes—brown that was almost black, under gold that was almost yellow.

Ryder had his mother's, Lewellyn eyes. They were canopy-leaf green, vibrant and startling in the light.

His Lewellyn eyes didn't make him any less Wolfe, though. But no one needed to know that.

"What're you doing here?" Jordan asked playfully. Her nose scrunched when she grinned, and she wrapped her arm around his shoulders to pull him into a hug. He'd forgotten how alike they sounded, raspy and graceless.

"I can't come see my sister?" Ryder mumbled.

Jordan's ashy blonde hair tickled his nose, swaying in loose curls over her shoulders. She smelled like lilies and blood. "You can, but you never do. What's up? What's going on?"

Ryder wanted to tell her, but everything lodged painfully in his throat. The reading. Liam. What it meant. If it even meant anything at all. His magic going nuclear more often than he was comfortable with. Him being a necromancer, but not. Him being a Fire witch, but not.

"Hey." Jordan sounded sad. She brushed her knuckles across his cheeks. "Hey, no, I don't like this. You feel like..." Her words were lost somewhere between them.

He stepped inside, and she closed the door. The loft was spacious and lulling. Candles were lit on the nightstand and the dresser. Runes and sigils were carved into the vaulted ceiling beams. A white-chalk circle decorated the floor beneath a round window on the far end of the room. No skulls, no rotting bodies, just odd purple plants, a stereo, and a rumpled bed.

Ryder paced back and forth, free to let his magic spark on the tips of his fingers now that he was with someone who understood it. "What happens if I choose to die?"

Jordan gave him space. She stood next to her bed, swathed in a long black dress. A fresh sigil was carved onto her arm. Part of it might've matched the one he'd seen on Thalia at the café earlier.

"If I go through with the Wolfe ceremony, if I die and come back, what then?" Ryder asked. He shrugged off his peacoat. It hit the floor, exposing pale, lean arms. His magic went every which way, abandoning the glamour he wore daily on his chest. The scars didn't bother him, but it didn't hurt to cover them either.

"God, look at you," Jordan said, exhaling on the end. "You look wonderful, Ryder."

"That's doesn't answer my question," he said. He stopped and stared at the ceiling, reining in the grate of his voice. "Thank you, yeah, whatever, but—"

"If you decide to die, you become a necromancer."

"And what happens to my elemental gifts?"

"I'm not sure. You're the first Lewellyn-born Wolfe we've ever seen."

The magic writhed against Ryder's bones. It thrummed under his skin, loud like gunshots inside him. "What would Dad say?"

"You can ask him yourself," Jordan said, her tone matter-of-fact. "I'm only a year older than you; it's not like he listens to me more than he listens to you."

"Yeah, okay, but you're..." Ryder gestured up and down, from Jordan's head to her toes. "You. You're the darling dark daughter."

Jordan rolled her eyes. "Are you going to tell me what's really going on?"

"I drew The Magician and The Tower today." He paused and licked his lips. "Liam pulled The Devil and The Lovers. Something came for us, and it was dark. Wolfe dark."

"Ancestors make appearances all the time with young alchemists. What's the problem?"

"We both felt it. I felt it, Liam felt it. We..."

"Tethered."

"Yes."

Jordan sat down on the edge of her bed. "Have you told him yet?"

"Which part?" Ryder sat down on the floor in front of her and hugged his knees to his chest.

"The part about you being fond of him?"

"Fond of him? Just say it, Jordan, Jesus Christ."

Jordan scoffed. "We're in a church, young man." Ryder choked on a pained laugh. The audacity. Jordan continued. "The part where you tell him you have feelings for him."

"He knows that."

"Does he know the extent of it?"

Ryder's magic thrashed about. It collided with Jordan's and the room heated. Steam leaked from between Ryder's lips, hot and scalding in his mouth. "I don't even know the extent of it!"

Jordan wasn't fazed by Ryder's outburst. "Has he acted on it?"

"Neither of us have! We haven't even talked about it; it's just there, all right? He... I don't know how to do this. I don't know how the fuck he couldn't know. But we're friends, and we've been friends for two years. I can't screw that up." Ryder swallowed a mouthful of steam and closed his eyes, hoping the unnatural magic coming to the surface would die down. "None of them know about me. I haven't told the circle."

Jordan went quiet. She slid off the bed and sat in front of him on the floor. Her lips parted and she reached out to touch his knee. "About you as in you, or you being a Wolfe?"

Ryder shook his head. "Neither."

She fidgeted. Her black painted nails clicked together, hands decorated in an assortment of jewelry and ink. "You still injecting once a week?"

Ryder held up two fingers. "Twice a week. I moved up eight months ago."

"And you're okay doing it by yourself?"

He shrugged. "It's been a while. I'm used to it now."

She gestured to his chest with a flick of her wrist. "Dad told me you healed up really well."

"That was two and half years ago, Jordie," Ryder scoffed.

Jordan's lips twitched into a smile when he used her nickname. "Yeah, I know, and I was dealing with my own bullshit back then. We haven't actually talked about everything, not since we were in high school."

Three years ago, Thalia had left. Six months after that, Ryder had top surgery. Another six months and he'd joined his own circle. Everything in between those specific markers was blurred and distorted, a mess of circumstances Ryder didn't want to pick apart. "Do we need to start now?"

Jordan shook her head and sighed, swiftly changing the subject. "You don't have to tell them about the Wolfe stuff until you've figured out what you want to do. But that—" Jordan gestured to Ryder's eyes. "—won't go away. Your magic will keep going nuts if you don't do something about it."

"What can I do?" Ryder pawed at one of his eyes with the back of his hand. Black fanned away from his pupils, covering the whites of his eyes. It took a minute, but slowly the inky black crawled back to the center.

"Practicing would help. You don't have to take life, but you need to at least work with blood on some level."

"Tyler would never approve of blood magic."

"Whether you choose to die or not, you're still the child of a necromancer. You'll always crave it."

Ryder nodded. He couldn't disagree with her; she was right. His thoughts circled the last few months, how quickly his necromancy had manifested within him. He couldn't tell her about the dreams he'd had, the ones that involved his teeth in Liam's skin and Liam's blood coating his tongue. He couldn't tell her how often he'd caught himself wondering what it might be like to feel Liam's heart beat in the palm of his hand.

"Can you translate something for me?"

"What is it?" Jordan tilted her head back against the bed.

"Latin for a spell Tyler and Donovan are working on."

"Donovan still can't cast?"

"Not well. He has a hard time focusing. He can't find his element."

Jordan barked a laugh. "He's Earth! It's right underneath him!"

Ryder's lips quirked into a smile. "I know, but he's just starting out. They want to give an offering to the woods and see what the trees have to say."

"Careful," Jordan purred. "Those trees will rat you out."

Ryder arched a brow questioningly.

"They call us bone benders," Jordan said. "Sometimes, darklings."

Ryder's magic settled. He could finally breathe without feeling like he was on fire, or going to start a fire. He noticed one of the basket plants hanging from the ceiling curl its tendril and sway back and forth. Their violet and teal leaves glowed prettily in the dark.

Jordan translated the part of the spell Tyler needed and made two cups of lemongrass tea. Since alchemists were the only clans who still used Latin for spells, they were typically the only ones who needed it. Jordan taught Ryder a few phrases and laughed at him when he couldn't pronounce *ignis*. The night quieted, and they sat in companionable silence for an hour, then another. It was half past eight before either of them mentioned leaving. Jordan worked in her grimoire. Ryder scrolled through his phone, avoiding Liam's social media at all costs.

Sometime during Ryder's second cup of tea, he realized how much he'd missed her. Just as Ryder's resolve crumbled, and Liam's Instagram loaded, Jordan grabbed her coat and keys off the dresser.

"Where are you off to?" He swiped the app away and slid his phone into his pocket.

"Thalia's meeting me for pizza," Jordan said. She smiled gently and arched a brow. "You can't avoid going home forever, Ry."

He nodded, a dark blush tinting his cheeks. "I'm not ashamed of it. The magic. Our magic. You know that, right?"

Jordan narrowed her eyes and held the door open with her foot. Ryder walked down the stairs while she trailed behind him. A nun dipped her fingers into a bowl of holy water by the last set of pews. She clutched her rosary and scurried toward the front of the church at the sight of them.

"I know that," Jordan assured. "But you're scared of it."

Ryder didn't answer. He didn't have to.

Jordan brushed past him. Her expensive perfume left a trail of vanilla and musky cinnamon. "As you should be," she quipped, rosy lips spread into a grin.

PORT LEWIS WAS a rainy little town on the coast of Washington. Ryder liked the way the streetlamps that lined the sidewalk illuminated the fog, and how mist dampened his face. He walked through downtown past the movie theaters and shopfronts. Water beaded up on the glass, and when he caught glimpses of himself, it was Jordan staring back at him.

He stopped in front of a deli. The glass window was dark, but the glow of the "closed" sign made it easy to trace the line of his nose, dainty like Jordan's, and his mouth, full like Jordan's. But there was no mistaking their striking differences: His buzzed head and stretched earlobes. His brow, as fair as hers, but stronger, the angled line of his jaw, more defined—harder.

You look wonderful, Ryder. Jordan's voice crept into his thoughts.

His peacoat wrapped around him and was buttoned tight up his chest, highlighting the cut of his shoulders. He shifted until his combat boots scraped the sidewalk, and ducked under an overhang as the rain started to fall faster. A taxi careened down the road toward the movie theater, and a few people hurried across the street to the 24-hour diner. He glanced at his reflection once more and kept walking.

Ryder trudged down Main toward his apartment building. Two left turns and a block past Crescent Coffee brought him to his neighborhood. He smiled at his neighbor Lucy who walked three yappy Chihuahuas, and fumbled with his keychain as he bounced up the stairs to his door.

A soft meow pulled his attention from his keychain to the entryway to his apartment.

Liam sat against his front door, his sweater replaced by a loose T-shirt, showcasing the bold oceanic tattoo on his left arm. Ryder's familiar, a yellow-eyed black cat named Percy, watched him from his place in Liam's lap.

"I've told you how cliché it is that you got a cat as a familiar, right?" Liam asked. His large hands stroked Percy's back, and the cat purred loudly.

Liam had teased Ryder about that weekly for two years.

"Once or twice," Ryder said. He swallowed hard and fiddled with his keys. His magic jumped under his skin, clawing its way through ligaments and joints to get to the surface. "It's not like an owl's any less cliché."

As if on cue, Opal landed on the railing of the outdoor staircase. She chirped at them pleasantly, ruffling her cream feathers to shake off the rain.

"He didn't mean that," Liam said to Opal. He lifted Percy into his arms and stood, gaze lingering on Ryder for long enough to make his heart beat a little bit faster. "You gonna stand there or can we go inside?"

Ryder offered his arm to Opal. She hopped onto his forearm, then his shoulder. "Do you want tea?"

Liam didn't answer. He followed Ryder into his dark apartment. The smell of sage and wax filled the space, left over from their reading that morning. Opal flew off Ryder's shoulder and landed on the bookshelf next to a thriving green fern. Percy's paws hit the wood floor. Ryder turned the lock on the door and hesitated, staring down at the doorknob while he tried to gather his thoughts.

There was breath on the back of his neck. Liam's energy squirmed around them, frantic and busy. Heat bloomed in Ryder's stomach, but he could barely control it.

When he finally mustered enough courage to turn around, Liam's wide hand hit his chest and shoved him against the door. Ryder reached for his magic and stitched it into a glamour, covering the pink scars that curved from his sternum over his ribcage on either side. A coat and shirt covered them, but his glamour was an old, comfortable habit.

Everything narrowed down to the sweep of Liam's dark eyelashes and his mouth tightening into a thin line.

"We tethered?" Liam snapped. A card was pinched between his thumb and index finger. He flashed it in front of Ryder. The Lovers. "I've pulled this fucking card three times today."

"It doesn't have to mean anything," Ryder said softly. He tried to look elsewhere, but Liam wouldn't permit it. Every time Ryder turned away, Liam leaned into his line of sight.

"Our reading isn't a joke. We're going to do something terrible together. Don't you get that?"

"How do you know it'll be terrible? What makes something terrible?"

"Why didn't you tell me?" A breath left Liam, winded and small. He pressed harder on Ryder's chest.

"You have eyes, don't you? C'mon, I wasn't that subtle." Ryder's blush betrayed his attempt at confidence.

"No, you weren't," Liam agreed. One brow quirked and he licked his bottom lip. Ryder pretended not to notice. "A fatal union, Ry. A shift in your magic, a partnership that will result in chaos or..."

"Or," Ryder purred and tried to smile.

Liam snarled. "This isn't as simple as that. We're going to... This is dark, Ryder."

"You scared?"

"Maybe."

"Of which part, me or the magic?"

Liam's lips pressed down and his brow furrowed. "Do you understand what this could mean? What you could be? What we're going to—"

Anger flared in Ryder. His magic burst from him, crackling in the air, turning the static energy upside down.

"What I could be?" Ryder hissed. A thousand cries and screams erupted beneath his voice. They slithered from him, haunting and horrible. The voice of a necromancer. He felt the moment his pupils bled over the rest of his eyes, showing the truth of him, the dangerous, wicked, unnatural part of him. Steam built in his mouth and drifted over his lips. "We're going to what, Liam?"

Liam's eyes widened. His magic surged like a crashing wave. It was cold and ancient, pure and protective. Ryder wanted to tear it apart. He wanted to hide, to push Liam out the door and lock himself in his room. Everything inside him twisted and roared, looking for a way out. He'd never wanted Liam to see this; he'd never wanted anyone to see it.

"You're..." Liam stepped back. His throat bobbed when he swallowed.

Ryder's chest was cold where Liam's hand had been. "Yeah," he spat. He shouldered past Liam and unbuttoned his coat with trembling fingers. The heat on his skin made his head spin. "Yeah, I am."

"But you're a Lewellyn," Liam whispered.

"My mom had an affair with Gerard Wolfe."

"Jordan's dad? So, Jordan's your..."

"Yeah." Ryder snapped his teeth down. He didn't bother turning the lights on, and draped his coat over the back of the couch once it was off. He walked past the kitchen, down the hall, and into his bedroom. Percy watched from the ottoman. Opal cooed curiously and flapped her wings.

Liam didn't immediately follow.

Ryder's lungs ached. His mouth quivered as he paced back and forth in front of his disheveled bed. Clothes were piled in the corner. A few plants sat in baskets next to the window. His altar was on the other end of his room, a repurposed vanity crowded with half-burnt incense, different colored candles, sage leaves, and open spell books. He snapped his fingers and the candles lit.

His skin still burned. "Fuck," Ryder panted. His magic raged in the room and inside him. He ripped off his shirt and tossed it away before snapping his fingers again. The tip of two incense sticks smoldered.

"Ryder." Liam's voice sounded from the doorway.

Ryder dipped into the attached bathroom and flicked on the light. The brightness stung. He winced at his reflection in the mirror, black-eyed, with steam rising from his skin. His palms hit the countertop and he exhaled a deep, hot breath.

Liam's reflection appeared behind him. His expression hardened and he tilted his head, eyes darting across Ryder in the mirror.

"Just go," Ryder said, whimpered and tender.

"Your magic is at odds with itself. The fire in you is fighting with the..."

"You can say it."

"Necromancy in you." Liam said *necromancy* carefully, sounding out all four syllables with the utmost respect. The carefulness was expected, the respect was a surprise. "Have you... Did you...?"

"No," Ryder whispered. "Do you see any sigils?" He gestured over his bare torso. "Jordan said if I don't start bloodletting, this will get worse." He blinked at himself and flexed his jaw.

Liam's water magic was fluid and coaxing. It drifted around them, rippling the energy. The familiarity made Ryder's shoulders droop. His body unwound and he decompressed, trying to even out his breathing as the darkness inside him continued to make itself known.

"Just go," Ryder repeated, exasperated.

The exposed bulbs above the mirror flickered. Liam's fingertips touched the base of Ryder's spine.

Everything was brilliant and blinding.

"When I pulled The Devil, I didn't think it'd be you," Liam said. His tongue ring clicked against his teeth.

Ryder's eyes cinched shut. His voice grew into a symphony of voices. "Fuck you."

Liam's hand crept along Ryder's vertebrae. "But then I pulled The Lovers."

His hands shook on the countertop, knuckles white where he gripped the edge. Ryder chewed on his lip and resisted leaning back when Liam's hand climbed up his spine.

"What do we have to do for the bloodletting?"

Ryder's eyes snapped open. "We don't have to do anything."

"We're tethered. I'm still your best friend, for one. And I'm your circle-mate."

Ryder caught Liam's eye in the mirror. The steam had dissipated, but Ryder's eyes were still ink black.

"We'll keep it between us," Liam added. "Tell me what I need to do."

"Cut me." The words edged between Ryder's teeth. His brows knitted, and he chewed on his lip until it hurt. The idea of Liam dragging a blade across his skin sent a shameful thrill through him. "Carve a spell into my skin."

"Dark magic," Liam said.

"The darkest there is. That's why I said you should just go."

Liam disappeared into Ryder's bedroom. Ryder's magic flared again. The lights in the bathroom popped and went out. His head spun as he stepped into the shadows of his room, elongated and flickering in the glow of the candles on his altar.

"Where?" Liam asked shakily. He held Ryder's black-handled athame, a curved silver blade, in his right hand. "Where do you want me to cut you?"

"Anywhere," Ryder said. He narrowed his eyes and glanced from Liam to the bedroom door and back. "You're serious?"

"Get on the bed."

"You don't have to do this with me."

"Get on the bed," Liam seethed.

Ryder sat on the edge of the bed. Liam knelt in front of him. Ryder had imagined this scene before, but differently. Desire pooled in his gut. Ryder ignored it.

The tip of the athame touched Ryder's hip. Desire bloomed into something far harder to ignore. Liam's whiskey eyes flashed to his face, and he asked, "Here?"

The blade was cold. It vibrated with purpose against Ryder's skin. He watched the tendon in Liam's neck flex, and nodded. "Sure, Princess."

Liam knocked him backward with one hand on his chest and dug the blade cruelly into Ryder's flesh. It stung. The darkness expanded around them. Ryder could hear Liam's racing heart. He listened to the sound of the knife cutting through his skin, smelled his own blood, coppery and rich and heady. Time paused to watch them.

"You should've told me," Liam hissed. He sliced another line across Ryder's hip.

"I didn't know how to. You're my best friend; how do I tell you something like that? Hey man, yeah—" He paused to suck in a sharp breath. "I might be in love with you. No big deal. Oh, and I'm a necromancer, also no big deal. And I'm—" Ryder stopped speaking altogether when Liam's mouth covered the bloody wound on his hip.

A strangled moan was torn from Ryder's throat. He threw his head back and tried to catch his breath, enduring the surge of shared power as Liam pressed his tongue against the new rune.

Fire set Ryder's veins ablaze. Liam ran his hands up his stomach, over his ribcage. One thumb traced the raised scar on Ryder's right side. His focus had been stolen, disintegrating the glamour, but he didn't care. His senses sharpened and his back arched off the bed. Everything became the movement of Liam's mouth and Ryder's blood coating his tongue.

The candles on the altar sparked. Ryder couldn't catch his breath.

"Stop," he said suddenly. He pawed at Liam's shoulders.

Liam stopped. He crawled over Ryder the same way Ryder had seen in dreams and nightmares and daydreams. His hands settled on either side of Ryder's arms and he looked down at him, handsome and powerful, with blood on his mouth and a pale tint to his eyes, his pupils and irises replaced by translucent gray.

"You have too many secrets," Liam said. His voice was every raindrop that had ever fallen, and every storm that had ever raged.

The athame sat on the bed next to them. Ryder grabbed it and pressed it hard against Liam's throat.

Liam craned into it, an encouragement. The tip of the blade nicked the flesh below his ear. He said, "You taste like power."

Chills coursed Ryder's arms. His stomach leapt into his throat. He pulled the blade back and tossed it to the floor. Liam leaned down, but Ryder turned to catch the cut on his neck rather than his lips. He pushed Liam onto his back and pinned him to the bed, teeth set around the cut, one hand clutching the sheets, the other pushed up Liam's shirt.

Liam's blood tasted like the ocean. It was clean and delicate, crowded with urgency and youth and vitality. Everything Ryder had kept at bay rushed from him. Every feeling became too potent, every ounce of magic became too electric. He licked across the cut, and Liam's breath hitched. Ryder dug his fingernails into Liam's ribs and Liam sighed.

"Ry," Liam whispered. "Ryder, stop."

Ryder didn't stop. He bit down until another spurt of blood warmed his tongue. Liam whimpered, and Ryder loved the way it sounded. He pressed his body down against Liam's, fit their hips together and nudged his thigh between Liam's legs.

"Ryder," Liam snapped. He wiggled his hand between them and tugged Ryder's jaw until he pulled back, only to be pulled in again.

Ryder didn't know if it started as a kiss. Their mouths met in a hurry, and Ryder's lips parted for the stroke of Liam's tongue, wet with his own blood. The stud was smooth as Liam licked into Ryder's mouth. It turned into a messy, rough, starved kiss that sent Ryder spinning inside himself.

Ryder had imagined kissing Liam every day for two years. His imagination couldn't have prepared him for this.

Their magic clashed. Cool water met a wildfire. Liam's elemental magic tangled with Ryder's necromancy. Their energy stitched together, weaving and tightening, and Ryder couldn't keep up with any of it. Not Liam's lips, insistent and demanding, not his heart beating fast in his chest, not Liam's hands low on his back, or Liam grinding shamelessly against his thigh.

Ryder wanted to sink his teeth into Liam's skin again. He wanted to tear his clothes off, and raise the dead, and set fires.

A hum built in Liam's throat and he moaned, breath hot in Ryder's mouth. Ryder wanted to hear it on repeat. He wanted to make Liam sound like that for hours, desperate and worked up and reckless.

It turned into Liam's mouth on his over and over, kissing that turned violent before it became tender. They bit each other's lips. Liam scraped his nails up the back of Ryder's neck and their teeth clanked when Liam tugged him down, forcing them to kiss harder and deeper.

The magic settled as they did. The quieter their breathing became, the calmer their magic was. Ryder's heat turned into a flush across his cheeks, and his eyes unclouded, the black sliding back to the center. Liam's hips pressed against Ryder's in slow, tentative rolls.

When the darkness dissipated, it left Ryder shaken. His body trembled. His lips slid away from Liam's and tried to catch his breath.

"You're..." Liam sucked in a breath and touched Ryder's jaw. His body stilled and relaxed into the bed. "Did you know you could do that?"

"Do what?"

Liam pushed Ryder onto his back. He leaned over him, hand firm on his chest. Ryder closed his eyes and felt the drag of Liam's hand down his sternum, across the flat expanse of his stomach, until it reached the line of his black jeans.

"Syphon power like that." Liam nodded toward the plant by the window. It was shriveled and wilted. His fingertips fluttered over the top of Ryder's pants and slipped between his legs.

Ryder's gasp was loud in the stillness. His hand shot down to latch around Liam's wrist.

He'd explained too much in one night to have to explain another secret.

"No," Ryder whispered. "I had no idea. I didn't mean to."

Liam took the hint and moved his hand to Ryder's thigh, then to his hip. The quiet was heavy, reminding Ryder that Liam could change his mind. That he probably would. This was just the magic, the leftover bits of it that made them hungry for anything and everything. Ryder had always been hungry for Liam, but he doubted Liam would stay hungry for him.

Even after tonight; even after what they'd done.

"They say it's addictive," Liam said.

"Magic like this?"

"Yes. We can't tell Tyler."

"We won't." Ryder sighed. "Don't worry; this won't soil your pristine reputation. No one has to know you did blood magic with a necromancer."

Liam's silence held weight. Ryder didn't have the courage to look at him, so he kept his eyes closed, and memorized the outline of Liam's hand on his hip and the taste of him in his mouth. He tried to focus his energy on the plant by the window. He reached for its life-force, for the pieces of it that still lingered inside him.

The flames atop the candles grew smaller and smaller until they faded. Ryder's energy drifted from him, as if he was shedding a second skin.

Liam stopped breathing.

When Ryder finally opened his eyes, he looked at the plant and watched it unravel. Its leaves filled with color, muted violet and dark teal. It was alive, but changed.

"You brought it back." Liam's voice was equal parts disbelief and awe.

"Looks like it."

Liam smoothed his palm up Ryder's side. His thumb stroked one of the scars on his chest. Before he could ask about it, Ryder slid off the bed and headed for the bathroom. He shook out his hands and glanced at his reflection. The symbol on his hip was a small upright triangle, the elemental emblem for fire. Half-moon indentions from Liam's teeth curved above and below it.

"I'm taking a shower." Ryder glanced over his shoulder.

"Do you want me to stay?" Liam adjusted his shirt as he got off the bed. He stood in front of the altar with his hands shoved in the front pockets of his blue jeans. He looked dismantled and beautiful and utterly confused, as if a thousand questions were ringing loud in his ears and he couldn't discern them. The tiny cut on his neck was covered by a blooming purple bruise.

"Do you want to stay?"

Liam shrugged one shoulder. "Up to you. Do you need some space?"

No. Ryder licked his lips. Space was the last thing he needed. "If you stay, there's tea in the kitchen. If not, I'll see you tomorrow."

Liam's jaw tightened and a pained smile twitched on his mouth. He nodded and looked from Ryder to the floor. One hand pushed his hair back, the other squirmed in his pocket. He blinked and gave another curt nod, as if he'd decided but kept it to himself.

The pipes groaned when Ryder turned the shower on. He sensed Liam as he stood under the water, but a few minutes later his energy was gone. Ryder wanted to be surprised, but he wasn't. He couldn't blame Liam for leaving. Ryder hadn't asked him to stay.

He scrubbed his body until his skin was pink, and stood in the shower until the water ran cold.

When he stepped out, Percy meowed at him from the entryway to the bathroom. His big yellow eyes blinked, long black tail swaying to and fro.

"Don't look at me like that," Ryder mumbled. The ghost of Liam's lips and fingertips and magic tiptoed across his flesh. "*He* kissed me."

Percy purred at him and flopped on his back.

Ryder swiped his hand across the fogged mirror so he could see his reflection. His body hadn't changed under Liam's hands. He was still lean and strong, with narrow hips and bare, soft skin between his legs. He was still smooth with tight muscles, and had the angled face of a Wolfe.

Now that he'd noticed it, he'd never be able to unsee his black eyes, his darkness. The necromancer in him had risen to the surface.

When he checked his phone, he had a message from Christy.

Bring beer tomorrow. And maybe the truth.

Ryder rolled his eyes.

He'd bring the beer.

Chapter Three

PERCY CURLED UP on his chest, but Ryder barely slept. He stared at the ceiling and scratched behind Percy's ears while the symbol on his hip continued to throb, reminding him that Liam had carved it there and drank his blood and watched him steal life from the plant under the window, and kissed him anyway.

His phone never rang.

Liam didn't knock on the door in the middle of the night, but Ryder hoped he might.

The only unexpected visitor was a jet-black crow who tapped on his bedroom window with an equally jet-black beak.

"River?" Ryder sat up, and Percy jumped off the bed to investigate. "What're you doing here?"

Jordan's familiar, River, cawed and tapped again. He ruffled his feathers and held up one foot, where a crimson ribbon was tied around it, holding a tiny cinched bag.

Ryder opened the window and held out his arm. "You're heavy," he said softly, sagging under River's weight. "What'd she send me?"

River nudged Ryder's cheek with his beak and nibbled on his ear. Percy yowled from the floor, winding around Ryder's ankles.

The note said:

Careful. It's sharp.
-J

Ryder waved toward his altar and the candles lit. He huffed a laugh when River walked up his arm to settle on his shoulder. "I've never seen one of these in person," he whispered, dropping the contents of the bag into his palm.

The silver reaver was slender and sharp. It fit over Ryder's index finger easily, armored like scales across his digit and pointed at the tip like a blade. Every necromancer had one of their own—a small, concealable accessory that could be used as a tool or a weapon.

He curled his finger and stretched out his hand. The metal was cool and grounding against his skin. River cawed at him, nuzzled his temple, and hopped onto the windowsill. A second later, River was gone.

"So, this is it," Ryder said. He glanced at Percy and shrugged. "I thought they only gave these to people after they were brought back."

Percy looked up at him and yawned.

Ryder slid the reaver off his finger and set it on his altar next to an almost burned-out candle. He sent a quick text to Jordan. *Thanks. Am I allowed to have this if I haven't gone through the ceremony?*

Our little secret.

Ryder had too many secrets, but one more wouldn't hurt.

THE NIGHT WAS charged with eerie newness. It clung to Ryder like a second skin and emerged all around him as he walked down the dirt road that led to Tyler's house, tucked away on the north end of the woods.

A full moon in Pisces meant aloofness and creativity. It also meant emotions, too many of them. They slipped around him like fish out of water, turning his thoughts back to the night before when he'd played with dark magic in his bed with Liam.

He fiddled with the reaver in his pocket and tilted his head back to look at the sky. Far away from the lights, on the outskirts of Port Lewis, the stars looked brighter next to the orange-stained moon above the treetops. These woods had seen sacrifices and death, Darbonne rituals and Thistle séances. They'd welcomed Lewellyn conclaves and went silent in the presence of cloaked Wolfe alchemists. He wondered if they knew what to do with a half-blood like him. He wondered if the trees could see his bloodline, how convoluted and ancient it was. If they knew where the boundaries blurred inside him. Fire burned in his bone marrow and stampeded through his veins. But darkness festered everywhere else.

The trees whispered around him in a different language, too otherworldly to be understood. He wondered if they knew the answer to all his unspoken questions.

If he died and came back, would his fire go out?

Could he burn away the darkness in him? Did he want to?

Voices sounded from Tyler's property. He saw sparks from the fire pit outside rise into the air. Shadows gathered around it, other young witches from clans across the Pacific Northwest. Some came to be surrounded by their own, others had moved to Port Lewis after Thalia ascended as the Darbonne clan matriarch. He didn't know many of them, but he still nodded to them as he walked by.

Tyler's one-story house was shabby and old, sitting on two acres that disappeared into the forest in every direction. The same tired, rusted car was in the middle of the pasture behind the house, yards away adjacent an abandoned barn they used exclusively for spirit board sessions.

Ryder walked through the open front door. Christy glanced at him from the couch and tilted her head toward the kitchen. Give me a sec, she mouthed. He weaved through groups huddled close to the walls, holding the six-pack of cold beer by his side. The kitchen faced the living room, next to a wide hallway that led to four bedrooms and two bathrooms. Tapestries hung on the walls, portraits of deities and energy grids, amid framed photographs and family trees. Ryder opened a beer for himself and put the rest in the fridge. He watched Christy meditate with a group of pretty girls, until one of them opened her eyes and blurted something in a different language. Christy had been working on her channeling skills for a while, but Ryder had never seen anything come of it until then.

The girls clapped and sighed, patted and cooed. Ryder could taste their energy, the purity of it. He continued to fiddle with the reaver, tucked deep in his pocket.

"Hey," Christy said. She eyed him with caution, as if he might grow fangs and snap at her. "You okay?"

"I'm fine. Why wouldn't I be?" Ryder sipped his beer and glanced around, hoping no one else could hear their conversation.

"I'm psychic," Christy hissed. Her hair was bundled into a colorful braid and a flower tiara sat atop her head like she was royalty. "You and Liam tethered. I felt it yesterday, and you didn't tell anyone, and I want to know why. What's going on with you two?"

"Nothing is going on. We tethered, yeah, over a stupid fucking reading that no one needs to worry about, all right? It's fine. We're working it out."

"What cards did you pull?"

"That's none of your business."

Christy pinched her small mouth. Her brow furrowed, and her energy prodded his thoughts.

"Stay out of my head," Ryder bit. His magic pushed back against her, hot and dangerous. Steam filled his throat, but he swallowed it down. "This isn't a circle problem; it's an us problem."

Liam's voice cut through their conversation. "You're here."

Ryder glanced from Christy to Liam, who stood just outside the kitchen, leaning against the wall.

"Liam will tell me," Christy said.

"We're dating." Liam sighed as he spoke. His shirt was pale blue and riddled with moth-eaten holes, and his jeans hung low on his hips like they always did, dark-washed and torn in the knee. "I pulled The Lovers."

Christy whipped around to look at Liam before she turned toward Ryder again. "And you tethered?"

"Yes," Liam snapped. "That's the big secret."

"Tyler doesn't think dating within a circle is a good idea." Christy eyed them both.

Ryder didn't know what to say. Heat flooded his cheeks and steam manifested behind his teeth. He kept his eyes averted to the floor in case they turned black. He didn't need a room full of witches pointing their magic at him, especially when he barely had control of his own.

"Don't tell Tyler then," Liam sang through a tight, sarcastic grin.

Christy tossed her braid over her shoulder and heaved a sigh. "It's just the full moon," she deadpanned, jumping back into her usual charm and positivity. "Everyone is really emotional right now, and I'm being a bitch. Just—" She flapped her hand at them. "—ignore me."

A couple of other people slid into the kitchen to pour shots. Christy smiled at Ryder, half-apologetic, half-suspicious, and floated back to her group of light-workers, the tail of her white dress fluttering behind her.

Ryder could barely breathe.

Liam closed his fingers around his wrist and pulled. He stumbled down the hallway after him, focus stolen by Liam's tight grip. His pupils dilated, and he squeezed his eyes shut, willing the charcoal that spread over his irises and fanned across his pupils to subside. It didn't.

"In here," Liam said.

Ryder let Liam push him into one of the bathrooms. The door shut. Ryder's heart raced. His stomach flipped and churned. When he opened his eyes, Liam was looking back at him. He exhaled a deep breath and steam poured from his mouth.

"You're okay," Liam whispered. He placed one hand on Ryder's cheek. The other rested low on his neck, thumb following the line of his jaw. "Breathe. Don't let it control you."

Ryder sucked in a deep breath and exhaled again. Steam dampened his lips and chin.

The bathroom lights were off, and Ryder was thankful Liam hadn't turned them on. The darkness let things be still. It shrouded them, contained them, softened by slivers of light that slipped beneath and around the bathroom door. Ryder could still see Liam's expression, the movement of his eyes and part of his lips. Laughter erupted from the bedroom next door. The house was filled with chatter and shouts. Loud, grimy electronica with a heavy, slow bassline rattled the air. Liam's hands on his face were gentle and steady.

Ryder reached past Liam and locked the door. "We're dating?"

"I had to say something," Liam growled.

Ryder snorted and rolled his eyes.

"You okay?" Liam kept hold of Ryder's face. Solid, fluid magic poured from his palms. Water flowed through Ryder, easing the tension that warred under his skin.

He caught the distinct outline of a small Band-Aid on Liam's neck.

"Since when have you been this affectionate?" Ryder teased.

"Since I've needed to calm down an unstable necromancer in our best friend's bathroom," Liam said, a low grate to his voice that Ryder recognized as impatience. His tongue ran along the back of his teeth. Ryder listened to the click-clack, click-clack of his tongue ring. "Are you okay?" he repeated, more pointedly. The hand on Ryder's neck fell to his waist and drifted under his shirt, fingertips tracing the symbol on Ryder's hip.

"I'm fine. It's just the moon," he said, mocking Christy in a swoony voice.

"Yeah, it's just the moon," Liam agreed. He sounded winded and sore, unlike Liam in a way that was very Liam after all.

Ryder felt Liam's heartbeat through the palm cupping his cheek. He tasted his magic, volatile and salty and alive. He wanted to kiss him. He wanted Liam to dig his fingernail into the cuts on his hip and break them back open. He wanted to be in control of something, anything. He wanted to make Liam moan and writhe and say his name.

"Did you set intention for tonight?" Ryder asked.

The darkness was thick around them. The full moon party went on outside the door, a cacophony of shouts and laughter and music.

Liam leaned back against the door. His hand fell away from Ryder's face, but the other stayed put on his hip, fingertips drifting back and forth, up and down, across one line, over another. "I did," he said. "But I don't think it'll matter."

"Why's that?"

"Because there's no going back now."

Ryder felt the sharp edge of the reaver against his finger. He withdrew his hand and slipped it on.

Liam held his breath. His gaze stayed pinned to Ryder's hand. Even in the darkness, it was easy to spot the silver pointed talon—a necromancer's blood-spilling tool. Liam didn't move when Ryder slid his clawed hand under his shirt; he just shifted his eyes to Ryder's face and waited.

Ryder scraped the tip of the blade lightly along the lines of Liam's stomach. He dipped it in the hollow beneath his hipbones, dragged it between each rib and over his sternum. Liam's eyes closed and he gasped, pushing against Ryder's hand. He stashed the sound of Liam's breath gusting from him away, memorizing the lift of his chest, the flutter of his eyelashes.

Someone banged on the door. Liam jumped and flinched when the reaver caught his skin.

"You done in there?" Another bang. "C'mon, hurry it up."

Ryder shoved the reaver back in his pocket, flicked on the light, and glanced at himself in the mirror. Normal eyes. Flushed. *Whatever, fuck it.*

"Ry," Liam hissed. He scrambled to grab Ryder's hand, but Ryder opened the door and slipped past him, sending Liam stumbling backward into the hallway.

The person who'd interrupted them said, "Hey, whoa, sorry guys."

Ryder grabbed the beer he'd left on the kitchen counter and darted through the living room toward the front door. He felt Christy's energy before he saw her. She ducked out of his way, a flurry of questions on her face. Her magic formed another shield. He glanced at her and shook his head, silently telling her to let it be.

A few of the white witches who had been channeling with her on the couch squeaked and gasped. One clutched her chest. Someone said, "Did you feel that?" Another replied, "That's dark magic. Who...?"

Ryder fled. He walked straight to the fire pit outside and focused on it, gathering enough energy to pull a patch of flames into his palm. He danced the glowing, sparking energy between his fingers in one hand. Other witches watched, either enamored or impressed or jealous.

He didn't need their envy or approval, he needed a distraction.

"No parlor tricks, Ryder," Tyler shouted from a bench he shared with Donovan. "You know the house rules."

The flame expanded before it fizzled out in his palm.

He flipped Tyler off, which earned him a lungful of laughter, and stalked around the side of the house. A couple made out beneath a window. Someone smoked a joint. A few people were doing a reading, encircled in burning white candles.

He dipped under the wire fence that divided the house from the rest of the property and walked through the yellow grass to the old rusted car. It'd been there for years, a junky mesh of metal, looming on its own in the middle of the pasture, at least half a football field away from the party and the partygoers. His muscles loosened as he put space between himself and the conjoined energies of so many witches. The voices from outside the house faded, along with the music and drums. He sipped his beer, and turned his reaver over in his palm like he had the flame.

Breathe. Ryder took a heavy, deep breath. He couldn't keep this secret for long. It would show itself in one way or another, in violence or blood or a burst of nervousness. He'd been keeping it for too long already, and now that it'd crept out, there was no way to force it back in.

The hood of the abandoned car faced the forest with the house behind it. Ryder sat atop it and looked at the sky. He replayed the sound of Liam's gasp again and again, and fished in the pocket of his coat for the maroon pouch he knew was there. Heat built low in his abdomen. He ignored it. Black magic tickled his throat. He ignored it. Ryder shrugged off his coat, hoping the bitter November air would cool him down. It helped, marginally.

"Give me something," Ryder whispered to the tarot cards as he shuffled them. "Anything."

Focus. He pulled the first card.

The Lovers.

"Fuck you." He shoved the card back into the deck. Shuffled. Shuffled. Shuffled.

C'mon. He pulled another card.

The Lovers.

Ryder fell back on the hood. There was no avoiding it or changing it or undoing it. He heard his mother's voice in his mind. *The cards never lie, sweetheart.* But the cards could lie. Sometimes they did lie. And this reading had to be a lie, because Ryder had wanted Liam for too long to be allowed to have him now. He blinked at the sky and picked out constellations, even as footsteps shuffled through the grass behind the car. Virgo. One step closer. Beetlejuice. Another.

"Pisces," Ryder said. He raised his arm and dragged it through the air, outlining where Pisces glowed against the night sky.

Liam leaned his hip against the car and nodded, arms folded tightly over his chest. "Where's Aries?"

Ryder pointed far to the left. "You can barely see it, but it's over there."

Liam hummed. He tapped on the deck next to Ryder. "What'd you draw?"

"What do you think?"

Liam's caramel eyes stayed pinned to Ryder. His hair was pushed off his face, and Ryder had a hard time not looking at him. He swallowed and kept staring at the sky instead, hoping his feigned disregard would be enough to send Liam back to the party.

"Was everything you said last night true?" Liam picked up the deck and shuffled it.

Ryder chewed on his bottom lip. "Does it matter?"

"Yeah." Liam flicked the card he'd drawn. It landed on Ryder's chest. "Especially when I can't pull a single card other than that one."

Ryder held it up. The Lovers. He slammed it down on top of the maroon pouch.

"Last night was circumstantial," Ryder said softly.

"For you or for me?" Liam's arms fell by his side. He moved to stand in front of Ryder's bent legs.

Ryder's nostrils flared. He closed his eyes and shook his head. "For you."

A hand circled Ryder's wrist and pulled him upright. The tip of his nose brushed Liam's cheek and their mouths hovered inches apart, breath warm in the autumn air. The full moon shone down on them, urging their magic to stitch together, to tangle and twist.

"We tether, I do blood magic with you, I kiss you, what more proof do you need?" Liam snapped the words close to Ryder's mouth.

Ryder swallowed hard. "I don't need anything..." Liam's hand on his leg stole the rest of what he wanted to say. The press of his fingers on the inside of Ryder's thigh was senseless and dizzying. The way Liam pushed until he opened his knees and slid between them caused the heat swelling low in Ryder's gut to pulse.

Liam's eyes narrowed. "What do you want then?"

That was a loaded question. Ryder wanted an absurd number of things, most unreachable, some in front of him. He wanted to get rid of his dark magic almost as much as he wanted to play with it. He wanted to set a fire inside Liam, and ask the trees if they could answer the riddle of his existence, spend more time with his sister and learn Latin. He wanted to be what he was without question or doubt. But mostly, Ryder wanted Liam, so he closed the space between them and kissed him.

It turned into Liam's hands under his shirt, and Ryder's hands on Liam's face, pulling him closer. They kissed like they had hours before, after their magic had calmed and the night was still—unburdened and deep and breathless. Liam was an exceptionally good kisser. Ryder had heard he was, but it was different being on the receiving end of his teeth and lips and tongue. He kissed slowly, like time was an irrelevant onlooker simply waiting for them to finish.

Ryder didn't think he'd ever finish kissing Liam. His thumb traced the seam of their mouths and he tried to steady his breathing, inhaling what Liam exhaled.

Liam dug his fingers into his ribcage and Ryder moaned, soft and encouraging between the parting of their lips.

"Tell me where I can touch you," Liam said against his mouth. His hand drifted over the top of his jeans, and slid between Ryder's legs, waiting.

Yes. Ryder nodded. *Touch me.*

"You have to tell me."

Desire pooled in his wrists and legs and kneecaps. Ryder's body begged him to keep going. "Fuck, just—yeah, yes, but I'm not, I don't—"

"Yeah, I know, I get it." Liam pinched Ryder's bottom lip between his teeth. "Just tell me to stop if I do something wrong, okay?"

"You have to start to stop, Princess." Ryder's hips canted, and Liam pressed the heel of his palm down, rubbing Ryder through his jeans. Distantly Ryder thought, *he knows.* He clutched the back of Liam's head with one hand and held himself on the car with the other. "Fuck, we're really doing this?"

Liam's hand was gone for a second, before he flicked the button open on Ryder's jeans, and slid his palm under the waistband of his briefs.

Heat rushed into Ryder's cheeks. He'd been touched before, but not in a while, and not by anyone he cared about. He'd had meaningless hookups after too many drinks, and one-night-stands with other witches. But Liam was different.

Ryder rolled his hips when Liam's fingers pressed against him, warm and careful. There was a moment of hesitation. Liam's hand stilled and his eyes narrowed, lips parting in something close to surprise, but not quite. Ryder chewed on his bottom lip and nodded, and Liam didn't stop. His back hit the hood when Liam pushed him down against it, and he opened his mouth when Liam kissed him, welcoming another hot breath and the smooth tease of Liam's tongue ring. Ryder moved against Liam's nimble fingers, his touches sure and firm, but they were gone too soon.

He didn't know what to say, if he should say anything at all, but before he could catch his breath, Liam's teeth sank into his throat, then his collarbone.

Liam crawled down Ryder's body, lips and teeth leaving a trail of vibrant bruises wherever they stopped. He pushed Ryder's shirt up and kissed his chest, bit the curve of his ribs and sucked hickeys on his stomach. When he made it to Ryder's hips, he was on his knees. It happened quickly. First, he was choking back a whimper while Liam chewed on his hipbone. Second, he was lifting his hips and Liam was tugging his jeans down. Third, he was arching off the hood of the car, gasping with his eyes squeezed shut.

The full moon beamed down on them and glowed on Ryder's skin. He felt it in the heat throbbing between his legs, in Liam's arm across his waist, in the softness of his mouth, hot and perfect, around Ryder's clit. He tried to keep quiet, but it was no use. Liam's tongue was clever and quick, and when his fingers slid inside him, Ryder cried out.

"Don't stop," Ryder sobbed, embarrassed by the weakness of his voice. He dug his fingernails into the back of Liam's skull and held him there, open mouthed and on his knees, taking Ryder's magic and body apart with the curl of his fingers and stroke of his tongue.

Liam's fingers twisted. He moaned against him—into him—and Ryder couldn't have dreamed a sound like that.

Desire coiled tight in Ryder's abdomen. Magic sped through him, around him, on top of him. A breath shattered the night—fast and whimpered and quivering, before warmth spread from the base of his spine into each of his limbs. It shot through his stomach, into his lungs and throat. Everything shook apart. Everything came together.

Steam gusted the air in front of Ryder's mouth and he went boneless beneath the light of the full moon. He stared at the night sky and counted each breath, three seconds in, three seconds out. His orgasm lingered, drawn out by Liam's persistent mouth, made painful, then wonderful, then painful, then blinding.

"Okay, okay," Ryder hissed, shifting his thighs off Liam's shoulders.

Liam slid up Ryder's body and set his hands on either side of Ryder's shoulders. His mouth was slick, lips swollen and overworked. "Why didn't you tell me?" he whispered.

"You didn't care two seconds ago," Ryder mumbled.

Liam's grin was sharp and playful. He shook his head and stifled a laugh. "I don't, but—"

"But nothing." Ryder pulled on the nape of Liam's neck until he leaned down to kiss him. Ryder tasted himself and smoke and power in Liam's mouth. "Now you know," he said, and dragged his lips across Liam's cheek. His hand snaked between them, over Liam's stomach, between his legs. Ryder gripped him through his jeans.

Liam's hips rocked forward, gasp muffled against Ryder's neck.

A voice echoed from the fence. "Ry? Liam?"

Of course, it was Tyler.

A frustrated groan drifted over Liam's lips. His dark lashes fluttered and he heaved a sigh. "We'll be right there," he called and pawed Ryder's hand away so he could stand up.

"You're like a well-trained puppy," Ryder said. He tugged his pants back up, and shoved his hands in his pockets, fiddling endlessly with the cold edge of his reaver. "We don't have to run whenever he calls, you know."

"Would you rather him come find us?"

Ryder blinked at the ground. He was still wet and pulsing between his legs. His hands still shook, his knees were still weak. He touched his neck with two fingers where Liam had bit him.

"Glamour it," Liam said. He bumped his shoulder against Ryder's and nodded toward the house. Music still thrummed in the air. People still beat on drums. The full moon was still high in the sky. Everything was up in the air, answerless and daunting.

"Why didn't you glamour yours?" Ryder grabbed his deck and beer and shrugged on his jacket.

Liam glanced over his shoulder as he paced toward the house. "I tried."

"And?"

"It didn't work. Water magic isn't used to cover things, you know that. Glamour isn't my specialty."

Ryder stayed quiet. He stitched a sheet of magic over his neck where the marks from Liam's teeth were, and slipped under the wire fence when Liam held it for him. Most of the partygoers had disappeared, but a few remained. A couple of girls pounded the smaller drums. The shouts and laughter had faded into soft chatter and lingering spell-work.

Tyler stood by the fire. He nodded to Ryder and Liam as they approached.

"We need to talk," Tyler said. He didn't seem angry, but worry flashed across his face. His gaze shifted around cautiously, from one person to the next. "My room."

They followed him inside. Christy stood up from the couch where she was surrounded by psychics and mediums. One of them, a girl with short pink hair, stared at Ryder, wide-eyed and skittish. Christy trailed after them through the last door on the left at the end of the hall. Donovan sat cross-legged on Tyler's bed, his auburn hair arranged messily, wearing a black hoodie and jeans. He picked at a bit of green nail polish on his thumb and heaved a sigh.

"Did you tell them?" Donovan asked. His gaze flicked from Christy to Tyler.

Tyler closed and locked the door. "There's a darkling here, or there was."

Ryder bristled. "You mean a necromancer?"

"A dark witch. One of Christy's light-workers felt black magic earlier, a lot of it. We don't know if it was a necromancer or not."

"Could've been me," Ryder said and shrugged. Liam's eyes widened, but he stayed silent. "I saw Jordan last night for a while. Everyone knows darkling energy sticks around."

"Yeah," Christy interrupted. She leaned toward Ryder from a few feet away. Her nostrils flared. "You smell like her—like you're covered in blood."

"She smells like Cartier, actually. But yeah, I get it. Could've just been residual energy." Ryder fiddled with the reaver in his pocket, passing it across his palm, feeling the tip with his finger. "Where'd you even hear that term, Tyler?"

Tyler's brow furrowed. "It's common in the Thistle clan. I heard them using it at Thalia's ascension when..."

"When the Wolfes showed up?"

The air thickened. Tyler's Air magic stirred uncomfortably. Donovan looked at his lap and Liam's gaze fluttered toward the walls, covered in scribbled spells and shelves filled with crystals—celestite, amethyst, apophyllite, selenite. Tyler's altar was clean and orderly on his nightstand beside the bed. The pale gray candles there flickered and sparked.

"Can we not fight, please?" Christy whined. She pulled the lace cuffs of her long-sleeves into her palms and twisted them.

"Who's fighting?" Ryder snapped. His magic flared, urging him on. "I'm not fighting."

"Ryder," Liam warned lowly.

"What's up with you, Ryder? They're darklings, they syphon energy, they practice unnatural magic. I'm sorry your babysitter's one of them, but it's the truth." Tyler's magic whipped the tension around. "They're thieves. They steal energy to redistribute it and they break every rule in the book when it comes to magic, you can't honestly—"

Ryder's pupils expanded across the whites of his eyes. He cut himself on the reaver in his pocket and winced. Anger turned his magic into a primal, vicious force. It ripped through him, fast and explosive. "I can't what, Ty?" His voice deepened. Screams and howls echoed underneath it. Steam leaked from his lips.

Control never had been one of Ryder's finer gifts.

Liam placed his palm on Ryder's stomach and gave a little push, urging Ryder behind him.

Tyler stumbled backward. Donovan pressed himself in the corner on Tyler's bed. Christy's lips thinned, as if she'd had an inkling and it'd just been confirmed.

"You?" Tyler spat. His eyes widened and he heaved in a deep breath. "Since when?"

"Ty, let it be," Liam hissed.

"Since birth!" Ryder's eyes stung. His hands balled into fists. "Jordan's my sister, by the way. She's not some..." His voice calmed, but something haunting still echoed around each word. "Twisted, unapproachable thing."

"You lied?" Tyler's voice sounded like a crack of thunder. His magic gusted between their bodies and blew the candles out on his altar. "You're not a Lewellyn?"

"You've met my mother; you know I'm a Lewellyn."

Christy inched toward the locked door. "His father is Gerard Wolfe," she whispered. "He practiced blood magic..."

Ryder whipped toward her. "Get out of my head, Christy."

"You knew about this? You..." Christy looked Liam up and down. Tyler's gaze followed.

Liam swallowed hard. "Everything happened really fucking fast, okay? I found out last night. But it doesn't change anything, we're still circle-mates. Everybody needs to cool it." He pushed harder on Ryder's abdomen. "You too."

Opal's white wings flapped outside Tyler's window. She screeched and pecked at the glass. Liam glanced at Ryder, then at the window. He asked questions with his eyes that Ryder didn't have the answers to.

Outside the door, partygoers went quiet. *Do you feel that? Dark magic. It's coming from Tyler's room.*

"Ty?" someone called.

Ryder warned Tyler with his narrowed, pitch-black eyes.

Christy's hand hovered over the doorknob.

"Don't," Donovan said quietly from the bed. "I mean... It's not... Thalia's dating a necromancer, isn't she? This is old world shit, guys."

"Calling necromancers 'darklings' is old world shit," Ryder snapped. "And she's dating my sister, so yes."

Power flooded the house. It happened within seconds. Ryder was snarling at his friends with Liam in front of him one instant, then he was listening to Thalia's sharp voice scold someone as she made her way down the hall.

"Let me handle this," Thalia growled. Her power surged. It made Ryder dizzy.

"Move."

Jordan's energy rushed in before she did. Black smoke leaked under the door. Christy moved back in enough time to dodge it as it was flung open. She floundered to the other side of the room and huddled on the bed with Donovan.

Tyler shriveled from the tall, cloaked woman with black fog whipping around her feet. He glanced once at Ryder, accusatory and unnerved.

Jordan raked her gaze from Ryder to Tyler. Her eyes were jet black. When she exhaled, steam dampened her chin.

"Are you all right?" Jordan asked softly, her hand outstretched toward Ryder. Her voice was as haunting as his, but more, somehow. The voices of everyone she'd ever killed and brought back stained her.

"What're you doing here?" Ryder hissed. "I'm fine!"

"You're not," Jordan mumbled. She glanced at Liam. "Your familiar found River while Thalia and I were meditating in the woods. She's a good bird. Not scared of necromancers."

"She's been around one for two years," Liam said softly. His fingers curled into Ryder's jacket, trying to push him back more.

Thalia stepped into the room next to Jordan. "Secrets," she said to Ryder, the same way someone would say I told you so.

Ryder looked at the floor. His eyes returned to their Lewellyn green, but his hands didn't stop shaking. He touched the top of Liam's hand and Liam's fingers laced through his, giving a slight squeeze.

"Are you scared?" Jordan hissed at the three huddled on the bed.

"Jordan," Thalia scolded.

"What?" Jordan's teeth snapped down and more steam trickled over her lips.

"Yes," Thalia droned, "of course they're scared."

"We're not evil." Jordan's magic lunged for them, twisting and bending above their heads. The heaviness of it almost made Ryder nauseous. He couldn't imagine how the others were handling it.

Thalia set her hands on Jordan's shoulders and gave a gentle push. "Take those two," she said calmly, nodding toward Ryder and Liam, "and I'll handle this."

"He's my little brother," Jordan seethed at Tyler. "Remember that."

Thalia's knuckles whitened as she pushed on Jordan's shoulders again, straining against her.

"Jordie," Ryder groaned. "Just stop. C'mon, I need a ride home."

Jordan pursed her lips. The black fog that circled her feet dissipated, but her eyes were still pools of midnight. She curled her top lip back in a snarl, a shared gesture between the siblings, and her mouth spread into a wicked grin.

"Christy, is it? You're the Carroway girl?" Jordan asked.

Thalia's power swelled. Christy stayed silent, but her eyes went wide.

"Bet your mother didn't tell you I put breath back into her lungs four years ago, did she?" Jordan's voice was chilling and deathly cold. "It's always easy to look down on magic you don't understand until you need it."

"That's not your place!" Thalia's eyes glowed gold. She shoved Jordan backward and waved her arm toward the hallway. Jordan's magic was virtually unshakable, but so was Thalia's. When they collided, it sent a ripple through the air that Ryder felt in his bones. Thalia said, "I'll meet you at the loft in an hour." It was a command, not a question.

Jordan stomped away, but not before grabbing Ryder's arm and hauling him with her. Ryder's fingers slipped from Liam's grasp, but Liam followed nonetheless.

"Really?" Tyler blurted. "You're going with him?"

Ryder glanced over his shoulder. Liam answered by slamming the door.

"Good choice, fish," Jordan said under her breath.

Liam's cheeks darkened, but he simply sighed and walked close to Ryder as they exited the empty house. The other witches must've fled after feeling the rise and clash in Tyler's bedroom. He didn't blame them. Jordan and Thalia's arrival was enough, but mix that with his magic, Liam's, Tyler's, even Christy's white light, and it turned into a cocktail of energy that was too tense to swim through.

Cool night air hit Ryder's face. It tasted like 2 a.m. Too late to be considered morning, and too early to still be night. The witching hours were weighed down with finality, and yet nothing seemed final. Ryder felt as up in the air as he'd ever been.

"Here." Jordan searched the pocket of her hooded black trench and handed him a joint. The paper was decorated with tiny yellow pineapples, which brought a smile to Ryder's face. She caught the roll of his eyes and lifted her brows at him. "It'll help." Her eyes faded to their normal dark brown. "Trust me."

Opal landed on Liam's shoulder and screeched at Ryder.

River circled above them, cawing and cawing.

"Yeah, hi, Opal." Ryder glanced from the owl to Liam. He saw the conflict on Liam's face, strewn across his brow and present in the hard set of his shoulders. "You didn't have to come."

They walked side by side, dipping into the woods to trail after Jordan. The trees seemed to shift around them, huddling close to whisper to one another. Ryder wondered what they said, if it was *bone bender* and *darkling* over and over, or if they were talking about his future, if he had one at all. Moss climbed their trunks, and clusters of gray-capped mushrooms popped up between their knobby roots.

Liam's jaw slackened. He shook his head and looked from Ryder's scuffed black boots to his nose. "Seriously? Even after tonight you're still skeptical?"

"You went down on me on the hood of a car," Ryder said through a sigh. He pinched the joint between his teeth and inhaled. The tip sparked and smoke filled his lungs. "Don't give yourself that much credit."

A few steps ahead of them, Jordan threw her head back and laughed.

"Has wanting you all this time been a waste?" Liam asked quietly.

"Lovers' quarrels after I drop you off, please," Jordan said over her shoulder.

Ryder's gaze shot sideways. Liam didn't look at him, he just tipped his head back to look at the sky and kept walking.

Jordan: *You're so mean to him.*

Ryder: *I'm not.*

Jordan: *You are. Did he really go down on you on the hood of a car?*

Ryder: *Is that a serious question?*

Jordan: *If the answer is yes then you should probably keep him.*

Ryder: *Lots of people would go down on me on the hood of a car.*

Jordan: *But none would stick around.*

Ryder frowned at his phone.

Jordan: *Since you have such a winning personality and all.*

Ryder: *Fuck you. Thanks for tonight.*

Jordan: *Yeah yeah. You need to talk to Dad though.*

Ryder: *Later.*

He placed his phone on the kitchen counter and waited for the kettle to start whistling. Percy meowed at him from the couch, perched comfortably in Liam's lap.

"Do you want tea?" Ryder asked.

They hadn't turned on the lights. The plants curled and swayed in the presence of their magic, tame and tempered. After the outburst of energy at Tyler's, Ryder wasn't surprised to find his magic sated under his skin. Jordan's pre-rolled helped too. Liam stroked Percy's back and nodded.

He strained the tea leaves and poured two cups. Everything was silent but for Opal's soft coos and Percy's purring.

"Here." Ryder handed Liam a cup. "I'm taking a shower."

Liam sipped the tea and nodded.

"Are you staying?"

"Do you want me to?"

Ryder's stomach lurched. His lungs tightened painfully, but instead of dodging the question, he nodded. "Yeah."

Liam didn't look at him. He just kept petting Percy and stared down at his lap.

Ryder stalked into his bedroom before he could say or do anything else to ruin whatever they'd started. Had anything started? Or was everything a mess of circumstances coming together soon to be dismissed or forgotten? Liam was there, in his apartment. Liam was there, offering to stay, and still Ryder's uncertainty crept between them. He turned on the shower, prepped a fresh syringe, and stripped. The heat fogged the mirror, obscuring his reflection. He waved a hand into his bedroom and the candles lit, then the incense.

A deep breath later and he was sliding the needle into his thigh.

"Does it hurt?" Liam asked. His magic stirred the air before he did, but Ryder didn't bother turning around.

"Yeah," Ryder said. He pulled the syringe back, capped the needle, and opened the cabinet to drop it in a red container. Embarrassment nagged at him, which was ridiculous considering what they'd done. Ryder resisted the urge to glamour himself. "Just like any other shot does."

Liam's fingers dusted the wing of his shoulder blade. "Can I ask you something?"

"Yeah."

Lips touched his neck, faint and timid. "Did you mean it?" Liam's mouth traced the shell of Ryder's ear. "When you said you were in love with me, were you serious?"

"We're in a circle. We all love each other," Ryder said. A hot blush dripped across the bridge of his nose.

Liam hummed. His pants hit the floor, followed by the rest of his clothes. He nudged Ryder toward the shower. "That's not an answer."

The water was hot enough to turn Ryder's skin pink and make Liam flinch, but neither of them bothered to turn it to a cooler setting. Liam's hands rested on Ryder's hips, his chest pressed along Ryder's back. *Were you serious?* He didn't know what to say—if there was anything to say. Yes, he did love Liam. Yes, he had meant it. But after tonight, he didn't want to get into the details of it.

Instead, he took Liam's hand from its place on his waist and pulled it to his stomach, slid it over his bellybutton, past his hipbones, between his legs.

Liam's fingers pressed against him, rubbing in slow, teasing circles. He smiled against Ryder's throat. "Still not an answer."

Ryder chewed on his bottom lip. His back arched and he dug his fingernails into Liam's wrist, feeling the tendons flex every time he moved. His other hand was firm against the shower wall, head bowed and eyes closed. Liam's free hand coiled around Ryder's chest and settled low on his throat.

"Do you need an answer right now?" Ryder bit back a soft moan when Liam's index and middle fingers pressed hard against his clit.

Liam shook his head. The hand on Ryder's throat crept below his chin, and Liam pushed his head to expose the long line of Ryder's neck. He bit and kissed, sinking his teeth in deep when Ryder's hips rolled against his palm.

Ryder whimpered when he came. He gasped and his spine bent, fingers scrambling to clutch Liam's wrist.

His heartbeat was a symphony. Magic buzzed contentedly under his skin. Fuck, why hadn't they been doing this for weeks or months or years? Why hadn't they taken showers together, or been in bed together, or fucked on old rusty cars, until the week Ryder's dark magic decided to go haywire?

He craned away from Liam's teeth in his neck to turn around. Water dripped off Liam's eyelashes and the tip of his nose. It clung to his lips and beaded up on his shoulders. He looked beautiful covered in his element, glimmering and powerful and relaxed. His eyes were half-curtained, dancing around Ryder's face.

Somehow, the shower hadn't gone cold. Ryder pressed his hand flat against Liam's chest and forced him against the white tiled wall out of the water's reach. He kissed Liam hard, because he could, and because they were alone, finally. Liam's tongue dipped smoothly between his lips, stroking against his own and clicking against the back of Ryder's eyeteeth. It went on like that, with Ryder sucking on Liam's tongue, and Liam panting into his mouth, until he reached between them and wrapped his fingers around Liam's cock.

Liam's breath turned shaken and weak. The sound of it, labored inhales followed by quivering exhales, brought a coy smile to Ryder's face.

"What do you want?" Ryder asked.

Liam's hand rested on his cheek. His thumb slipped into Ryder's mouth, and he hummed appreciatively when Ryder flicked his tongue against it.

He kissed Liam's palm, leaned forward and kissed his lips, then dropped to his knees.

Liam traced Ryder's cheekbone, his jaw and bottom lip, and he sucked in a sharp breath when Ryder's mouth dragged along the underside of his cock. He tasted like the sea, like melted snow and fresh rain.

"Is this okay?" Liam gripped his chin and tugged him, pulling Ryder where he wanted.

Ryder glanced at him from under his lashes and gave a curt nod. Two of Liam's fingers pressed between his lips, and Ryder opened his mouth, sucking hard until his throat flexed.

"Do you know how many times I've thought about this?" Liam asked, voice low under the sound of water splattering the shower floor.

Ryder scraped his teeth across Liam's digits, kissed his hipbones, bit his inner thigh, and then closed his lips around Liam's cock.

A deep, gritted moan echoed in the shower. Ryder loved it. He loved the roughness, and the little bit of pain. He loved the weight of Liam in his mouth, the way his throat fluttered when Liam pushed on the back of his head. He watched Liam through his lashes and fought another jump in his throat when Liam's hips jerked and he slid deeper, grip tight on the nape of Ryder's neck.

He held onto Liam's legs and flattened his tongue, sucking hard whenever Liam pulled back and gave him room to breathe. Ryder's jaw was sore, but he didn't care. Liam's gasps and whines were clipped and breathy, softer than Ryder imagined they would be. He swallowed around Liam until his eyes watered, and pulled his magic to the surface. Heat filled his mouth, and Liam choked back another moan. He was slick between his legs, but he was too over-sensitive to touch himself.

"Fuck, Ry," Liam whispered. A low groan rumbled in his throat. He dug his fingernails into Ryder's skull, the only warning he was given before Liam pulled back and came on his face, across his mouth and jaw and cheek.

Ryder rested his forehead against Liam's hip and caught his breath. He felt used and dirty and light, the sexiest he'd ever felt. He closed his eyes when Liam's shaky hand stroked the back of his head, sighed when Liam thumbed come off the side of his mouth and cupped his face.

Liam had moved the water, bending it to his will until it lifted from the showerhead and poured down on them. It was lukewarm, verging on cold. Ryder pressed his lips to Liam's hip, kissed the tight skin stretched across his abdomen, and trailed his mouth to his chest and collarbones as he stood.

Liam's head was tilted back against the shower wall. His gaze rested on Ryder, lips parted, cheeks flushed, vulnerable in a way Ryder hadn't seen him before. Their small piece of the world was quiet, shadowed by a dark apartment and a darker magic, waiting for them to move or breathe or break it apart.

Ryder reached back to turn the shower off.

Liam leaned forward and caught his lips in a quick, fluid kiss.

There was still an air of caution between them. Their uncertainty watched from the corners, blinking from the darkness, waiting for the chance to convince one of them to flee. Ryder didn't know if the reading had pushed them to each other, or the darkness, or his long-term feelings, or Liam's hidden fondness.

Maybe they were just going through the motions like two people would when they'd been put in a situation like theirs.

Maybe it would pass and they'd stay friends, and never speak of it again.

They dried off and Ryder gave Liam a pair of clean briefs to wear for the night. Opal bounced into the bedroom and perched on the top of the vanity. Percy slept on the windowsill while rain pitter-pattered the glass.

Ryder stared at the ceiling as he lay in bed next to Liam. He felt eyes on him, but didn't have the courage to look. So much could be said in a glance, and Ryder didn't know if he'd say the right thing if he took the chance to gaze back at Liam after what they'd done together—to each other.

The quiet turned into the rhythm of Liam's soft breath as he slept, rain on the window, a breeze rustling the tree branches outside, and Ryder's magic stirring restlessly in his chest.

Chapter Four

SUNLIGHT BEAMED THROUGH the window. Sleep peeled off Ryder in layers. He inhaled a deep breath. The short hairs on the back of Liam's neck tickled his mouth, and his chest lifted and fell beneath Ryder's arm. Sometime while they slept, Ryder had fit himself against Liam's back, resulting in the tangle of their legs under the comforter and the dips of their bodies curving into each other.

Percy jumped on the bed in front of Liam and meowed. Liam stroked the cat's back lazily and hushed him. "You're so loud," he whispered, voice sleep-rasped and lulled. "Even Opal's quieter than you, Percy."

Ryder moved his hand from where it rested on Liam's sternum and scratched behind Percy's ear.

"Thought you might be awake," Liam said.

He pressed the bridge of his nose against the back of Liam's neck. "You sleep okay?"

Liam hummed. "Yeah, you're like a furnace, though."

His lips curved into a smile, and he pressed them against Liam's shoulder. "Fire witch, remember?"

"Necromancer," Liam corrected gently.

"Necromancer," he agreed, "but still Fire." He pressed his hand against Liam's chest and his magic pulsed, sending heat under Liam's skin.

"You did that last night," Liam mumbled, playfulness threaded through his words. He twisted around to face Ryder, expression hazy in the morning light. "Will you lose it if you…"

"Die?"

Liam's hand smoothed up Ryder's side and he nodded.

Ryder traced the lines of Liam's tattoo with his fingertip. A crashing wave, a set of swirling clouds. "I don't know. Jordan didn't know either."

"If you choose not to…"

"You can say it," Ryder bit. "Die. And I don't know what'll happen if I go through the ceremony. If I do it, one of my family members will slit my throat, bring me back, and I'll be declared a necromancer. If I don't, my magic will keep freaking out."

Liam's eyes narrowed. His thin mouth pressed down and his nostrils flared. Anger looked strange on Liam, like he was conflicted over the feeling itself. His fingers dug into Ryder's ribs. "I don't like thinking about your death, all right? What about the bloodletting? I thought that was supposed to help."

"It did—it will, but that won't stop my dark magic from surfacing. Look at what happened at Tyler's. I got mad, my dark magic took over, and now everything's fucked up."

"Not everything," Liam said. He tilted his head, bumping the tip of his nose against Ryder's. He went quiet for a moment, mouth open as if he grappled with what to say. "I've had to be careful with this," he confessed. He snaked his hand around Ryder's back. "I never drank around you, I never dated anyone for long, because I'd have to introduce them to the circle, and then they'd have to meet you." He paused to give a short laugh. "God forbid."

"I thought you didn't like commitment?"

"I didn't, I liked you."

"I've been staring at you for two years, and you're just now telling me this?" Ryder arched a brow. Liam's breath on his mouth made it hard to concentrate.

"Well-trained puppy, remember?" Liam's tongue darted across his bottom lip. "Tyler would've lectured me daily until we broke it off."

"He still might."

"I've had your blood in my mouth," Liam said nonchalantly, as if it dismissed their consequences. "And things weren't as simple as I thought they were. You aren't..."

"A white witch?" Ryder teased. He let his pupils expand, black pouring across his eyes.

Liam's breath hitched. His gaze flicked from Ryder's eyes to his lips. "No, you're definitely not."

"Speaking of blood in your mouth," Ryder whispered. His lips parted against Liam's. They kissed deep and slow, the kind of kissing that vibrated in him, wet and breathless and unhurried. Steam trickled between the parting of their lips.

Liam winced and pulled back, unable to inhale the steam without burning himself.

"Sorry," Ryder mumbled.

Liam shook his head and pressed closer, chest to chest. "Don't be," he said softly, leaning in to slot their mouths together again.

A loud knock splintered the silence, annoying, and halted whatever the morning had in store, more annoying.

Of course.

"Feel that?" Liam said through a sigh.

"Sure do." Ryder could recognize Christy's fluttery, positive energy anywhere. "Get dressed. I'll—" he flung an arm toward the door "—deal with this."

"Be nice to her," Liam said. He slid out of bed and gestured to the dresser. "Can I borrow something?"

"Go for it." Ryder didn't bother with a shirt. He grabbed his jeans on his way out of the bedroom and tugged them on. Percy paced behind him.

Willow was already inside. The little white mouse peered up at him in from the floor and wiggled her nose, beady red eyes flashing from Percy to Ryder and back again.

"It's a little early," Ryder said to Willow.

Her whiskers bounced and she sat on her haunches to clean her face.

Ryder pulled the door open to find Christy on the porch with her hands clutched tightly in front of her. She blinked at Ryder and her brows drooped, lips pulled back in a grimace.

"What're those...?" She glanced at his chest.

Ryder reached for his magic and stitched a glamour across his scars. The curved pink marks faded. "You've never seen a hickey?"

Christy huffed an annoyed sigh. "You don't have to glamour for me, Ry. It was just a question. I know what those are." She jabbed one of the mouth-shaped bruises on his stomach with her finger.

"It's a question I'm not answering. Hi, good morning, what're you doing here?"

"Good afternoon," she corrected. Her hair was bundled into a thick bun on the back of her head, and an assortment of protective pendants hung around her neck, dangling over a strappy pink top. "Can I come in?"

"Liam's here."

"I know," Christy said pleasantly.

Ryder held the door open and Christy walked inside. She cleared her throat, glancing from one end of the tiny living room to the other.

"Tea?" Ryder asked.

"That'd be nice." She knelt and held out her hand for Willow to climb into. "How are you today? Are things... better?"

"I'm not going to kill anyone," Ryder said. He filled the kettle and set it on the stove. "And even if I did, I could bring them back if I tried hard enough."

Christy's energy was a thin bubble around her, protective and bright. "Yeah, I guess you could, huh?"

Ryder handed her a cup filled with ginger tea. Their fingers brushed and she winced. An image flashed behind Ryder's eyes—Liam's tan torso stretched in front of him, dripping wet, and Ryder's mouth climbing his stomach.

"That's not something I ever needed to see," Christy sang. She stepped back and closed her eyes, gesturing between them with a flick of her wrist. "I'm psychic, you syphon energy, that means—"

"Yeah, I get it. That was an accident." His cheeks burned hot. He nodded toward the couch. "What'd Thalia say last night?"

Christy heaved a sigh. She sat on the couch but left space between them, her on one end, him on the other. "I didn't come here to talk about what Thalia said; I came here to apologize to you, and if I get started on something else I won't be able to stop talking about it, so first off, I'm sorry." She took a deep breath and stared at the couch cushion between them. "This can't be easy for you, and all your friends just..."

"Freaked out?"

"Yeah," Christy breathed.

"Not all your friends," Liam said. He walked out the bedroom and into the kitchen.

"You did a little bit." Ryder glanced over his shoulder to get a glimpse of Liam wearing his clothes. The faded black band tee Ryder had owned since high school fit a little tight, but looked good on him. "There's tea if you want some."

Liam nodded and poured himself a cup. His bare feet padded the wood floors, as familiar as they always were. He rounded the side of the couch and set his hand on Christy's shoulder. "Hey," he said softly.

Another image blinded Ryder. It came and went, like a lightning strike or glass splintering. Ryder stretched across the hood of the car, shirt rucked up and his bare thighs over Liam's shoulders. The long line of his throat extended, his voice gasped and spent saying *don't stop*.

"Jesus fucking Christ—seriously?" Ryder hissed.

"Can you guys stop thinking about each other naked for two seconds!" Christy whined, squeezing her eyes shut.

Liam cocked his head, confused.

"Stop syphoning, Ryder! That's why this is happening. You're taking my energy and that's amplifying whatever images I'm pulling from you two—images that would normally be in the back of my mind where I can't see them!" Christy sipped her tea. Her face was three different shades of pink. She looked around the apartment instead of at the boys, and chewed on her bottom lip.

"What just happened?" Liam asked. He sat on the ottoman and glanced between Ryder and Christy.

"You gave Christy access to a memory of us having sex," Ryder said, voice clipped. There was no going around it or making it sound better. He shrugged one shoulder and lifted his brows.

Liam grimaced and his cheeks flared red.

"Yeah, on the car! Do you guys know how many people have had sex on that car? That's gross—you're gross," Christy groaned. She made a mock-disgusted noise and sipped her tea. "Anyway, I was in the middle of saying I'm sorry. Necromancers have a bad reputation, but that doesn't mean Tyler should've said what he did last night."

"What did Thalia say?" Ryder asked again. His gaze was pinned to the floor, but when he braved a glance up, Liam was looking back at him. His eyes flashed to the floor.

"And what did everyone else say?" Liam added.

"Thalia said we needed to be careful, and that we shouldn't jump to conclusions." Christy stared at her lap and pressed her legs tight together. "She also said that you have the potential to be dangerous..."

The room went quiet. Tension battled with anger beneath a thick layer of hurt. Ryder tried to steady his nerves, to rein in the disappointment from showing outright. But it was already there, and Christy was already fumbling over herself to make up for it, and Liam was already getting up from the other side of the coffee table.

"Ryder." Christy said his name sadly, pitifully. He hated it. "We'll figure this out. It doesn't mean that you are dangerous. I don't think you'd ever hurt us, and I don't think anyone would ever assume you'd—"

"You should go," Ryder said. His eyes stung. His throat was scratchy and tight.

"Ry, c'mon." Liam knelt in front of the couch. "Thalia's a matriarch, she can't sugarcoat things."

Christy placed her hand on Ryder's arm. He looked at her and she flinched back. "Sorry. No, Ryder, I didn't..."

"I scare you," Ryder hissed. He didn't know if he was crying or not, but his face was hot, everything was hot. His black eyes burned and his mouth quivered. He wanted to hide or run or rip something apart.

"You scare yourself," Christy whispered, surprised.

Ryder had barely felt the slide of her energy against his thoughts. "Stay out of my head!"

"Christy," Liam warned. "Maybe you should go."

"I didn't mean to... I'm just not used to your eyes, Ryder. It's..." Christy stood up and took a step back.

"Terrifying, I know," Ryder bit. Sarcasm filled his mouth along with a cloud of steam.

"I'll go," she said gently. "If you need anything, though..."

"I need you to tell me what the others said," Ryder interrupted.

Christy shifted from foot to foot.

Percy hopped onto Ryder's lap, bristled and wide-eyed. He rubbed against Ryder's chest and yowled at him, ears tucked against his skull like they always did when they shared emotions. Ryder inhaled a deep, long breath and stroked Percy's back, grateful for his familiar and the sudden redirection of his anxiety.

Liam rested his hand on Ryder's leg.

"Donovan thinks it's fine, and he wishes you would've told us sooner. Tyler..." Christy paused to gnaw on her bottom lip.

"Tyler what?" Ryder asked. He swallowed the lump in his throat and pawed at his face with the back of his hands. His cheeks were wet and Ryder's top lip curled, embarrassed that he'd let himself get worked up.

"Tyler was angry. He yelled at Thalia when he found out she'd known about you, and Thalia cut off his air supply for two minutes while she lectured him. It wasn't pretty. Tyler almost passed out. I left after that, but Donovan texted me and told me Tyler was still pissed."

"Thalia Sith choked him?" Ryder asked through a laugh.

Christy's head listed and she rolled her eyes. "Yes, asshole. She did. Will you guys meet me and Donovan for dinner tonight?"

Liam sighed. "Without Ty?"

Christy nodded.

"Sure, yeah, whatever, but I need to talk to my sister at some point about getting the other alchemists ready for the ceremony." Ryder stood up. He noticed Christy take another step back. He ignored it, but her fear still stung. "Where are we eating?"

"Archy's?" Christy offered timidly.

"Yeah, see you tonight." Ryder glanced at her.

She held eye contact with him for a moment, as if she wanted him to know she could. "Seven?"

Ryder nodded. Christy glanced at Liam before she closed the door. Her shoes smacked the concrete stairs as she barreled down them.

His friends were afraid of him. His circle-mates were afraid of him. Ryder rested his hands on the back of the couch and closed his eyes.

"You're doing it?" Liam asked.

"Yeah," Ryder said quickly. "I have to do something, don't I?"

"Dying isn't something."

"Jordan and my dad will bring me back."

"And if they can't? What if something goes wrong?"

"Then I stay dead," Ryder snapped.

Opal ruffled her feathers from the bookcase. Percy hissed.

Ryder tried to dip out of the living room, but Liam caught him by the arm in the hallway. His back hit the wall and steam gusted from him, lungs heaving as Liam grabbed both his wrists and slammed them above his head.

"That's not an option." Liam's voice was a tidal wave. It sounded like a waterfall crashed inside him. His brown eyes were gone, replaced by gray, ghostly orbs that stared at Ryder under a tense brow.

Black smoke coiled defensively around Ryder. It was the first time he'd ever conjured it, and it felt sticky and unmade, like time cracked apart as it drifted from under his feet. "Get off me."

"I'm not scared of you," Liam snapped.

Ryder tasted the words before he said them, bloody and thick. "You should be."

Liam's magic thrashed, a storm in Ryder's ears. His grip loosened on Ryder's wrists, but he didn't let go. They were too close. Liam's nose brushed his cheek, his breath smelled like ginger tea, but was unnaturally cold under the weight of his magic. A strand of dark hair fell over his brow and he exhaled sharply when the black smoke wrapped around his legs.

"I could hurt you," Ryder said.

"I'd let you." Liam leaned against him. His Water magic circled them, sinking into Ryder as he reached for it, beckoning it into his skin, his mouth, his lungs. He hadn't realized it until his heartbeat accelerated, and he thought back to Christy's shrill voice minutes ago. *Stop syphoning, Ryder!* The act of the spell came naturally, as if Ryder had been doing it for as long as he'd been breathing. The truth of practicing dark magic rushed to the surface.

No wonder people say it's addicting.

It felt like drugs—like snorting a line of coke, or smoking too much weed, or peaking on ecstasy. *Oh*, Ryder thought, *this is what it's like.* He pulled on Liam's magic until it sank into his bones, until it surrounded him, broken apart and pieced back together. He recognized every particle of it. The living, breathing essence of Liam expanded and compressed: mist on Ryder's face, the shock of an icy river, the comfortability of warm summer rain.

He pulled on Liam's magic, dug his claws in and sighed when it met the Fire inside him.

"Careful," Liam whispered. He dropped his hands. One rested on Ryder's face, the other gripped his hip. "Don't get greedy."

"I'll give it back," Ryder whispered. His voice was haunting and rich, unfamiliar even to himself. "What does it feel like?"

"Like you're inside me," Liam said.

Ryder's eyes fluttered closed. Heat flared at the base of his spine. "You can't say shit like that right now."

"It's the truth."

"I barely have control as it is," Ryder gritted.

"Let it go." Liam's lips dusted Ryder's mouth.

"I could kill you," Ryder seethed. He kissed Liam and pushed the magic back where it came from. It was charged and electrified and hot. It rushed between them, inhaled through a ragged gasp that Liam barely tried to contain. Ryder sank his teeth into Liam's bottom lip. "Don't you get that?"

Liam made a wounded sound, one that brought chills to Ryder's arms and made him ache low in his abdomen. He clutched Ryder and opened his eyes, their translucence gleaming and pretty surrounded by Ryder's black smoke.

The energy calmed. Ryder let out a breath. Liam rested his forehead on Ryder's shoulder.

"Feel better?" Liam asked.

"Yeah, you?"

"I was fine before, but I'm better now."

"I need to talk to Jordie." Ryder sagged against the wall, and Liam leaned heavily against him. "Because that—" He paused to sigh. "—is the dangerous shit Thalia was talking about."

"You're not dangerous," Liam whispered.

Ryder nosed at Liam's neck. "I felt your heartbeat," he said shakily. The echo of it lingered in his palms. "It was like I had my hand wrapped around it, like I could've pulled it right out of your chest if I wanted to."

Liam nodded.

"That's dangerous," Ryder repeated. He pushed on Liam's waist and slipped away from him. His hands trembled. His heartbeat stampeded. Adrenaline raced through him. His senses were heightened, making every creak in the apartment and rustle of Opal's feather sound closer. "Maybe you should talk to Tyler while I'm with Jordan."

Liam leaned against the doorframe of the bedroom with his arms folded across his chest. "Without you?"

"Yeah." Ryder put on a different pair of jeans and a black long-sleeved thermal. He watched Liam push his hair back, caught the restless flick of his eyes and twitch of his fingertips. They were both electrified, overdosed on magic. "He trusts you. He might listen."

"He trusted me," Liam corrected. "But yeah, I can give it a shot."

Ryder pulled a beanie over his ears. "I'll see you tonight."

Liam stepped in front of him when he tried to walk through the doorway. They were almost the same height. Ryder was an inch or two shorter. His gaze wandered over Liam's face, from the lingering blush on his cheeks to the fluctuation of his pupils, swelling and compressing over and over.

"Is the ceremony exclusive to alchemists?" Liam asked.

Ryder parted his lips. He considered the question carefully. "It's not something I'd want you to see."

"That's not what I asked."

"Then yes, it's exclusive," Ryder rasped.

He tried to step around Liam but was blocked again. Liam kissed him hard and deep. Ryder tilted his head and closed his eyes, relishing the weight and softness of Liam's mouth on his. He broke away and headed for the door a moment later. Percy followed by his feet.

Liam's voice sounded distant when he blurted, "You don't have to do this."

Ryder closed the door and headed down the stairs.

Chapter Five

RYDER HESITATED. HE stood on the porch of Gerard Wolfe's house, situated in a cookie-cutter neighborhood that overlooked the ocean. The air was lighter. It smelled of the sea and harbored an ever-present chill the Washington coast was known for.

The front door was painted dark red. A wind chime dangled from the overhang, jingling in a salty breeze. Ryder lifted his fist to knock but hesitated again.

This is my home. He closed his eyes. *Why am I scared of it?*

The door opened before he could knock.

"Hey, kid." Gerard's voice was warm and rough. He had the face of a Wolfe, so much like Jordan's, so much like Ryder's. His jaw was strong and his cheeks were dusted with faint freckles. Light, blonde hair was slicked back. He clasped a hand over Ryder's shoulder. "Were you gonna stand there forever?"

"I might've," Ryder said. His lips twisted into a smile. "Sorry."

"It's all right. I've been waiting for you to come inside for ten minutes, but your energy is a bit..." He tilted his head to the side, dark, golden eyes narrowed playfully. "Predictable."

"Is Mom here?"

"Yeah, Jordan too."

"I think..." Ryder inhaled a deep breath. He looked away from his father and shifted his weight from one foot to the other. "I went at this too fast. It's only been a couple days, but it's getting worse and worse."

"C'mon." Gerard tugged on his shoulder. "We'll talk inside."

The Wolfe household was just as he remembered. The wood floor was stained dark cherry, covered in throw rug after throw rug. High ceilings opened the space, highlighting a chandelier crafted out of antlers and portrait paintings framed on the wall. A staircase on the right led to the second floor, but they headed left toward the living room.

Jordan sat in front of a brick fireplace, wearing a ratty T-shirt and tattered blue jeans. River was perched on her shoulder, and Moon, Gerard's familiar, was coiled over her lap, around her arms and legs. Moon's tongue flicked out, tasting the air. She lifted her head and looked to Ryder, scales patterned prettily and tail red as ever.

"She's gigantic," Ryder said through a laugh. He grinned and his brows relaxed.

"Boas can get up to twelve feet long, she's only eight. Still got growing to do." Jordan pouted her lips at Moon. "Ellen's in the kitchen making coffee."

Ryder wrinkled his nose.

"Tea for you," Jordan added quickly. "Coffee for the rest of us."

"I'll help her bring the cups in," Gerard said.

Jordan waited for their father to slip into the kitchen before she pinned her gaze to Ryder and lifted her brows. "You've been syphoning. I can feel Liam's magic on you."

Ryder glanced over his shoulder. Anxiety hummed in him alongside the magic, Liam's magic and his Fire and his darkness. His nostrils flared and he tried to steady his breathing. "It was an accident."

Jordan narrowed her eyes. "Is he okay?"

"Yeah, he's fine. We're fine. But—"

"But it scared the shit out of you," Jordan snapped.

Ryder shuffled over to the fire and sat down beside her. Percy crawled into his lap and meowed at Moon. "I don't know what to do. One day I'm doing a reading with Liam, the next he's going down on me on the hood of a car and I'm sucking his soul out of his body. What the fuck, Jordan? What do I do?"

"For one, I hope you sanitized that nasty car—"

"Can you not, right now? Honestly?"

Jordan's full mouth split into a grin. "Most necromancers start to notice their magic early, but your Lewellyn blood must've put things off. This is normal, it's just happening at an inconvenient time."

"And at an accelerated rate." Ellen spoke like flowers bloomed, slowly, gently. She set a teacup on the table in front of Ryder and sat beside him on a patterned, colorful rug. Her skin was milky, and she had hair that turned gold in sunlight, but white under the moon. She ran her fingers along the side of Ryder's face. "You okay, sweetie?"

"Not sure," Ryder mumbled, hoping his mother hadn't heard any more of their conversation. "What does Margo think of this?"

"The Lewellyn matriarch has no say in it," Gerard interrupted. "You're a Wolfe."

"They don't have a say." Ellen's tone was soothing as she shot a stern glance at Gerard. "But they did offer their support. If you decide to do the ceremony, Margo will recognize it."

"What about my magic?" Ryder glanced between his parents. The flames sparked in the fireplace. He looked at the photos lined up across the mantel above it. He recognized one of him and Jordan from when they were small, wearing matching outfits. "And my circle?"

"Necromancers are solitary for a reason." Gerard leaned back on the couch and kicked his ankle over his knee. "I don't know how progressive things have really gotten with Thalia in charge of Port Lewis, but…"

"It'll take time," Jordan said. "But we haven't run into any problems yet."

"It's only been a few weeks, Jordie," Ryder whispered. "Tyler and his parents won't change, you know that."

"The Lis are purists." Ellen flapped her hand dismissively. "The world is changing around them and they're standing still. What does everyone else think? The Carroway girl, what's her name, Kelly?"

"Christy," Jordan piped. She grinned and poked Ryder's leg with her bare foot. "I didn't tell you—she sent me flowers yesterday. Flowers. With an I'm-sorry-thank-you note."

Ryder arched a brow. That was something Christy typically would do, but he didn't think she'd have the courage to go through with it. She didn't do well outside her comfort zone. As much as Ryder wished Christy would've apologized to Jordan face-to-face, the gesture warmed him.

"Christy, that's right. And Liam, the cute one," Ellen said. Her small nose twitched on her round, full face.

"The cute one," Jordan whispered, prodding Ryder with her foot. He swatted her.

"And the Were!" Ellen exclaimed. "How's he doing?"

"The what?" Ryder asked. "You mean Donovan? He's an Earth witch."

"Donovan Quinn?" Ellen blinked at Ryder, her wide green eyes upturned and clever.

Gerard cleared his throat. He shared a look with Ellen that spoke of secrets. "We should be talking about the ceremony, shouldn't we?"

"Yes, yes," Ellen said. She sipped her coffee and smoothed out the wrinkles in her long, colorful dress. "Have you been practicing, Ryder?"

Ryder nodded.

"With anyone?" Gerard asked.

Ryder swallowed hard. "Yeah, with a circle-mate."

"Bloodletting only?" Ellen's voice hardened.

He glanced at Jordan and she tilted her head, egging him on with a lift of her brows. Ryder whispered, "No."

"You syphoned someone?" Gerard scooted to the edge of the couch and set his elbows on his knees, pulling Ryder's attention. "I thought I felt Water magic, but I couldn't be sure. How badly?"

"It's fine, Liam's fine, it was quick and I ended it before it could get worse." Ryder felt Jordan scoot closer to him. Moon slithered onto his shoulder. "What will happen to my elemental magic after I die?"

Gerard and Ellen went quiet. Jordan's hand rested on his knee.

"Right. No one knows," Ryder mumbled. "That's great."

"You're a powerful Fire witch," Jordan said matter-of-factly. "I doubt it'll go anywhere."

"And what about Percy?" Ryder stroked Percy's back and she arched into his hand with a contented purr.

"Moon will handle that," Gerard said. "He'll be the first life you bring back. You know that. Your sister had to do the same with River."

Moon flicked her tongue at Percy and he meowed at her. The thought of Moon wrapped around him, squeezing the life out of him, made Ryder's throat clench and his chest tighten.

"When can we do this?" Ryder asked.

"As soon as tomorrow," Gerard said. "This is usually where I'd tell you to wait, take your time." He paused and exhaled a deep breath. "Think it through. But with how quickly things are happening, I think it's best if we do this now."

"Now as in tomorrow," Ryder whispered.

"Now as in before you kill someone."

The room went quiet again. Ellen held her breath. Ryder felt her eyes on him, tender and patient. Her Fire burned as hot as his, but when it warmed his skin he closed his eyes. Her magic had always been a lullaby.

He knew what he was capable of, but that didn't make anything easier. His phone buzzed in his pocket and he ignored it. It buzzed again, and he whispered a curse before digging it out.

Liam: *Tyler just needs time.*

Ryder: *I don't have any time. It's happening tomorrow.*

"Can you give me a ride to Archy's?" Ryder glanced at Jordan. "I took an Uber here."

"I would've picked you up," Jordan said. "But yeah, of course."

"We'll take care of you, Ryder." Gerard reached over to curl his thumb under Ryder's chin. "Jordan's a great teacher. You've got me and the rest of the clan behind you too."

Ryder nodded. He wanted to believe it—that everything would be all right, that his magic wouldn't rip him apart, that after the ceremony he'd be as confident in his abilities as Jordan was. But his nervousness made it impossible to be anything other than terrified.

He kissed Ellen on the cheek and hugged Gerard. Jordan did the same.

As they were walking out the door, Ryder heard his mother's voice, shaken and small. "Gerard, what if something goes wrong...? What if you can't bring him back?"

"We'll bring him back," Gerard assured her, a whisper he thought Ryder and Jordan couldn't hear. "I'll make a deal if I have to."

"We don't make deals," Ellen snapped.

Gerard hushed her.

Jordan tugged on Ryder's arm, pulling him out the door and into the driveway.

We don't make deals.

He replayed those words again and again as he slid into Jordan's old truck.

"Put your seatbelt on," Jordan said.

He put his seatbelt on.

Ellen's voice kept echoing in his mind. *We don't make deals. We don't make deals. We don't make—*

"It's not common," Jordan said, as if she'd read his thoughts. "But the rumors are true."

"You..." Ryder's heart raced fast in his chest. His head spun. Everything tilted. Nothing made sense. "Demonology? You make deals with demons?"

"I prefer to call them deities," Jordan said and stepped on the gas.

CHRISTY, DONOVAN, AND Liam sat in one of the red-upholstered booths that lined the window at Archy's Pizza.

Ryder watched them talk through the rain-streaked glass. Christy spoke with her hands, smashing her index finger against the table again and again. Donovan kept shaking his head. Liam chimed in once in a while, the force of his words bitten and harsh.

Jordan stood beside Ryder, leaning against the truck bed. "I'll make sure it goes okay," she said.

"By making a deal with a demon?"

"By asking for a favor. What do you think these are, Ry? Scribbles?" She held out her arm, covered in scarred sigils. "Some of them are spells, some are runes, but these..." She pointed to an intricate design on her wrist. "These are demonic. That doesn't make them more or less; it just makes them different. Like us."

"If I don't come back—"

"Don't," Jordan snapped. Her voice clashed with other voices.

Ryder exhaled sharply through his nose. "If something goes wrong—"

"I said don't," she seethed.

Downtown was crowded by umbrellas and scented with coffee, pumpkin spice, and vanilla. Uncomfortable silence swelled between them. A few people walked by on the sidewalk, chatting pleasantly about a movie they'd just seen, others hurried to their cars or dipped into cafés. Rain misted down on them, dampening his beanie. Ryder could barely think straight. When he wasn't focused on the ceremony, his mind drifted back to Liam.

"What do I tell them?" Ryder glanced at Jordan, and she looked back at him, her jaw slackened and brows knitted.

"The truth," Jordan said. She drew him into a tight embrace, arms around his shoulders, cheek against his temple. "Tell them you'll still be you."

If I come back.

He nodded. She pressed her lips against his forehead.

They didn't say goodbye to each other. Ryder didn't think Jordan would stand for it.

The truck roared to life. He glanced at her as she drove away. She tried to smile, but it was forced. He watched her go, saw the outline of her through the back window. Her hand slammed against the steering wheel. She wiped her eye with the side of her hand, grabbed her cellphone, and lifted it to her ear.

"Hey," Liam said.

Ryder turned around. Christy and Donovan watched them through the window. Liam stood in front of him, hands shoved in his pockets.

"We got fries. The wedge ones you like." Liam regarded him, hair pushed back like it always was, face sculpted into an expression that sat between concentration and assurance. His tongue ring clicked against his teeth. His hands squirmed in his pockets. He was still wearing Ryder's shirt.

Now or never, maybe.

"I don't know when it happened, but sometime in the last two years I fell in love with you." Ryder exhaled a quivering breath. "It happened fast, like this." He gestured to himself, to the darkness, hoping Liam understood. "One day, I was looking at you, wondering if you'd ever look back, and I realized how bad it was, how absolutely fucked I was."

"Tell me this tomorrow."

"I'm telling you now."

Liam shook his head. "I don't accept that."

"You have to," Ryder said through a short laugh. "Because tomorrow—"

"You'll die." Liam's mouth tensed and he rolled his lips together, eyelashes sweeping up and down as he glanced around Ryder's face. "And you'll come back."

"I didn't know if it would go away. For some reason I thought it might, like I'd been compelled, like you were some bullshit Fae with an unshakable hold on me, and then I realized it wasn't compulsion or a spell. I was done for. It was you and you were all I was ever gonna be able to look at." The words rushed from Ryder's mouth clumsily. He wished he could've picked them up and swallowed them back down. "You wanted to know. There. Now you know."

Rain hit the ground, slow and then fast, light and then in quarter sized drops. Ryder wondered if Liam had been the cause of it, if his magic had reached into the clouds and initiated a downpour.

"Guys...?" Christy held open the door to the pizza parlor and peeked around it. "The pizza's getting cold and you're getting soaked."

"Food's getting cold," Ryder mumbled. He brushed past Liam as he walked by and followed Christy to the table.

Donovan paused midbite of a greasy piece of veggie pizza when Ryder sat down. "Hey," he slurred. "We got the weird barbeque ranch for you."

"Thanks." Ryder tried to smile, but the conversation outside with Liam mixed with the conversation he'd had in the truck weighed it down. "Sorry if I scared you last night."

"You didn't," Donovan said. "I've seen worse. You okay?"

Liam slid into the booth next to Ryder. His energy was heavy and chaotic, buzzing on Ryder's skin like a thousand wasps.

"I'm fine." Ryder grabbed a piece of pizza and the side of barbeque ranch that no one else would touch.

"You gonna tell them or not?" Liam snapped.

Ryder chewed on the inside of his cheek and picked jalapeños off his pizza. Christy's magic drifted across his thoughts, testing a poke here, a prod there. He stayed still and allowed it. Her energy wrapped around a few things, information he'd kept to himself. She lingered over the conversation with Liam and then moved on, which he appreciated. As soon as he felt her snag the word *demonology*, he pushed back, burning her.

Christy flinched. "You're choosing to die?"

"And come back, hopefully," Ryder said. He swiped a fry through a puddle of ketchup and chomped on it.

"Hopefully," Liam echoed under his breath.

"And it's safe?" Donovan asked.

Ryder stifled a laugh. "Nothing's safe. We're witches."

"Demons definitely aren't safe," Christy mumbled.

Ryder's magic cracked like a whip. It undulated around them, dark and fiery and horribly thick. The table went silent. Even Liam held his breath.

"What'd Tyler say?" Ryder asked. His magic retreated.

Liam swept his gaze sideways. "That he thinks our circle would be compromised if we let a necromancer stay connected to us."

Typical. Ryder took a bite of his pizza. Somewhere underneath the anger, it hurt.

"But he can also go fuck himself, so..." Liam grabbed the discarded jalapeños off Ryder's plate and put them on his pizza.

"Ty doesn't really feel that way," Christy stressed. She sighed and shook her head, nudging Donovan with her elbow. "Right?"

"You're the psychic," Donovan said.

"He's just scared and traditional and he doesn't like change, but you know him better than the rest of us, so..." Christy looked down at her half-eaten pizza and her lips thinned into a knowing smile. "What has he said to you?"

Donovan shot her a deadly glare.

Ryder caught the distinct, private look on her face. He caught Donovan's blush too.

"That's not fucking fair," Liam snapped. He gestured between Christy and Donovan. "You're telling me, hey, look at me—" He snapped his fingers in front of Christy until she looked up. "You're telling me Donovan and Tyler are screwing around?"

"You don't have to say it like that," Donovan growled. "Don't blame me for your—" he gestured between Ryder and Donovan with a wave of his hand "—petty bullshit. No one was stopping you two!"

"Actually," Ryder sang, "someone was, but whatever. Good to know Tyler can have what he wants, and no one else can."

"It hasn't been going on long," Donovan said softly. "It just... happened."

"Guys, can we not," Christy said through a sigh.

Thunder cracked outside. Ryder was almost sure Liam had spurred it on.

"Okay, we're done with secrets." Christy waved around the table, gesturing wildly to everyone. "Donovan and Tyler are a thing, you two" —she pointed to Ryder and Liam— "are a thing, and I" —she laid her hand over her chest and offered a wide, sarcastic grin— "am disgustingly single. This is literally the least of my worries right now seeing as Ryder is going to die tomorrow."

His cheeks were hot and his magic still crackled around them, but Ryder couldn't help the small smile that pulled his lips upright. *You two are a thing.* The words played in his head again and again. It felt good to have something out in the open for once.

"What happens if...?" Donovan didn't need to continue.

Christy looked away as if she'd seen something gruesome.

"If I don't come back?" Ryder asked.

The table went quiet. Christy played with her long braid and looked at her lap. Liam didn't move or breathe or say a word. Donovan picked at the pizza crust left on his plate and nodded.

"Then I stay dead," Ryder said matter-of-factly. "That's it."

Donovan's expression dropped. "And there's no way to know for sure?"

"No."

"What about—?"

"Donovan," Ryder snapped. He swallowed around the jagged lump in his throat. "I'll be fine, all right?"

Tension looped around them and pulled tight. A flash of lightning lit the window. Wind whipped around them, energy they all knew but hadn't expected. Ryder didn't look up. He didn't move from his place against the wall. His heart raced and his thoughts overlapped. Everything kept colliding too quickly for him to grasp, details flying by in the blink of an eye. He was going to die tomorrow. Liam's lips were softer than he ever imagined. Jordan had made pacts with demons. Donovan was something. Christy knew about Ryder's other secret and hadn't said a word. Liam had been looking back at him for two years.

Nothing was sedentary. Everything was too fast, too soon.

Tyler walked toward them with confident strides, like he always did. Ryder glanced at him without moving. A scarf was wrapped around his neck over a plain sweatshirt. His wet shoes squeaked against the tile.

"You're going through with the ceremony?" Tyler asked. His palm slammed against the table. "You're really doing this?"

Liam's magic flared. Ryder gripped his thigh under the table.

"I have to," Ryder said. He locked eyes with Tyler and his mouth tightened into a line. "I won't risk anyone's life. I do this, I get control over it, and I move on."

"Or you stay dead." Tyler sounded like he cared, which was surprising.

"Tyler, c'mon," Donovan said softly. "Enough."

"You should've told us," Tyler whispered. "About the reading, about your magic, about everything."

Ryder's top lip curled back and he rolled his eyes. "I'm not a white witch," he teased. "I don't have to abide by your rules."

Tyler's magic whipped toward him. "That's not my point!"

A few people looked up from the other tables. Christy hushed Tyler and slid down in the booth.

Liam took Ryder's hand and pulled. "We're leaving."

Ryder didn't argue. "See you tomorrow," he said to everyone and no one.

Donovan said, "Wait," while Christy said, "Hold on."

Tyler grabbed Ryder's elbow, stopping him in his tracks. When Ryder whipped toward him, his eyes were black as night.

"Will you?" Tyler asked. He chewed on his bottom lip and sighed through his nose. He didn't waver, not for Ryder's black eyes or his slithering, upside down magic. "Because we're still a circle."

"Now we're a circle?" Ryder bit. He yanked out of Tyler's grasp and headed for the exit, gazing at the ground to conceal his eyes from the rest of the people at the pizza parlor.

The nerve. Ryder's hands shook. Heat spiked through him, burning and unyielding. *The absolute fucking nerve.* He stepped into the night air and welcomed rain on his face. A chilly breeze kicked through the trees and Port Lewis smelled like home. He inhaled as much of it as he could, because he might not get to again.

"Where's your car?" Ryder asked.

Liam laced his fingers through Ryder's and tugged. "This way."

Chapter Six

RYDER CLUTCHED HIS reaver in his palm, smoothing across its delicate ridges with desperate strokes of his finger. Rain splattered the windshield and Liam's thumbs drummed on the steering wheel. A string of beads swayed from the Subaru's rearview mirror. One of the cup holders was filled with polished stones, and a vial of essential oil was stuffed in the compartment of Ryder's door.

Liam's car smelled like him—crisp and clean, with hints of rosemary and citrus. Ryder had sat exactly where he was sitting many times before, foot propped on the dash, watching Liam out of the corner of his eye while music drifted from the speakers. Everything was different now. Everything was evolving and accelerating, and it could be ending before Ryder even understood when it'd begun in the first place.

The woods were a safe haven, even in the storm. Especially in the storm.

Ryder glanced at Liam and their eyes met briefly. The intent between them was palpable.

Liam directed the car down a dirt path toward a familiar meadow nestled in the trees. The forest stirred. Critters crawled onto branches to watch, as if they'd been anticipating their arrival. Ryder heard the trees whisper in a different language.

Darkling. Storm wielder. Bone bender. Water conqueror.

Liam put the car in park. The headlights went out, shrouding them in darkness. They sat there, listening to the rain come down and the forest come alive, until Liam unclicked his seatbelt and sighed. "Ry…"

"C'mon," Ryder said. He kicked his shoes off, his socks, and slid out of the car. Soft grass cushioned his feet. He curled his toes and closed his eyes, pulling his elemental magic to the surface. Heat pulsed around him, warming the rain as soon as it hit his skin. He took off his shirt and threw it to the ground.

"You don't have to do it." Liam's voice was muffled by the rain and the trees. "We can find another way to make this work."

"Until I kill someone," Ryder said.

Liam walked around the side of the car. Thunder rolled across the sky, each loud rumble in tune with his footsteps. *Until I kill you,* Ryder thought.

The forest stirred delightedly. *Sea sorcerer. Alchemist.*

Liam stood in front of him. His brown eyes were masked gray and white, and his lips were parted, chest heaving in breath after breath. He shook his head, and Ryder looked at all of him, every bit of him. His gaze wandered the slope of his neck, along his shoulders and down his arms. The raindrops clung to Liam, while steam lifted off Ryder's bare skin.

"If I come back—if I make it—can we do this?" Ryder flicked his wrist between them. "Me and you, us, can we be something?"

Liam shook his head. His hands latched around Ryder's hips and pushed him backward. "We're already something," he said.

Ryder stumbled, almost tripping over his feet. The rain poured down on them and the night felt endless. The forest chattered and whispered, and Ryder's eyes squeezed shut when Liam crushed their mouths together. Their lips were slippery, and Ryder could barely keep up with each step, with the part of their lips, every shared inhale and exhale, the grass around his ankles and on his back.

It happened in segments. Ryder's head spun and heat built in him. Flames licked across his bones, coiled around his joints and ligaments, hummed in his muscles. He clung to it—to the Fire inside him. They'd landed on the grass somehow. Ryder tripped or Liam pushed him; either way, it didn't matter. The meadow was cool on his spine, soft and grounding, and the air smelled like pine and magic, like every spell they'd ever attempted to perfect in these woods, like every afternoon spent lying in the sun with his grimoire open, surrounded by his circle-mates.

Liam kissed him harder, longer, with intermissions of steamed breath drifting between them, and Liam's teeth set in Ryder's lip. Pain radiated in the indentions left behind from Liam's canines. Want ached behind Ryder's ribcage and between his legs.

"Off." Ryder tugged at the bottom of Liam's shirt, guiding it up until Liam pulled it over his head and dropped it beside them. "Tell me to stop, okay?" Ryder's reaver was snug around his index finger. He dragged the tip of it through the water on Liam's stomach, across his hipbones and up his side. "If it hurts, just—"

Liam's fingers closed over Ryder's hand, guiding the point of the reaver into the flesh stretched across his bottom two ribs. Another flash of lightning splintered above them. Fog turned the moon hazy and blurred the stars, clung to the treetops and snaked between their gnarled branches. Blood soaked Ryder's fingertips and pooled in the hollow of his reaver.

He dragged the bloodied point across his tongue and Liam watched, transfixed. Vitality tasted like sea salt and honeysuckles. Ryder focused on it—the emotions, the power—and let his pupils bleed over, allowed his Fire to burn hot and his magic to be present and unrestrained.

Liam's fingertips dipped under the front of Ryder's jeans. "What's it like?"

"Your energy or you touching me?"

"Both." Liam's fingers moved slowly, sending shivers across Ryder's arms and down his legs.

"You feel like a storm." Ryder lifted his hips off the forest floor, chasing sensation. "It's like drowning, but not. Like I'm being held under water until it hurts." He shifted his hips until his jeans slid lower, and he kicked them off, followed by his briefs. If it were any other night, with any other person, being bare in the woods would be unthinkable. But it wasn't any night, and Liam wasn't any person. "C'mon," Ryder rasped. He fumbled with the button on Liam's pants. "Like our ancestors used to."

Liam laughed against Ryder's mouth. "Witch jokes?"

"Yeah, Princess, might as well laugh about it while I can."

"You're coming back," Liam said and tossed the rest of his clothes away. Ryder shoved him onto his back. The trees whispered through the rain. *Wildfire. Death dealer.* He slid his thighs over Liam's hips and watched the rain bounce off Liam's chest. It streamed over his shoulders and gathered on his cupid's bow. Liam's lips quirked at the edges. "And stop calling me that."

Ryder leaned down to kiss him. Moonlight bent through the mist and sharpened the dark hollows of Liam's collarbones, the faint dip of muscle on Ryder's stomach. He sucked in a sharp breath when Liam sat up, hands steady on Ryder's hips.

It was a halted, tilting moment—Ryder looking at Liam and Liam looking back. The forest went quiet, listening, and the rain slowed, waiting. Liam nodded, hooked his teeth over Ryder's clavicle and bit, pulling a gasp from deep in his throat.

Ryder gripped Liam's jaw until he let go, and sliced the edge of his collarbone open with the reaver. Liam surged forward. He bit down again, and wrapped his arms tight around Ryder's back.

The rain froze in place. Ryder clutched the back of Liam's head with one hand and dug his nails into Liam's shoulder with the other. Emotions rushed between them. Every stint of eye contact, every day spent practicing his spell work with Liam in his apartment. Liam's head resting on his stomach last summer, out there, in the same woods— the dread and anger and hopelessness that spiked through Liam when Ryder said he'd chosen to die. The elation and excitement of their first kiss, bloody and messy and overdue. Liam's unyielding, absolute fear that Ryder might not come back.

It was quiet and still. Ryder stayed present in the shared emotions for as long as he could, enduring the whiplash of their energies and magic. Liam's lips hovered over the wound and he dipped his hand between Ryder's legs, two fingers sliding into him without pause.

"You sure?" Liam's mouth was bloodied and warm on Ryder's jaw.

Ryder tried to say yes, but Liam's thumb circled his clit, and the word skidded out of him in the shape of something else, wounded and steep.

Liam replaced his fingers with his cock, and Ryder couldn't breathe. He tilted his head until their lips met. It was kissing and moving, and then it was Ryder's lungs catching up with their actions, breathing into Liam's mouth, eyes open, watching Liam from under his lashes. It was Ryder's hips rolling, and Liam pressing up into him, the tender sound of their bodies meeting, chased breath and fluttering, shaky moans. Ryder's magic flared; the Fire in him rushed to the surface. The rain fell again. The trees around them chattered and howled.

It was unlike any dream or daydream or nightmare, because when Ryder dreamed, he dreamed of his brutality, of blood and sacrifice—and when he dreamed of light, of Liam, it was never as good as this.

The grass cushioned his shins and knees. His reaver curved delicately over Liam's cheek, the bite of Liam's evening stubble harsh on his palm. Ryder's eyes returned to their Lewellyn green. His body trembled, hips grinding down again and again. Liam's fingers dug into him, the storm ceased, and his gray eyes turned golden brown.

Ryder's name slipped from Liam, and Ryder swore he felt both syllables slither between his ribs.

Their energy hovered around them. Something wicked watched with a thousand eyes—the same something from their reading. The air parted. Everything sped away and came back, compressing around them. Ryder felt it like a free fall. Autumn wind cut through the trees, rustling copper leaves and ivy vines.

Liam swiped his thumb over the fire rune etched into Ryder's hip. The hazy moon looked down on them, highlighting Ryder's pale skin and making Liam appear otherworldly against the darkness. The whisper of the forest died down. Heat thrashed in Ryder, pleasure building and building. He kissed Liam hard, his mouth opening wide for deeper, longer, fiercer kisses.

Time turned over.

Ryder felt like a king or a god or a magician.

Liam made the darkness in him feel like a gift.

Ryder trembled when he came. He gasped, body tightening in spasms and jerks and tremors. Liam moaned prettily into Ryder's mouth, stilling inside him and digging his thumb into Ryder's hip hard enough that Ryder pawed at him, telling him to let go.

The trees rambled again. This time Ryder understood them.

The Magician. The Tower. The Devil. The Lovers.

Liam's eyes were half-lidded. He hummed when Ryder leaned into him, their chests pressed together, bodies spent and shaking.

"To ravage," Ryder whispered, resting his cheek on Liam's shoulder.

Liam ran his fingers along Ryder's spine. "A dark partnership."

The fog lifted and moonlight dripped across their bare skin.

Chapter Seven

RYDER DIDN'T SLEEP.

His lips dusted Liam's shoulder, and he stared at the altar where Percy was perched atop a pile of books, lit by waning candles.

After the meadow, they'd climbed into the backseat of Liam's car, and after an hour spent in the car, they'd finally made it to Ryder's apartment. Ryder remembered the sounds Liam made, every heaved breath and shaken cry, his back arching off the bed with Ryder's fingers inside him. He remembered Liam's bruising grip on his thighs, Liam's relentless mouth between them, and Ryder coming apart at the seams as he clutched the sheets.

The night was over, though. Sunlight peeked through the slots in the blinds. Ryder listened to Liam wake, the draw of his breath coming faster.

Liam lifted his head off the pillow and glanced over his shoulder. His eyes softened and he sighed. "I thought you'd left."

"No, not yet," Ryder rasped.

Liam rolled onto his back and stared at the ceiling. Ryder's gaze followed the staircase of bruises from his hips to his shoulders, mouth-shaped, shadowed by teeth marks. The small cut from the reaver shone dark against his olive complexion.

"Have you checked your phone?" Liam asked.

Ryder shook his head.

"I bet they've been trying to get a hold of us."

"Probably."

"I want to be there."

"Liam—"

"Please," Liam whispered. He closed his eyes and tilted his head against the pillow, reopening them to meet Ryder's gaze. "I don't want to fight with you about this, but I will."

"You really wanna watch them slit my fucking throat?" Ryder bit.

"No," Liam snapped back. "But if it's..."

"If this is about you seeing me for the last time, remember me like this."

Liam's mouth twisted. His eyes hardened and his jaw flexed.

He dragged his mouth across Liam's cheek. "C'mon," he purred, "don't fight with me." He was sore, but it didn't matter. He was exhausted and more awake than he'd ever been. "Don't fight with me," he whispered again, pressing a kiss against Liam's mouth.

His phone buzzed on the nightstand. He ignored it. Liam's phone buzzed next. He ignored it.

Liam kissed him slowly, his tongue ring dragging across Ryder's bottom lip.

A shrill caw erupted outside the window.

Suddenly, all Ryder wanted was more time. More of this. He gripped Liam's waist. More of everything.

Another screech. The sound of wings flapping and claws against glass.

Ryder kissed Liam hard and rubbed his thumb across Liam's cheek, hoping the quivering in his chest hadn't crept to his limbs yet.

"You don't have to go," Liam said weakly.

Three hard knocks rapped the front door.

Ryder slid out of bed and got dressed. He grabbed the reaver off his altar and slid it over his index finger. His room was the same, except not. Watermarks of Liam stained the bathroom, the shower, the wall by the dresser, the floor, his bed. He hesitated in the doorway and steadied his breathing.

"I've loved you the whole time," Liam said. "Now. Then. I've been looking back since the beginning. You know that, right?"

Ryder glanced over his shoulder. Liam sat on the edge of the bed, clutching one of Ryder's small amethyst geodes in his palm. His pupils expanded, turning his eyes inky black. Percy trailed him to the door.

"Ryder." Liam's voice was pleading and soft. His bare feet padded on the wood floors.

Ryder didn't have the heart to look at him.

"If you don't..." Liam choked on the rest of what he wanted to say and skipped it. "You better haunt me, asshole. You understand that, Ry? You come back and you haunt me."

A small smile curved Ryder's lips.

He closed the front door behind him and brushed past Jordan toward the stairs.

JORDAN STAYED QUIET for most of the drive.

Finally, she asked, "Were you guys up all night, or—"

"Yes. Almost. He fell asleep at four."

They were stopped at a red light. Jordan cocked her head and raised a pierced brow. "Remember that one time you caught Thalia and I in the laundry room?"

"On the dryer, yeah," Ryder quipped. "I also remember you threatening to throw my laptop out the window if I told Dad."

Jordan made a *pssshhhh* noise that turned into laughter on the end. It fizzled out. The light turned green. Everything was still again. Ryder focused on the places he still felt Liam, the sore spots under his clothes that he would take into the afterlife, and hopefully bring back to this one.

"I thought the ceremony happened at night," Ryder said.

"It does." Jordan nodded. "Time warps when we altar life and death. When you die, you'll come back and it'll probably be late—ten, maybe eleven."

The thought of being dead for that long turned Ryder's stomach. "Where does it take place?"

"The woods."

"People hike out there during the day." Ryder furrowed his brow and his jaw slackened.

"Not where we're going," Jordan assured him.

They took the curvy road to the coastal side of the woods and turned down the two-lane highway that cut through the trees. He glimpsed the giant bottom of elder trees out of the window and followed the mossy blanket draped across the forest floor, decorated in an assortment of pale autumn flowers. A dirt road to the left flashed by. He remembered driving down it the night before in Liam's car.

The further they drove, the larger the trees became. Ryder caught sight of a dangling sign on a branch—a sphere with a wolf's jaws painted on it, red as blood. Jordan turned the wheel, and the truck rumbled down a rocky, overgrown path.

Percy napped in Ryder's lap, purring softly.

Ryder's heart was beating fast in his chest. He wouldn't be surprised if Jordan could hear it.

The road turned from dirt, to grass, to dirt again. The trees were close enough to the window that leaves scraped the glass.

"Where are we...?" They bounced over the last of the rocky path and joined a row of other vehicles parked in front of a tall, wrought iron gate. He recognized his father's Jeep, but the other two cars were new to him. "A cemetery?"

"Sort of," Jordan said.

The iron gate reached at least ten feet, curved at the top to meet jagged spires and thick arrow-points. It matched the fence that surrounded a fairly large plot of land. The canopy folded over them, as if the trees had leaned together to umbrella the hidden Wolfe cemetery. Beyond the gates, headstones in different shapes and sizes littered the grounds.

"Did you bring your reaver?" Jordan asked.

Ryder nodded.

"I told Dad I gave it to you, so—" She shrugged. "You can wear it if you want."

He slipped it on and watched Jordan do the same. Her reaver was longer than his, thinner and feminine. Where his resembled a claw, hers was a bird-like talon. Percy hopped off Ryder's lap when he opened the door, and bounded off into the cemetery. Chatter came from the alchemists inside the gates, but their voices hushed as Jordan and Ryder approached.

"Will it hurt?" Ryder asked under his breath.

"For a moment," Jordan said.

"How bad?"

"It's hard to describe. Death is different for everyone."

"Was it bad for you?"

"I was eleven," Jordan said plainly. "But I was ready, I had to be. I can't remember the extent of the pain, only that it was present." River landed heavily on Jordan's shoulder and she stumbled, hissing at him to be careful. "You have to welcome it."

Ryder pushed one side of the gate open. It creaked and howled, clanking loudly behind them when it shut. Headstones weren't the only things scattered throughout the cemetery. Two mausoleums stood close together where the alchemists and his mother stood, watching him expectantly.

Ellen stood out in a sea of black, swathed in a rich orange dress. She clutched a dark bundle in her hands and offered a lopsided smile to Ryder. He hadn't realized he'd stopped walking until Jordan pressed her hand on his lower back and gave a gentle push.

Gerard and the other alchemists wore their cloaks. Each one was specially made, tailored to the necromancer who wore it. Jordan's was floor length with a deep, wide hood and tight sleeves. Gerard's was short, styled like a coat with a smaller hood. The others varied in size and shape. A person with cropped teal hair regarded Ryder with a flick of their eyes, features smooth and androgynous. Their cloak was tight-fitting, buttoned up the front and clasped beneath their chin.

"Ryder," Gerard said and held out his hand, motioning Ryder closer. He gestured to the woman on the end, wrapped in a simple black dress. She had a mane of brunette curls and dark bronze skin. Her striking green eyes set her apart from the necromancers. "This is Margo Lewellyn. She's here as a witness for the other clans."

"I've heard about you," Margo said. She had a voice that sparked like a wood-wick candle. "The Fire witch with necromancy in his veins. We've never seen one like you before."

Ryder didn't know what to say. He nodded and glanced from Margo to the other two witches.

The person with teal hair dipped their chin to him. "Vassa," they said. "They, them if you'd be so kind."

Ryder nodded. The side of his mouth twitched into a half smile. "He, him."

"Noted," Vassa said. They winked playfully.

"I'm Stefan," the other witch said. He had a rugged, scruffy face, with kind, dark eyes. "I've been your father's friend since we were kids."

"Cousins," Gerard clarified. "Stefan and Vassa are here to assist, but mostly to witness. Jordan and I will be the ones dealing your death."

"Jordan," Vassa purred. "Good to see you."

"And you, Vassa," Jordan said politely. An inkling of shared history lingered between them. Jordan steered her attention to Ellen. "Did you finish it?"

"I did, yes." Ellen tucked a piece of silky blonde hair behind her ear and unfolded the bundle in her arms. "I'm no seamstress, but it's done."

The cloak was knee length, and more a coat like Gerard's than a draped piece like Jordan's. Black clasps climbed one side, matching loops on the other, and the collar was short and trimmed, perched around a wide hood. Red satin lined the inside, which he could only guess was a nod to his Fire magic.

"I added these," Ellen said. She flicked one of the triangular loops. They matched the symbol etched into his hip. "And the inside, but the cloak has been yours since you were ten. We never knew if you'd use it, but..." She shrugged. "Here we are."

"Here we are," Ryder echoed.

The forest whispered around them.

Darklings. Bone benders. The unmade. Thieves.

"We should get started," Gerard said. "You'll get your cloak once you wake up."

Ryder's stomach was knotted and tight. His chest hurt. His throat started to close.

"It's all right," Jordan whispered. She pressed her hand on his lower back again. "I've got you."

Ellen chewed nervously on her lip. Margo watched, wise curious eyes flicking from Ryder's feet to his face.

"Vassa," Gerard said.

Vassa nodded. They reached onto one of the headstones and grabbed a dagger. Its blade was stained red, jagged and uneven, with a white handle displaying the Wolfe clan's emblem, a set of fanged jaws. They handed Gerard the weapon and stepped back.

"Stefan," Gerard said.

Black smoke floated beneath Stefan's feet, tendrils of it expanding out, over the cobblestone and grass, like veins. He handed Jordan a hooked needle and a strand of thick black thread.

Ryder looked at the thread questioningly.

Jordan met his eye and said, "To stitch you."

Ryder swallowed hard. He resisted the urge to touch his throat, but did manage to take a step back. The black smoky vines wrapped up his calves and held him in place. Panic built in his stomach and arms and chest. His wide eyes must've alerted them, followed by smoke of his own lashing out from beneath his feet. Heat blistered on his skin. Steam billowed out of his mouth.

"Sweetheart, it's okay—" Ellen stopped when Gerard flashed his palm to her.

Ellen's magic spiked, hot and familiar.

Margo rested her hand on Ellen's shoulder. "Ellen," she said firmly, "let it be."

Time stopped and restarted. The forest shivered in the wake of the darkest magic—unnatural and sticky, the kind of black magic that dripped like sap. It weighed down Ryder's shoulders, vicious and powerful and chaotic.

"Now?" Ryder blurted, voice shaky and wrecked.

"Yes, now," Gerard said.

Ryder's pupils bled over the rest of his eyes. Instinct took over and his magic lashed out, thrumming around him, trying to shield him. It clashed with his father's, then his sister's, biting and clawing at their energy.

"Ryder," Jordan warned. "You have to accept it."

His Fire burned in him. The air turned dry and hot. If he had a flame—any flame, he could surround himself with it. But there was nothing. His gaze darted around in search of something, anything. The black tendrils dug into his thighs and held him tight. He barely felt them curl around his wrist, and suddenly he was bound and unable to move. Flames burst in his palms, but he couldn't focus enough to direct them. The fire burned and burned and then faded.

"Jordie," Ryder whimpered. His heart raced. Percy hissed somewhere nearby. His gaze whipped to the left, where Moon's huge body was curled around the base of a stone cross, her tongue flicking out, upper body poised to strike. Percy's back arched, his ears flat against his skull. Black smoke billowed around Ryder, cutting off his vision of Percy and his mother and the cemetery altogether.

Percy yowled and hissed. It was like a knife to Ryder's gut. Moon's teeth in his throat and his stomach and his legs—he felt Percy scrambling to stay alive, heard his claws in the dirt and felt his lungs being crushed. Tears burned Ryder's eyes. His Fire twisted around him and inside him.

It happened quickly.

The black smoke bent around Jordan's shape, making room for her in front of him. She lifted the dagger to his neck and pressed its teeth against his flesh.

"Don't fight it," Jordan whispered. She placed something in his hand. A match. And dragged the blade across his throat.

Blood filled his mouth and lungs. He clung to vitality—to life. But it was no use.

The forest got louder and louder, until all Ryder heard was a whirlwind of languages he didn't speak. He tried to breathe but couldn't. He tried to keep his eyes open but couldn't.

There was a hand on his face. Jordan's hand.

"Belial," she whispered, "I need a favor."

RYDER OPENED HIS eyes.

He inhaled as much air as he could and pawed at his neck. He'd expected to find blood, but his smooth skin was unmarred and intact. Blackness pulsated around him, a nether rich and unwavering. The afterlife, the in between, or something else.

"Okay, guys, bring me back," he said through gritted teeth.

Anytime now.

His heartbeat was steady. Good. He lifted his hand and looked at the reaver curved over his index finger. *Am I...?* He slid his thumb across the pointed tip and winced. Blood beaded up from the tiny cut. *Not a ghost.* A relieved sigh fluttered over his lips.

He fiddled with the match in his palm.

Jordan's voice replayed in his mind. *Belial, I need a favor.*

Ryder knew that name. He'd heard it before during hushed conversation at his father's house, and he'd seen it scribbled in Jordan's grimoire. He knew the name like he knew any demon's name—as something that never belonged in his mouth.

He swallowed hard and sat up. There was nothing, just emptiness and more emptiness. His energy reached out, only to come back cold and alone. He tested the name to himself, sounding it out again and again. *Bel-i-al. Belial. Bel-ial.*

"Belial," he called. "I require...assistance? Fuck, okay, I'm new to this. I need help, I think."

The darkness didn't move or change. He looked left, right, to the floor which was as black as everywhere else, and to the ceiling, if there was a ceiling at all.

He sighed and pulled his knees to his chest, resting his chin atop them. He twirled the match in front of face and opened his mouth. *Be there.* He reached for his Fire. *Be there.* His lips rounded and he blew gently across the match.

To his surprise, it lit.

Ryder closed his eyes. Elation bloomed in him. His magic brought the Fire inside him to the surface. The tiny flame on the match stretched into his palms, wrapped over his body, and hovered around him. He kept it close, allowing his magic to lift it and pull it, coaxing the flames into a slender, snake-like form.

He felt the energy shift before he saw it. The same unruly, heavy energy from the reading with Liam manifested. It was more. It slid against him, blisteringly hot. His head spun, and he closed his eyes again, pulling his Fire closer. His magic buckled down, fierce and nervous, pulsing around him in tight bursts. Whatever energy had made an appearance before, it was the same and different. It hummed at Ryder, a deep, rough growl.

Anytime now, Jordan. Any-fucking-time.

When Ryder opened his eyes, a being knelt in front of him. All the breath in his lungs rushed out. His Fire moved faster, circling him again and again, a figure eight, circles, an infinity sign, a hexagon, circles again. He couldn't move, and his heart pounded in his chest, body and mind stuck between terror and intrigue.

It shone gold, as if sunlight was trapped beneath its flesh—armor. It wasn't skin Ryder was looking at, it was a suit of armor. Horns sprouted from the top of a helmet, white like daybreak. Eyes hid somewhere under scales of golden metal, warm and clear, human in a way Ryder hadn't expected. Something sharp slid under Ryder's chin, a curled index finger. More knuckles. Longer. *Oh*, Ryder thought. Its name surrounded him.

Ryder closed his eyes. "Be not afraid, right? That's what you're supposed to say."

Belial hummed again, and it sounded like it might've been a laugh. Belial's gloved finger under his chin was sharp and smooth. It fell away and was replaced by the tip of a sword.

Ryder's fire whipped and thrashed.

The sword dug into his throat.

He heard it in his own mind, around him, above him.

An unusual one. The voice wasn't his own. It was every flame that'd ever sparked, every lightning strike that hit the ground and volcano that erupted. A peculiarity.

Belial's sword pierced Ryder's throat.

You, Belial said, voice smooth and not, loud and not, silent and not, *belong in my Order.*

Ryder squeezed his eyes shut. He thought of Jordan and Ellen and Gerard, of his circle-mates, of Liam.

Belial's sword retracted. A wide, gloved hand pressed against Ryder's chest, and he felt the world shift.

Little Darkling.

"BACK UP!" JORDAN shouted.

Ryder's eyes flung open. Life didn't take its time—it filled him all at once. His lungs expanded. His blood rushed. His Fire, *his Fire*, leaped from him. Flames burst from between his fingers and surrounded him as he tried to catch his breath. Everything hurt. His legs were sore, his stomach lurched, his back ached. He tried to take a breath and gagged, choking on a puddle of stagnant blood.

The world came into view in two blinks. Everything was vivid and startling. The night sky looked down at him, filled with an abundance of stars and distant galaxies and the moon's white smile. He recognized the trees curved over the cemetery, open in the middle in a perfect circle.

He turned and coughed, spitting mouthfuls of blood onto the cobblestone.

Steam filled his mouth. Black smoke mingled with the flames shielding him, a balance of Fire and necromancy. It was as if someone had reached inside him and turned the volume up, as if he'd been living his life half inside himself for twenty-one years. *This is what it's like.* He curled his hand into a fist. Dark magic boiled in him, desperate to be used.

"Ryder! Calm down, you're here, you're back," Jordan called.

He focused on the Fire until it died down, and realized how fast his breath was coming, shaky and loud.

Margo said, "Interesting."

Vassa laughed, impressed, and clapped.

He smelled blood, his own and someone else's. Once the flames around him were gone, Ryder saw Jordan standing across from him, wrapping a white bandage around her forearm. Gerard stood beside her, a confident smile perched on his lips.

Ryder gripped his throat and winced. The wound on his neck was stitched with black thread. He felt it fading, the thread turning to smoke as his flesh merged again, leaving his throat looking untouched. He coughed again and spit globs of blood on the ground.

Something was different. Everything was different.

"You still have your elemental magic," Jordan said. The fresh sigil on her arm was covered with a white cloth, but Ryder could see the outline of it, familiar in a way he couldn't place. "Which means the king of flames probably met with you in the afterlife, yeah?"

"Belial?" Ryder asked.

Ellen made a disapproving noise. Margo sighed.

"I had to do something," Jordan hissed over her shoulder. Her gaze shifted back to Ryder. "What's it feel like?"

"I want to tear something apart," Ryder gritted.

"Good," Gerard growled haughtily.

"How about you put something back together first?" Jordan nodded to the left. "Percy would probably like to join you in this life. Focus your energy, the newness inside you—" She tapped on her chest. "—the part that's almost too heavy, and syphon it into Percy. His bones are broken. You'll have to set them too."

Ryder grimaced. "How...?"

Gerard cleared his throat. "It'll come naturally, Ryder."

Ryder could barely focus. The air vibrated around him. Time was disheveled. It was night, but it'd been day minutes ago. He'd died, and he was alive again. His heart thundered. There was the newness inside him, and there was something else, something ancient and powerful, an unknown that Ryder had felt before. It reconstructed itself inside him—the energy from the reading with Liam, from out in the woods, from the afterlife. Belial filled him like smoke.

Help me out here, Ryder thought.

To his surprise, Belial's energy spiked.

Ryder scooted toward Percy. Blood was working its way to each of his organs and muscles, resuscitating him in shocks and jolts. His wrists jerked. Tremors wracked his body.

Percy's lithe form was twisted and bent. Ryder's top lip curled back, and he sighed when he caught sight of Moon, perched on the stone cross, watching him. "It's not your fault," he mumbled.

Moon flicked her tongue and inched her nose toward Percy, tasting the air again and again.

Ryder reached for Percy's energy. He closed his eyes and sifted through thought, emotion, memories. Liam's smile pressed against his lips. Liam's hands on him. Liam's Water, and his turmoil, and his love—*stop*. Ryder squeezed his eyes shut tighter. He let images slip through his fingers and emotions drift around him. Concentrate. He imagined Percy alive and clawed through himself to find pockets of Percy's energy. One by one, Ryder put the pieces together. *There.*

Percy twitched.

Ryder's energy surged and he reached into Percy like he had Liam, clawed through bones and ligaments, stitching here, fixing there, until Percy's body snapped and popped. A loud yowl cut through the silence.

"Percy?" Ryder sat back on his heels.

His familiar shot to all four paws in a way only a cat could do. Percy's tail was bushed and straight, his black fur standing up on end. He hissed at Moon before bounding over to Ryder.

"It's done," Gerard said.

"It is," Jordan said through a sigh.

Underneath the bustling magic, Ryder was exhausted.

A cloak—his cloak—was draped over him. Ellen smoothed her hands over his shoulders, and Ryder slipped his arms through the sleeves. He scooped Percy into one arm, tucking him safely against his chest, and took his mother's hand when she offered it. Ellen hauled him to his feet and steadied him, nodding with her lips pursed. Green eyes flicked across his face, down his torso, back to his face.

"You attached?" Ellen asked softly.

Ryder shrugged. "Is that what it's called?"

"Yes. It's rare for a white or elemental witch to form a bond with a deity."

"I still..." Ryder conjured heat and exhaled a deep breath. "I still have my Fire. But I'm..."

"A necromancer," Margo interrupted. She regarded Ryder with skepticism, but her lips curved into a smile. "A necromancer who has elemental magic and is favored by a fire king. A fine addition, Gerard." Her fierce eyes pinned to his father. "Keep him in line."

Ryder's top lip curled back in a snarl. "That's it? We're done?"

"Yeah," Jordan quipped. "That's it. You die, I spend an hour carving Belial's sigil into my goddamn arm, he likes you, which is fucking ludicrous because you're the most unlikeable person I've ever—"

"Fuck off, Jordie. Get to the point," Ryder snapped.

"I'm kidding," she rasped. "You attach, wake back up, you proceed to wake your familiar back up, and ta-da" —she waved her hand up and down in front of Ryder— "a necromancer is born."

"I thought I'd have to eat a skull or something," Ryder teased. "Drink a chalice full of blood, cut my palm open and chant."

Gerard narrowed his eyes. Jordan barked a laugh.

"You need to sleep," Vassa said. They tilted their head down in a polite nod. "Your magic is a mess right now, I know. It may not feel like it, but some rest will do wonders."

"They're right," Jordan said.

Ryder nodded. His eyelids hung heavy despite the rabbit-fast beat of his heart. "And a shower, yeah. Can I go? Am I certified or whatever?"

"You'll start training with your sister in two days," Gerard said.

"What about this attachment?" Ryder asked.

"You have one, your sister has one, I know a couple other dark witches who have them. It isn't common, but it happens." Gerard waved dismissively. "We'll talk about that another time."

Belial stirred comfortably in the air. Every time Ryder inhaled, Belial warmed his lungs. Every time he exhaled, the demon shifted inside him.

Ellen kissed Ryder's temple and settled her hands on his cheeks. "He'll protect you," she whispered.

"Dad?"

"Yes," Ellen mumbled. "But I was talking about Belial." She sounded his name out mindfully. "He'll protect you, and he'll hold you to certain standards."

Ryder swallowed hard. "I'll be careful."

She sighed and dropped her hands. "Come by more often." A golden-feathered eagle circled overhead—Ellen's familiar, Darby. The eagle screeched at River, and both birds swooped over the woods toward a white puff of feathers in the distance.

"Yeah, I will, Mom." He followed the birds as they swept around each other in the night, one more prominent than the other two against the darkness. "Opal..." Ryder glanced through the trees and caught a flash of brick-red fur. A fox dipped between the trees, and scaled up branches until it could focus on Ryder. "Castle?" He tilted his head. The fox, Castle, tilted his head the same direction. "Castle! Where are they?"

Castle's ears twitched, and he took off into the woods.

"That was Tyler's familiar," Jordan said and lifted a brow.

Something tiny scurried up Ryder's boot, and then his jeans. Willow climbed until she hit his coat sleeve and followed it to his shoulder.

"Your circle-mates are close?" Margo asked.

Ryder eyed Willow with a small smile. The white mouse cleaned her whiskers and ears, squeaking pleasantly. "I guess so."

"A necromancer with a circle?" Vassa hummed.

"A Fire witch with a circle," Ellen corrected.

"A circle of assholes," Jordan snapped. "Except for the psychic, she's okay."

"And the cute one," Ellen added.

Darby screeched. River cawed. The night grew fierce. Trees whispered in urgent chirps and windy hisses. *Bone bender. Thief. Black fire.*

"I'll be watching," Margo said. Hooves cut through the wailing forest. A horse with a silky brown hide trotted along the gate, eyes pinned to the Lewellyn matriarch.

"Still need a ride?" Jordan asked.

"Yeah." Ryder nodded toward the other end of the woods where the birds hovered above the tree line. "To the meadow."

RYDER LISTENED TO Jordan's tires crunch down the path that led out of the woods. He stroked Percy's back and set the cat on the ground. Percy stretched and yawned. Willow crawled down his arm and into his palm. He placed her on a tree branch and she scampered off into the darkness. His phone buzzed.

Jordan: *Text me if you need a ride.*

Ryder: *I won't.*

Jordan: *Just in case.*

Ryder: *K.*

Soon enough, Opal's pearl feathers flapped close to Ryder's face. She chirped and cooed, landing heavily on his shoulder. A pair of dark eyes watched from a bush close by. Castle inched his nose toward Percy, ears upright and twitching.

The darkness crowded around, as if the night wanted to hear what the trees gossiped about.

Necromancer. Air Magician. Seer. Instinct. Storm Wielder.

"Come on out, Castle," Ryder said gently. He knelt and held out his hand. "I'm still me."

Castle's bushy tail flicked. Percy meowed and licked his paw, content with Castle's hesitation.

"Ry?" Christy's voice called shakily through the trees. She quieted and cursed. "That's his energy, I know it is."

"It could be another necromancer." Tyler sounded skeptical.

"It's too... I don't know how to explain it, but Christy's right," Donovan said. "It feels like him. Ryder, are you out here?"

Energy swelled and pulsed.

"Liam, wait!" Christy hissed.

Opal ruffled her feathers. Castle sank into the bushes.

The darkness rippled around Liam's shape. Ryder knew his footsteps. He knew the beat of Liam's heart, the quickness of each inhale and exhale. Ryder crept around a thick oak, under a knot of branches and stood at the tree line, looking out into the moonlit meadow.

Liam stopped abruptly. He stood a few feet away, illuminated by white light, handsome and brutal and unchanged. Ryder stared at him, restless in his own skin, tired and deadly and changed. A year could've gone by, and Ryder would've stayed there, with Liam looking at him like that, and Ryder looking back.

Christy, Donovan, and Tyler stood behind him. Tyler held his arm out, signaling for Christy and Donovan to stay where they were.

Opal shifted on Ryder's shoulder. The purred chirp of a fox sounded by his ankles, followed by Percy's rough meow.

"You feel different," Liam said. His eyes trailed Ryder's face, his chest, his legs.

"I'm still me," Ryder offered. "Just more of me."

Opal chirped at Liam and flew to a nearby branch.

"Yeah, I can tell."

"From all the way over there?" Ryder tried to sound playful, but his voice shook and quieted on the end. He swallowed and shifted from boot to boot, playing with the buttons on his cloak. "What were you guys doing out here?"

"Protection spell," Liam said. He took a step forward.

Ryder's magic reached for him like flowers reach for sunlight. "For the circle?"

"For you. Against death, or a solid ending, or something...Tyler came up with it."

"I unmake death," Ryder said. "I don't need protection from it."

Liam's jaw set tight. "Come into the light."

Ryder stepped into the light. He looked down at himself. His reaver was still snug over his index finger on his right hand. His cloak was buttoned and smoothed, hood pulled up over the back of his head. Blood stained the shirt underneath, and crusted spots darkened a few places on his jeans. He watched Liam carefully and heard the hitch in Tyler's breath when he came into view.

"Ryder..." Christy whispered, somewhere between shock and relief.

Ryder touched his throat where the thread had been. There was no mark, but he felt their eyes on it, like the wound was still there, gaping and terrible. It wasn't. His flesh had stitched itself back together, and his organs had started working again, and his heart still beat.

Liam took another step. He was within reach, but Ryder didn't know what was allowed and what wasn't.

"What happens now?" Liam touched the top of Ryder's hand with his fingertips. His thumb brushed the tip of the reaver. He tilted his head and pressed harder on Ryder's knuckles, then grasped them tightly. A tender, confused expression knitted Liam's brows together. "You're warm."

"I'm always warm," Ryder mumbled. He flushed and glanced at the ground, suddenly bashful again, as if he hadn't been in Liam's lap the night before. "Fire witch, remember?"

"He kept his magic..." Christy slid the words quietly to Tyler. Christy shuffled around Ryder's head, poking and prodding, until everything went quiet and Christy's energy flared, startled and frightened and thick. "And an attachment," she added.

Liam didn't let go of Ryder's hand.

"I would've stayed dead," Ryder whispered. The thought got stuck in his throat, prickly and jagged. He swallowed around it, eyes and nose burning. "It was subconscious. I didn't know I'd attached until I was back, coughing up my body weight in blood."

Liam flinched. His tongue ring click-clacked the back of his teeth. "Did it hurt?"

Ryder nodded. "Like a bitch, yeah."

Donovan sighed through his nose. Christy glanced around, from Tyler to Ryder and back again. Tyler's gaze was glued to Ryder, narrowed and defensive.

Liam still didn't let go of Ryder's hand.

"Take me home," Ryder whispered. He felt his eyelashes dampen and his throat turn to sandpaper. "I'm too fucking tired for this."

"If you leave, I leave," Liam said.

"No one's leaving," Tyler said.

Ryder closed his eyes. His magic bristled, but he hadn't lied, he was too tired to be angry.

Liam shot a hard look over his shoulder. "Ty—"

"We're a circle," Tyler interrupted. "We're still a circle. We'll figure this out together. Agreed?"

Christy hesitated, but nodded. "Yeah."

Donovan said, "Of course."

"Yes," Liam said.

Ryder let out a long breath. He glanced at Tyler and didn't quite find an apology, but something close enough. "Take me home," he repeated. His eyelids were heavy, and if he could've, he would've curled up at Liam's feet and gone to sleep. "I still have blood in my mouth, and I need a shower, and I just..."

"Yeah," Liam mumbled. He glanced over his shoulder again and nodded to the three behind him. None of them approached. It hurt, almost. But Ryder ignored it. "They're just..."

"Scared, I know."

"Thanks for the protection," Ryder said. He eyed Christy and Donovan and Tyler. "Maybe Belial came to me, because you asked him to."

"Doubtful," Christy piped, but it was playful enough to put Ryder at ease. "We have exams in the morning, Liam. Set an alarm."

Ryder turned when Liam tugged on his hand. "You don't have to stay, Liam. You can just drop me off."

Liam didn't bother saying anything.

They got in the Subaru, Liam in the driver's seat like always, Ryder with Percy in his lap and his foot propped up like always.

Chapter Eight

THE MORNING APPEARED in the form of sunlight beaming through the slots in the blinds. Ryder shifted on top of the comforter. Percy slept soundly on the floor next to the altar. The apartment was silent—the kind of silence that was broken apart by familiarity, which made it something else entirely. A tea kettle whistling. Bare feet against wood floors. A rustle of feathers. Car tires on wet asphalt outside. Ryder was alive. Alive.

The night before was surreal. Ryder had fallen to sleep on the way to his apartment. He'd let Liam half carry him up the stairs, took a shower, brushed crusted blood out of his mouth, and crawled into bed. Liam had stayed awake, a book in his hands, Ryder's head on his lap, and stroked Ryder's neck until he fell asleep again. They hadn't spoken a word to each other until Liam woke before sunrise and whispered that he'd be back in a few hours.

Ryder wondered about himself. About what he was, what they were, and what was going to happen now that he was half of something acceptable, and half of something not. The morning warmth turned into midmorning heat, comfortable and sleepy, with sunlight striped across the bed.

Everything slowed. Everything felt at odds with itself, as if Ryder might close his eyes and wake up in the blackness of the afterlife again, skin cold and sunlight gone. He heard Liam coo at Percy and kept his eyes closed, even as Liam set two teacups on the night stand, even as he let out a gentle, timid breath.

Ryder turned to face him. Liam's shirt was petal white. His tie fastened properly, a deep navy, the same color as the sea at dusk. He traced Ryder with a patient gaze, his expression unreadable.

What was there to be said? Ryder was above the covers, shirtless, in a pair of boxers, wondering if they would ever be more than what they were. He was more than what he'd been—a Fire witch, a dead witch, a necromancer, and something else entirely. But they were two boys who kissed and got ahead of themselves and slept in the same bed and had done terrible, wonderful things to each other.

Ryder had seen life and death. He'd unmade death itself. Still, he knew nothing. Not with Liam standing over him, smelling like brine and tea leaves and brown sugar.

His arms were above his head, one hand resting over his mouth. For some reason, it caused him to flush—the gust of his own breath against his knuckles, knowing his mouth was empty and he wanted to fill it with Liam's tongue and skin and fingers and blood.

Liam kept watching him.

Ryder swallowed and slid his hand away from his mouth. How was class? *Just ask. Ask him. Be done with this silence.*

But the silence moved. It shifted around them, waiting, pondering. Sunlight warmed Ryder's stomach and chest. He listened to the silence take shape, heard it break around the bed dipping under Liam's hands and knees as he crawled over Ryder.

Ryder opened his mouth, but there wasn't room for words. His lips just parted, and he tilted his head back, hoping to find Liam's soft mouth, his sharp teeth and hot breath. Liam kissed him. He dipped his tongue into Ryder's mouth and stroked it against Ryder's, the kind of kissing that was too slow, too deep, too wet. Ryder tried to breathe, but he could barely find a reason to. Not with Liam tilting his head, not with their lips pressing and pulling, the easy slide of their tongues between shuddered breaths. Ryder tried to inhale, but ended up playing with Liam's tongue ring. He tried to exhale, and Liam bit his lip.

Liam kissed his jaw. He followed strips of sunlight down Ryder's chest, his lips soothing sharp nips from his teeth. Ryder tried to sit still, to let his body unwind with Liam pulling the strings, but his hips kept shifting and his eyelids kept fluttering and he couldn't concentrate. The room was too hot. It was too good and too quiet.

When Liam's lips pressed lightly against his hipbone, Ryder said, "I'll never let you die."

Liam paused. He set his chin on Ryder's belly and blinked at him. "Never?"

"Never," Ryder whispered.

Liam got off the bed, and Ryder closed his eyes. *I shouldn't have said that.* But Liam's energy was calm and moving, it rolled off him like waves licked the shore. Ryder listened to shuffling on the altar, to Percy meow, and Liam cluck his tongue. A minute later, Liam's thighs slid over Ryder's hips.

Relief shaped his mouth into a smile, and Ryder opened his eyes.

"Let's see what the cards have to say, darkling," Liam said. There was a fine dusting of stubble on his cheeks and jaw. His eyes lifted at the edges when he grinned.

Darkling sounded good in Liam's mouth, and something hot tightened in Ryder's abdomen as it dripped off his tongue. He replayed the sound again and again as

Liam shuffled the deck. *Darkling. Darkling.* The syllables only came together that effortlessly when Liam or Belial said them. The thought of the demon slumbering inside him came and went.

Liam handed the deck to Ryder. He shuffled them and handed them back.

"Off the top," Liam said.

Ryder took the card off the top.

"The bottom."

Ryder pulled from the bottom.

Liam set the two cards on Ryder's stomach and said, "Flip them over."

Ryder flipped the first card.

The Magician.

Liam smiled at him.

He flipped the second.

The Sun.

"Ownership of oneself. A magical revelation," Liam purred. He tapped on The Magician, then The Sun. "Good fortune. Vitality."

"Looks like my luck's turning around," Ryder said, smugness lingering in his sleep-rasped voice. With one hand, he gripped Liam's waist and walked the other up the neatly fastened buttons on his shirt. "What do you think you'll draw? The Devil?"

Liam's eyes narrowed playfully. "Don't need to," he said. His hands settled on either side of Ryder's head. "I've got a devil right here."

Ryder looked at Liam. Liam looked back.

"Darkling," Ryder corrected softly.

Liam tilted his head. "Darkling," he agreed.

Ryder's eyes turned black. He snatched Liam's tie, pulled him down, and kissed him hard.

UNDERTOW

Chapter One

THE OCEAN SWEPT around Liam's ankles. Night hovered over the water, turning what was left of the day into a washboard of dusty rose and deep violet. Sea foam dampened his calves. He rolled a smooth, gray stone in his palm.

Magic made itself known, a current wound tight in his core, churning blood and flexing bone. Uncertainty misted his cheeks, stung his eyes, and even when he willed it away, it clung to him. All magic was different—Fire, Earth, Air— but Water was something else entirely. It waited for no one. When it took, it took completely. When it gave, it gave until it hurt. Liam wasn't used to being volatile, but tonight his magic thrashed within him, whispering lies about power and promises about the deep.

Storm Wielder, the ocean said. *Come closer.*

Port Lewis was a beautiful, awful place full of beautiful, awful things—the ocean and beaches, the unyielding storms, and wet weather-beaten sidewalks. Liam Montgomery often wondered if he was one of those beautiful, awful things too. Full of rage and antiquity; powerful and unknowable.

Warm fingertips followed the ridge of his knuckles and slid over the stone he kept worrying in his right hand. Ryder's energy blistered and taunted. Its darkness had an unmistakable heartbeat, a tantalizing, insidious taste that Liam still wasn't quite used to. A hot breath hit Liam's neck and he closed his eyes.

"You're still out here," Ryder said. His lips touched the shell of Liam's ear and Liam was reminded that unknowable was a useless label with Ryder Wolfe, who knew him like clouds knew rain and foxes knew forests.

Ryder was one of those beautiful, awful things. He might've been the most beautiful. The most awful.

Liam leaned back until his spine met Ryder's torso. "Where else would I be?"

"I can think of a few places." Ryder's lips curved into a smile against Liam's neck. A long, pale index finger traced the veins in his wrist to his thumb, over his knuckles and back again. "Labradorite." He touched the smooth surface of the stone and hummed appreciatively when Liam let him pluck it from his palm. "The stone of transformation?"

"Yeah, figured it might be worth a try." Liam tilted his head until Ryder's lips were close enough to catch. He kissed him gently, a soft press and nothing more. "How's Jordan?"

"Ruthless," Ryder said through a groan. "I didn't think being a necromancer would be this difficult *or* require a fuck-ton of studying. How's the ocean?"

Liam smirked. He flicked his gaze to the sea and said, "It's ruthless too."

"Anything new out here?" Ryder's chin settled on Liam's shoulder. "Merfolk stealing babies in the night?" he mused playfully. "Selkies and sirens arguing over meals?"

"Selkies don't eat people," Liam corrected. "And no, there's nothing new out here. Not yet, at least."

"Not yet," Ryder teased. His mouth dusted Liam's jaw, following the line of it to his cheek. "C'mon, Water witch, we've got a circle meeting."

"Joy." Liam would've stayed at the beach with Ryder and the ocean for hours if he could've. He would've stripped down to nothing and dragged Ryder into the water with him, touched and been touched, let moonlight drape over their skin. But the ocean sang too loudly tonight, and if Liam let it have him, he might not make it back to shore. "Are we at least eating?"

"Yeah, of course. You think I'd agree to a circle meeting *after* training with my sister if Tyler didn't promise to bring pizza?" Ryder stepped in front of him, the fine angles of his face sharp and pronounced. His shaved head was covered by a beanie that slouched over the back of his neck, and a black peacoat was snug over his broad shoulders.

It had been weeks since Ryder decided to become a necromancer. Since his Fire magic battled with the darkness inside him, since a King of hell took residence in his body, since he died and came back as this—a powerful, wicked darkling. It'd been weeks since Liam and Ryder cut through the red tape wrapped around their friendship and fell into bed together.

Everything still felt new, somehow.

"Are we going to the house?" Liam asked.

Ryder laced their fingers and tugged. His palm radiated heat. "The barn, actually. But yeah, we're going to Tyler's."

They walked toward the banks at the edge of the beach. Roots sprouted from the dirt, tickling the sand. Giant trees that had fallen years and years ago littered the place between beach and forest, home to crabs and critters, overgrown with odd teal moss and sprinkled with beige mushrooms.

Somewhere far off, an owl hooted. Somewhere closer, a creature screamed.

It echoed from the water, a gurgled, awful howl, torn and pained, as if it'd ridden the backs of waves for miles and miles. The sound looped through gusts of wind, splintering around them.

Liam had heard it before. Once. He whipped around at the same time Ryder did, fingers buckled in Ryder's iron grip. Ryder's magic surged. Heat blistered the air, lashing out at the unknown.

"What the fuck was that?" Ryder shifted in front of Liam. Black tendrils snaked over the ground beneath his heavy combat boots.

"A kelpie," Liam whispered. He watched Ryder carefully, the way his jaw tightened, the way black drifted over his eyes like ink on a canvas. "Chill out, Ry. Put that shit away."

"Fuck off," Ryder hissed. "I don't need some water horse biting a chunk out of my neck tonight, all right? Since when have they come this close to shore?"

The shrill, sudden call of the kelpie echoed until it faded, replaced by waves crashing, wind careening through tree branches, and Ryder's steady breath beside him.

"They don't—they *haven't* in a long time," Liam said. He squeezed the heel of his shoes in his free hand. "It's unusual. It means..."

"It means we're leaving," Ryder snapped. He tugged Liam's hand until Liam stumbled along, glancing over his shoulder as he went.

The ocean looked back at him, whispering, wanting.

The kelpie's call meant something was coming for him.

Liam swallowed hard. He kept hold of Ryder's hand and listened for another scream, for the sound of hooves, but they never came. He climbed into the driver's seat of his old Subaru and stared out the windshield, hand tight around the steering wheel.

Mist clouded the glass, but he could still see the black ocean yards away, the white foam on dark sand and the moon's smile rippling on the water.

Ryder climbed into the passenger seat. "Hey," he rasped. "Princess."

Liam tore his gaze from the sea. Ryder's sharp eyes melted back to their jungle green and picked him apart, long eyelashes sweeping up and down. His lips thinned, and he reached over to brush his knuckles over Liam's thigh.

"Don't call me that," Liam mumbled. "I'm fine. It's just the moon."

Ryder scoffed. His hand stayed put on Liam's thigh, and Liam was grateful. "It's just the moon," Ryder parroted sarcastically.

The car rumbled to life. The headlights cut a path through the darkness as they drove to the canyon outside the Port Lewis woods.

Liam watched the ocean disappear in the rearview mirror, but he knew it would follow him.

TYLER'S FAMILY LIVED in a large, one-story house in the middle of the woods. They'd been there for three generations, cooking up spells, talking to the dead, hosting full-moon parties once a month, and Liam had spent days, weeks even, exploring the property.

The barn on the outskirts of the empty pasture had been plucked out of a horror movie. It was typical and haunting, painted dark, earthy brown, with a sturdy roof and two giant doors. Their circle of young witches had gathered there for the last few years—calling spirits, doing readings, inviting creatures from other realms to join them.

Tonight was no different.

Ryder walked through the door, coat open and billowing around him. Liam kept hold of his hand, even when Tyler's jaw tightened at the sight of them. No matter how many weeks went by, no matter how many circle meetings they attended, Tyler was still unnerved by Ryder's necromancy, and even more frightened of what it might do to Liam.

Liam squeezed Ryder's fingers when they slackened in his grasp. "Ignore him," he whispered.

Ryder snorted and rolled his eyes.

The barn was lit by strings of white lights looped over eaves and wrapped around pillars. A couple of lanterns hung on braided ropes and blankets were strewn on the ground amidst hay bales. Tyler filled a kettle with water, his long, lean frame covered in a tight navy sweater and blue jeans.

Christy's dark hair hung over her shoulders, tickling her grimoire. She flipped a page and sighed. "Sorry, Donovan. No luck on the unearthing Earth magic front."

Donovan frowned. He was perched atop a hay bale across from her. His ginger hair caught the light, along with his orange freckles and petite, pink mouth. "Hi, Liam." He nodded to Liam and Ryder. "Eaten any souls lately, darkling?"

Ryder snickered. "Fuck off, baby witch."

Liam plopped down beside Christy.

"Oh, hi," she cooed. She tucked her hair behind her ears and glanced at him. Necklaces weighed down by crystal pendants ringed her neck over a loose white top. "How was the water?"

Ryder's magic bristled, crackling the air. Liam's jaw flexed.

"A..." Christy's breath caught. The tickle of her magic prodded his thoughts. "A kelpie? That's—"

"I could've just told you," Liam said. Sometimes having a psychic in their circle was bothersome. "No mind-reading necessary, Christy."

Her violet lips pulled down in a grimace. "Sorry, bad habit. But that's what it was? You're sure?"

"I heard it too." Ryder strode toward Tyler and snapped his fingers. The kettle started whistling at the touch of his Fire magic, spewing steam, and vibrating in Tyler's hand. "Careful, don't get burned."

It was a good thing Tyler held the kettle by the handle. He glared at Ryder and shook his head but went to work filling short, round teacups rather than scolding him.

"Kelpies don't come to shore anymore," Tyler said. "They haven't in years."

"I don't know what else it could've been," Liam said. His eyes fluttered to Ryder, tracking each movement as Ryder slipped off his coat.

"The tea might have something to say," Donovan said. His lips twitched into a half smile and he shrugged. "Or maybe it was a fluke thing."

It wasn't. Liam still wore chills from the sound of the kelpie's scream. The echo of it had stayed with him, cutting cold and merciless through his skin. He smiled back at Donovan anyway and nodded. "Yeah, maybe."

Tyler passed out the cups and sat cross-legged on the ground with his back against Donovan's hay bale. Christy straightened her back, shoulders pulled tight and chest elevated. Ryder leaned against one of the wood pillars, stirring his hot tea with his pinky finger. Liam stared into his own cup, watching, waiting.

Christy's lips moved quickly. Her frenzied whispers came on long, winded breaths, fading into each other until her voice was one layered chant. She waved her hand over her cup, slender fingers stretched toward the steam. She opened her eyes and they were ghostly white.

"Drink," she said.

Liam gulped his tea—clean, green jasmine—and covered the top of his cup once he was done.

Tyler did the same. Donovan sipped his until it was gone. Ryder tossed his back like a shot and settled his pitch-black eyes on Liam, closing one in a wink. Liam glanced away before he made a fool of himself.

"All right," Christy chirped. She grinned at her cup and wiggled restlessly in place. "One by one, please. Donovan, you first."

Donovan slid off the bale and handed Christy his cup.

"Hmmm…" She squinted and cocked her head. "Two mountains. A journey is ahead. The first one is small and…" She traced the shape of the leaves with her index finger. "Predictable, maybe? But the second will be hard. Harder than you think."

"That sucks," Donovan said through a laugh.

Christy wrinkled her nose and grinned. "It doesn't! Journeys are good for the spirit. Tyler, c'mon. Your turn."

Tyler scooted forward and handed the cup over.

"Your leaves are as stubborn as you," she said. Her eyes narrowed. Concentration furrowed her brow. "Pain," she whispered. "Something… Some*one* is going to hurt you soon." Christy's gaze flicked to Tyler. "Is everything all right?"

"Yeah," Tyler blurted. His elegant, sharp features morphed into confusion a little too late. Liam had seen it, the acceptance, the knowing, before Tyler had smothered it. "I don't… It's probably just something stupid. I bet I'll fall down the stairs tomorrow."

Tyler attempted a laugh, but no one else joined him.

Ryder cleared his throat. "Or maybe you'll get another gift from your old man."

Liam closed his eyes. His chest tightened. Tension filled the room like smoke, dipping in and out of their magic in clumsy, fast jolts. When Liam looked at Ryder, his hard gaze was unapologetically fixed on Tyler.

"Tyler..." Christy touched Tyler's hand.

"Get out of my head," Tyler snapped.

The tension shattered. Christy's magic flared: A crisp, protective bubble.

"Ty, c'mon," Donovan whispered. "It's fine."

"Bring up my dad again." Tyler slid his attention to Ryder. "And you'll have to resurrect yourself."

"Don't fight," Christy whimpered. "C'mon, please."

Ryder hummed. His smile was mean and distant, and he traced the line of it with his reaver, scraping the tip across his bottom lip. Despite the challenge in his eyes, Ryder wasn't wrong. They all knew it. Tyler's father had never been kind, and the bruises Tyler brought back with him after fights at home were enough to solidify the circle's suspicion.

Still, Tyler never admitted it.

"Oh yeah, Wind witch?" Ryder smirked.

"Ryder," Liam growled—a warning.

Donovan cleared his throat. "Tyler, enough."

"Listen to your lovers," Christy mumbled. She raised her brows at Tyler and Ryder. "They're both pulling on your collars for good reason. Ryder..." She nodded to him. "Stop pushing. Tyler..." She handed him his cup back. "Be nice."

Liam sighed through his nose. They didn't talk about certain things—Liam and Ryder. Tyler and Donovan. It would end in an argument, jabs at each other over Tyler's insistence that no one in the circle should date while he'd been sleeping with Donovan for weeks without telling them. The whole thing was ridiculous, but it was sore and new, an unspoken secret that lingered just beneath the surface.

Tyler's father, though. That was a wound that kept festering.

"Your turn, Ryder." Christy held out her hand expectantly.

Ryder tapped his reaver against his cheek, glaring at Tyler.

"Ry," Christy snapped. Ryder pushed off the pillar and walked past Tyler to hand Christy his cup. "Okay, let's see." Christy jumped into her usual self, upbeat and charming, wearing a smile that was half-faked and half-true. Slowly, the thick, syrupy tension dwindled. "Transformation, maybe? Or—wait... Yes, that's it. Transformation through trials."

"Lovely," Ryder droned.

Liam handed Christy his cup. "And last but not least," she said and offered him a smile before turning toward his tea leaves.

A choked, sharp gasp cut through the barn. It was shrill and warped, a noise that usually accompanied bad news. She clutched Liam's cup between both hands and heaved in great, pained breaths. Her head whipped around, glancing from each of them before she looked back into Liam's cup.

Everything was still. Everything was quiet.

Liam heard his blood running fast through his veins.

"What is it?" Ryder said, voice clipped and serious.

Christy opened one hand and tipped Liam's cup over. A cluster of leaves fell into her palm.

"Dry leaves," Christy whispered.

Liam swallowed hard. He stared at the leaves, dry as they'd been before they were brewed, and remembered the sound of the kelpie's scream. "Murder... Conquest." The words felt alien in his mouth. He ran his tongue stud across the back of his teeth, chasing them away. "That's... I don't understand."

Footsteps hit the ground close to Liam's legs. Ryder knelt beside him and clasped a hand over Liam's knee. He didn't speak, but his presence alone was comforting.

"You heard a kelpie tonight," Donovan said softly.

Liam nodded.

"And your leaves are dry..."

Liam nodded again.

"Something is coming for you. Something is coming to..."

"Kill me," Liam said.

"We don't know if it was a kelpie." Tyler shook his head, feigning confidence. "And dry leaves don't just mean murder—conquest could be defeat; it could be annihilation. This reading might be pointing at something else, okay? Everyone calm down."

Christy curled her fingers around the leaves. "Yeah, you're right... It's probably just... We shouldn't jump to conclusions. Witch 101: Don't overreact."

Ryder's hand was steady on Liam's knee. "Doesn't matter if it's true," he said, voice rough and low, close to Liam's ear. "You know that."

"We should...eat, or something. We should do literally anything else besides this," Donovan said.

Christy placed Liam's dry tea leaves in a drawstring pouch. She cleared her throat and nodded. "Donovan's right. Let's eat. We'll consult the cards later and go from there."

A tiny, white mouse scampered across the barn and into Christy's lap. Willow, Christy's familiar, blinked red eyes at Liam, translucent whiskers twitching next to her nose.

A second later, talons curled over Liam's shoulder. Opal, a barn owl who had been with Liam since his magic manifested years and years ago, nudged his cheek with her beak. Their familiars must have sensed the unrest and came to investigate.

"Hey, Opal," Liam whispered. He craned his neck to make room for her and didn't brush her away when she nibbled on his jaw.

Tyler cleared his throat. He stood and walked to the other end of the barn where the pizza was. Donovan trailed after him. Their voices were low and quick, words hissed and sighed in hopes that Liam wouldn't hear them. They walked on eggshells, careful not to be too loud, but Liam still caught a few words. *Kelpie. Water. Murder. Ryder. Demon.*

"We should go," Liam said.

Ryder's eyes had faded back to their bright, forest green. His nostrils flared, and he nodded.

"No, Liam, please stay," Christy said. She scrambled for his ankle, but he pulled away. "They don't mean it—guys, would you *stop!*" She aimed the last bit at Donovan and Tyler. "We need to figure this out and we can't if we don't stay together..."

Liam walked away. His chest ached. Tyler's words stung, whether he'd meant for them to or not. "I need to sleep on this, okay?"

Ryder snatched his coat from one of the hooks on the wall.

"Liam, wait!" Christy called.

"Let him go," Tyler said.

Opal clung to Liam's shoulder until they got to the car. As soon as he opened the driver's side door, she took off into the sky. Ryder slid into the passenger's seat. His eyes were hard and unwavering, fixed on the dark forest outside the pasture. Liam couldn't tell if Ryder was hurt or worried or thoughtful or scared.

Liam was all those things, though. He was everything at once.

"They think I'm gonna kill you," Ryder said.

Liam turned the key in the ignition. "It doesn't matter what they think."

"Then why'd we leave?"

A heavy, lucid quiet slipped into the car with them. The night watched, starless and black, until Liam turned the headlights on and drove toward the sea.

THE OCEAN CRASHED yards away. Dark waves licked the sand, and Liam could've sworn he saw fingertips in the water, dragging like claws through white foam, trying to crawl onto land. Somehow, the sea had grown twice as powerful on the night when Liam had grown twice as fearless.

"Liam—" Ryder reached for him, but Liam slipped out of the car before he could be caught.

He stripped off his shirt and kicked his shoes away. Whatever was out there, whatever was coming for him, he needed to find it first. He hopped from the bank onto the sand. "Come get me if I'm not back in ten minutes."

"What the fuck are you doing? *No.* You're not... Liam!" Ryder grabbed his wrist, halting him in place. "You're not getting in that water tonight."

Cold, dark water slipped around Liam's ankles. His magic pulsed, vibrating under his skin, urging him to take another step, to let the ocean have him. Another wave crashed. Slimy, wet hands slid along his bare feet, and wind whispered against his cheek.

Storm Wielder, it said. *Come closer.*

Ryder's fingernails dug into his wrist. "Seriously," he rasped. "Come on, don't do this."

"I need to know what's going on," Liam said. Another wave lapped against him and he closed his eyes. "This is my element. It won't hurt me."

"No, but the kelpie who happens to *live* in your element might."

Liam tugged his wrist out of Ryder's grasp. He took a step. Ryder protested with another breathy snap, "Liam, seriously!" But Liam kept going and going, wading into the water until it covered his shoulders. His heart raced, adrenaline overrun by the elemental magic throbbing inside him. The ocean cradled his arms and legs, dark as the sky above and haunting in ways Liam couldn't express. It knew him. It wanted him.

He closed his eyes and concentrated, palms open beneath the water, reaching for answers to questions he hadn't spoken aloud.

What's happening to me? What's coming for me?

Something old and brutal twisted in him. It was his magic, but it wasn't—like understanding a word in a language he didn't know.

Fingertips pressed on his palm. They were ice cold. Liam's magic lulled him, making room for those fingertips to slip between his knuckles. Something brushed his stomach. The ocean sang and shushed. *Rain born.* Liam watched a man appear—a boy, maybe—somewhere between the two. He rose from the water inches from Liam's face. His skin was ghostly pale, violet veins webbed over too-pronounced cheekbones and down a slender neck. Water dripped from his eyelashes and sharp chin, off strands of black hair and almost-pointed ears.

"Liam Montgomery," the kelpie said. "The ocean sings about you."

Liam's voice was somewhere on shore, lost to him.

"It tells me you you're a witch." His eyes were the color of abalone. His fingers left Liam's hand and he ran them across Liam's abdomen, over his chest. The kelpie slithered closer, his body lithe and strong in the water. "Tell me, Liam the Water witch, what secrets do you keep?"

"I..." Liam's eyelashes fluttered. The kelpie tilted his head, mouth wet on Liam's cheek. "What do you want from me?"

The kelpie moved like the ocean, slow and then fast. Liam had never pondered how *not* to kiss a person back—he'd never been faced with the issue before. But here he was, in the ocean, and a kelpie was kissing him. The kelpie's lips were slippery and soft, his mouth tainted by seaweed, salty and rich. A webbed hand pressed on the nape of Liam's neck, drawing him closer.

Images flashed behind Liam's eyes. Blood between teeth. Hooves beating damp sand. A hand around his throat—Ryder's hand. A sigil carved into flesh. Blood on his lips. Candlelight. The dry tea leaves in Christy's palm. Lightning splintering the sky. Ryder's mouth shaking around a gasp.

Liam's eyes closed. His chest ached. His head fell beneath the water; the ocean roared above and below him, a magnificent, sentient thing. The kelpie's tongue rubbed against Liam's, sure and slow, before he pulled away and stared at Liam through the dark, dark water.

Ancient, strange magic squirmed in Liam's stomach. It burrowed into him, slipped over his bones like the kelpie's hands had slipped over his skin, and Liam found himself helplessly, hopelessly drowning in it.

"The ocean does not need to make a weapon out of love. It is, in its own right, born a weapon already." The kelpie's mouth didn't move, but Liam heard his voice. "Water is only patient when it needs to be. Remember this, Liam Montgomery."

The kelpie's figure cut through the water, growing smaller and smaller the further he swam. Liam lost sight of him as he broke for air, gulping in breath after breath. He let the waves carry him to shore, kicking until his legs were numb and burning the kelpie's words into his memory.

The taste of him—old, like wet leaves and sea spray—lingered.

"I was this close—" Ryder pinched his fingers together. "—to fighting the ocean if it didn't give you back." He ripped off his coat and draped it over Liam's shoulders. "Aren't you cold? Jesus, Liam. What happened? Did you figure anything out?"

"You were gonna fight the ocean, huh?" A fond smile stretched across his mouth. Despite it being after midnight, neither the water nor the wind bothered him. "I met the kelpie... It was..." He watched Ryder's expression tighten. "I'll tell you in the car, c'mon."

"You met the kelpie and it didn't drown you? Or eat you?" Ryder stayed close to Liam, shoulders hunched and hands stuffed in his pockets, enduring a blast of chilly wind.

Liam tossed Ryder's coat to him and squirmed in the driver's seat. His wet jeans clung to his legs, sopping and heavy.

"No, he didn't drown me—well, he almost drowned me. But it—he kissed me," Liam said, listing his head to the side. It still didn't make sense. None of it.

Ryder barked a laugh. "You kissed a water horse?"

"No, a water horse kissed *me*, and he wasn't a horse, he was a guy, or he'd taken the shape of a guy or...something. Anyway—oh, c'mon, don't look at me like that. It's not like I initiated it." Liam turned the key in the ignition. His face flushed, and he chewed on his lip, ignoring Ryder's arched brow and wry smile. "He showed me things, but none of it made sense. I don't know if it was the past or the future, or what it was."

"Did he say anything to you?" Ryder smirked. "Or were you too busy pulling his mane—"

"Fuck off, oh my God," Liam hissed. "He told me that love was a weapon and that the ocean isn't patient. He also said that the ocean sings about me."

"Oh," Ryder purred. "A-plus flirting."

Liam shoved the car into drive and ignored him. "He showed me you."

Ryder went quiet. He stilled, all of him suddenly fixed on Liam, listening intently.

"He showed me *us*. Bloodletting, our magic, things we haven't told anyone."

"Was this before or after he said love was a weapon?"

"Before. I just—I don't understand. I don't get what any of this means. A kelpie comes to shore for the first time in decades and talks to me in fucking riddles, and my tea leaves say murder is in my future."

Ryder tilted his head back against the seat. His eyes were faraway, somewhere out the window or further, even. "A kelpie showed you images of me, the tea leaves said someone is going to kill you," he mumbled, a strange, alien sadness filling his voice, "and you're still trying to put the pieces together?"

They were on the winding road outside Port Lewis between the forest and the sea. Liam clicked his tongue stud along his teeth. Headlights lit the fog.

Liam didn't know what to say. He stayed quiet but rested his hand over Ryder's wrist and held on.

Chapter Two

LIAM DREAMED OF the kelpie.

He dreamed of wet lips and opalescent eyes, of a voice that turned time inside out and the slide of a webbed hand over his chest. His dream was as blurry as any other dream, a loop of movements and words that didn't make sense. The kelpie sang to him in a language he didn't understand. He teased the tendon in Liam's neck with his teeth and slipped his hand down the front of Liam's jeans.

"Don't be scared, Water witch," the kelpie whispered.

Liam gasped awake. He stared at the ceiling and shifted, earning an irritated meow from Percy, Ryder's familiar, who was curled by his feet.

Ryder slept soundly, bare skin warm against Liam. They hadn't spoken—not a word. Once they'd gotten to the apartment, Ryder made tea, Liam took a shower, and when Liam was dressed again and ready to talk, Ryder had already been in bed, asleep or pretending to be.

They hadn't talked about the kelpie or the tea leaves, or the persistent, nagging thought that Ryder would be the cause of Liam's death.

The circle had thought it. Liam, despite trying not to, had thought it. And Ryder, as confident and powerful as he was, had thought it too.

But thinking and believing were two very different things.

It wasn't quite morning. Darkness blanketed the apartment. It turned the witching hours into a mix of navy blues coming through the blinds, shadows stained by muted, cloud-covered moonlight. The dream faded. Times like these, when the night wasn't quite night, turned movement into poetry and breath into artwork.

Ryder stirred against him and Liam swallowed, paying mind to Ryder's slender hand settled on his stomach, to Ryder's mouth hovering over the top of his spine and his thigh pressed innocently between Liam's legs.

Times like these, when morning was far enough away to be ignored, Liam remembered that he was allowed. To have. To touch. To cast spells with his body. To not let empty prophecies frighten him. To ask for things.

He pushed his waist back until his ass met the warm, soft jut of Ryder's hipbones. Ryder's fingers twitched on his stomach. His breath deepened into one long inhale and Ryder exhaled gently as he asked, "You okay?"

Liam felt the brush of his eyelashes, the drag of lips on his nape and the lift of Ryder's chest against his spine. He grasped Ryder's wrist and tugged it over his sternum, between his collarbones, up the column of his throat to his mouth. Ryder's thumb stroked his jaw and Liam closed his eyes when Ryder curved around him, guiding his thigh higher, coaxing Liam's legs open.

"It's..." Ryder probably meant to say *early*, but Liam took two of his fingers into his mouth and Ryder trailed off, words stuck somewhere in the back of his throat, disintegrating into a low groan when Liam's tongue stroked the underside of his knuckles.

Blood rushed fast in Liam's veins. His heartbeat skidded, dancing behind his ribs where his chest was tight. His cheeks heated, and he closed his eyes, taking Ryder's fingers deeper until his throat flexed.

Ryder's breath hitched. His teeth scraped the soft flesh behind Liam's ear, followed the echo of his pulse. He bit down, and Liam whimpered. "Tell me what you want," Ryder said, sleep-rasped and quiet.

Liam's stomach jumped. It shouldn't be difficult to articulate, but the space between morning and midnight, between what had happened at the ocean and what was happening now, made him hazy and light, weighed down with desire and unable to get the words out in the order he wanted them. He settled for slipping Ryder's fingers from his mouth and placing them below his tailbone, under the waistband of his boxers.

Everything was slow until it wasn't. Liam gasped when Ryder pushed him onto his stomach, when he tugged Liam's boxers down and fumbled in the nightstand, returning with slick fingers and a hot mouth on the nape of his neck. Ryder's fingers were nimble and bony, rubbing hard and slow over his hole.

Liam jerked, dick trapped against the bed, and closed his eyes, allowing the shadows bent at odd angles around the bedroom to disappear. He clutched the sheets and canted his hips back, grinding shamelessly against the heel of Ryder's palm. The same fingers that were in his mouth moments ago curled deep inside him, pulling winded, bitten sounds from Liam's lips.

Ryder's breath halted on his neck and Liam felt him pause. He squeezed his eyes shut and rolled his hips. *Keep going, don't stop, don't make me beg—*

"Can I..." Ryder stopped and swallowed hard, wrist digging into the swell of Liam's ass.

Power rushed into Liam. It squirmed and writhed, tugging on Liam's Water magic until it surfaced. Ryder's breathing turned choppy, his necromancy present and palpable in the dark. Liam let him syphon—he gave and gave until he couldn't. Until his muscles twitched and his hips stuttered, until Ryder's fingers grew relentless and rough, until he felt the magic flood back into him, repurposed and energized, dark and thick.

Ryder's weight holding him down was the only thing that kept Liam from arching off the bed. He muffled a hoarse cry and twitched away from Ryder's hand. His orgasm lingered in his shuddered breath and shaking limbs, body raw and oversensitive.

"Stop." The word gusted from him. "Ryder, enough."

Ryder's magic retreated. He put space between them, rolling off Liam and onto the other side of the bed. Liam listened to Ryder hold his breath. He heard his own heartbeat ricochet off his bones, the tail end of their shared magic bursting and sparking inside him.

Liam wanted to stay in this darkness, the space cracked open by their graceless desires. He wanted to take Ryder apart and eat him alive, he wanted them drunk on magic, bare and unyielding. He wanted to become what he was capable of being, as beautiful and awful as Ryder.

"Liam..." Ryder placed his hand on the small of Liam's back.

Liam heard the apology building in Ryder's mouth and turned over in time to stop it. He grasped Ryder's cheek and pulled until their lips met, until Ryder was beneath him, his briefs pushed out of the way with Liam's palm between his legs. His fingers slipped through slick, wet heat, stroking and massaging until Ryder's legs fell open and he ground into Liam's hand.

They'd kissed plenty of times before—rough kisses and messy kisses and long, deep, unhurried kisses. But none of them competed with this. Ryder surged against Liam. He kissed as if he was drowning, unapologetic kissing that accompanied soft moans and stirring hips. His teeth scraped Liam's bottom lip before they sank in.

The night was almost gone. Liam was drunk on Ryder, quivering in the wake of dark magic with the ghost of pleasure burrowing beneath his skin.

Ryder gasped, head thrown back, thighs clamping around Liam's hand as he twitched and trembled.

"*Fuck*, good morning to you too," Ryder mumbled. He turned away to catch his breath, the line of his cheekbone sharp in the darkness. One moment Ryder's eyes were pitch black, the next they were lively green. The rise and fall of his chest slowed. He took Liam's slick fingers from between his legs and lifted them to his mouth, nipping at them.

"It's not morning yet," Liam said. He tugged his hand away from Ryder's mouth and leaned in to kiss him, accommodating the bump of their noses and their wandering hands shifting over bare shoulders.

Ryder swallowed another deep breath. "You could've told me."

Liam's brows quirked.

"That you want me to fuck you." Ryder kissed Liam's mouth, his cheek and jaw. "I've gone down on you, I've gotten you off plenty of times, why didn't you just say something?"

"I didn't—it's not..." Liam huffed. He found Ryder's eyes and stayed there, trapped in them. "I like fucking you. I like you fucking me. I didn't know we had to talk about it."

"You didn't know I had a dick," Ryder corrected, smile coy and fanged.

It was the truth and it wasn't. Liam hadn't known, but he also didn't know how to ask. His chest tightened, and he sank into the comforter, allowing Ryder to crane over him, nose against cheek, lips brushing. Liam felt the sizzle of Ryder's magic stir in him, the echo of necromancy fresh between his bones.

Ryder's smile split into a grin. His hands skated Liam's chest, down his sides and back again, pressing lightly on his shoulder until Liam flopped onto his back and let Ryder crawl over him.

"It's your lucky night, Princess," Ryder purred.

Liam rolled his eyes. "Apparently not since you won't stop calling me that."

Ryder's deep chuckle sent chills down Liam's arms. "Roll over and stay there. I'll be right back."

The knot low in Liam's abdomen squirmed, desire coiling around his insides, turning his magic in circles. He did as he was told, lip pulled between his teeth, heartbeat skittering fast in his chest. Darkness enveloped him. The room was thick and quiet. Liam pushed the thought of the kelpie far away, the thought of the ocean, of his tea leaves, of what was to come, and focused on Ryder. An incense stick on Ryder's altar sparked and smoke drifted from it, sending wafts of patchouli through the air. A drawer opened and closed. Ryder hummed. Something was pulled tight.

Liam closed his eyes when the bed dipped. Ryder's mouth dragged across the back of his knee, his thigh, climbed his vertebrae. Warm, slick fingers slipped between Liam's legs.

"Can I?" Ryder asked. Heat filled Liam, unspooling from Ryder's fingers buried deep inside him.

A soft curse fluttered over Liam's lips. Back bent, he clutched the sheets, nodding as best he could while Ryder's Fire magic pulsed hotter. Ryder's teeth met Liam's shoulder; his knees nudged Liam's legs further apart. He whispered, "Breathe, babe," against Liam's throat and replaced his fingers with his dick.

It was too early to be considered night, but it was too late to be considered morning. The place they were in, suffocated by magic and heat, stood still.

Ryder wasn't careful with him, and Liam loved it. He loved the fit of their bodies, the way Ryder curled over him, the slow, deep rock of his hips, the heavy weight of Ryder's dick inside him, Ryder's hands on either side of Liam's shoulders, the glint off the reaver curved over Ryder's index finger.

Ryder's breath played on the shell of his ear. "Just a little," he whispered and lifted the silver talon to Liam's throat.

It was hard to think, to keep his gasps quiet when Ryder nicked the skin below his ear and sealed his mouth over the cut.

"Ry—" Liam's breath stuttered from him, caught between a moan and a whimper. He reached back to touch Ryder's thigh, and trailed his fingers along the thin, leather straps wrapped around his hips.

Ryder bit down harder. Pain radiated in Liam's neck, but he didn't care. He was too busy being held down, with Ryder on top of him, inside him, and he was too caught up in Ryder leaning over his shoulder, finding his mouth and kissing him with bloody lips.

Liam couldn't comprehend a damn thing. Not the coppery taste of blood in his mouth. Not the soft sigh against his cheek, or the way his body tensed before he came. He trembled and gasped, voice hoarse and winded when he said Ryder's name. Dark magic played on his skin. Fire lurked inside him, mingling with his volatile Water magic, coaxing and prying.

Ryder eased out of him. Liam stayed still through the aftershocks and tried to put his magic in order. His body was raw and alive, and his heart was sore and fluttery. Something hit the floor beside the bed. Hands pawed at him until he rolled over and then Ryder was there, kissing him, tongue red and warm with fresh blood.

Images flashed again. The kelpie's kiss. Ryder's trembling mouth. The tea leaves. Black hooves. They came and went, there one moment and gone in the next.

Distantly, Liam thought it was too much—Ryder cutting his tongue, the blood passed between them during urgent, breathless kisses—but he couldn't deny the way it felt to drag his tongue along the roof of Ryder's mouth, to swallow Ryder's blood and get high off it.

This was magic they shouldn't be playing with: Dark, ancient, unstable.

The ocean does not need to make a weapon out of love.

"This is dangerous," Liam whispered. He gripped Ryder's bare hips where the straps had been moments ago. "Blood magic is one thing—"

"It's all the same," Ryder growled. Liam pulled him, and Ryder had to catch himself on the headboard when his body bent forward, thighs sliding around Liam's ears. "And you're not stopping, so..." The rest of what he was about to say was trampled by a throaty moan.

No, Liam wasn't stopping. He was letting their magic push them. He was putting his mouth on Ryder, scraping his teeth along his pelvis, and fitting his lips around Ryder's clit. He was gripping Ryder's waist with both hands and listening to him come apart, to his whimpers and gasps, to the soft, barely there whisper of Latin on his lips.

Blood magic was one thing. Sex magic was another.

Ryder's energy locked around Liam's bones. It tightened and ached, pulling Liam's Water from the depths of him, the wildest parts of him, the wickedest places. Ryder syphoned until he was a trembling, sobbing mess, until he was squirming in Liam's grasp, oversensitive and overpowered. Liam didn't let up, he kept Ryder in his mouth, under the pressure of his tongue, until Ryder's magic faded.

Liam felt hollow. His magic loomed outside his body, transfigured into something darker, something worse than it should've been. Ryder swatted Liam's hands off his waist and flopped on the bed, heaving in breath after breath.

Water energy sank through Liam's skin, back into his blood and bone and spirit. His eyelashes fluttered, and he endured the heart-pounding, bone-humming, sickeningly sweet high that came from magic torn apart by emotion, stripped from him during intimacy, and syphoned by a necromancer. It was like drugs. It left them without a proper hold on things.

Ryder touched Liam's leg. "You good?"

"I don't know," Liam said. His eyes slipped shut.

A clipped laugh cut through the room. "Did you *feel* that?"

"Yeah, I felt that," Liam mumbled. His breathing steadied. He didn't move when Ryder scooted closer. "You took..." He paused when Ryder's cheek rested on his shoulder. "You took a lot."

"I felt your heartbeat all over me," Ryder whispered. He pressed his lips to Liam's collarbone. "I gave it back, didn't I?"

"Yeah, you did, it just..." Liam didn't want to say it scared him. It hadn't. When Ryder syphoned like that, when the bloodletting turned into spell-casting, their magic became interchangeable.

Ryder had swallowed pieces of Liam.

Liam had inhaled parts of Ryder.

They'd chewed on each other from the inside.

"It's reckless," Liam whispered.

Ryder stilled beside him. He pushed Liam's jaw to the side with two fingers. Their noses brushed. Ryder's onyx eyes peered at him, gaze tempered and honest. "The kelpie...and the tea leaves," he whispered. Liam's eyes softened. Ryder shook his head. "I get it. I do. But I'd never hurt you, Liam. Not on purpose, at least."

Liam kissed him. Their mouths were stained with blood and each other.

"Do you trust me?" Ryder's fingers curled around the back of Liam's neck.

"I do," Liam said. "But sometimes I don't trust *us*."

"We'll figure this out." Ryder swung his leg over Liam's waist and loomed over him. His lips brushed the side of Liam's mouth. "And if something comes for you, if something tries to take you from me..." He kissed Liam's jaw, trailed his lips to his ear. "I'll rip their heart out."

"Did you see it? When you gave me your blood I—"

"Yeah, I saw it." Ryder rested on his elbows, nose against Liam's nose. "That kelpie was *into* it—"

"Be serious for two seconds," Liam said, biting back a laugh. "It was your skin... The sigil that I saw—that was your body and your blood."

"And?"

"And the kelpie wouldn't show me that just to show me. It means something."

"Did you recognize the sigil? I didn't."

"No," Liam said. He tilted his head against the pillow and stared at the ceiling. Ryder rested his cheek on Liam's shoulder, limbs heavy and body relaxed. "Think Jordan might?"

Ryder made a dismissive noise. "I'll ask her. Hey, sis, Liam made out with a kelpie, we had sex after, and surprise, we shared a blood-vision about it. Neat, huh?"

"Are you actually mad about the kelpie?" Liam lifted his head to try to find Ryder's eyes.

"No." Ryder snorted. "I'm mad that my boyfriend is talking about my sister ten minutes after fucking me."

Liam's heart swelled. A smile pulled his lips upright. He shifted, moving them until they were on their sides. He kissed Ryder softly—slow, mindful kisses that grew deeper and longer. Ryder's fingers trailed the ink on Liam's arm, and Liam's palm smoothed along Ryder's vertebrae.

"I'm sorry that our extremely important conversation got in the way of us cuddling." He kissed Ryder again and pulled him close, melding their bodies together. Blood and incense and sex scented the room, and the sun was beginning to rise outside the window.

"You should be," Ryder teased. He rested his palm on Liam's cheek and leaned back. They watched each other, close and unhinged, still buzzing in the aftermath of dark magic. Ryder bumped his nose against Liam's. "I won't let anything happen to you," he said. An air of seriousness formed between them. "You get that, right? I won't let anyone hurt you."

The unknown was restless and horrible. It surrounded them, a being with too many eyes and too many teeth, waiting to rip them apart. Somehow, Ryder was still more dangerous than any unknown and any kelpie and any other witch.

Liam pressed his lips to Ryder's again. "I know."

THE DAY WENT by quietly.

Once Ryder left for work in the early afternoon, Liam went home. *Home* was technically a guest house on his aunt's property, but house was probably too big a word for it. The studio was across an acre-long yard behind the Montgomery estate, elevated with a set of wooden stairs that led to a front door. The paint was chipped and sometimes the roof leaked, but it was cozy enough.

He tossed his messenger bag on the ground next to a lumpy beanbag and glanced at the window. Opal peered back at him, ruffling her white wings as she balanced on the wooden perch attached to the windowsill. "Sleepy?" Liam asked.

Opal screeched at him.

"Sorry I asked."

The bed pushed beneath the window had been with him since he was sixteen. It had seen many different bodies and beings. A nymph once, Christy's younger sister, a boy whose name he couldn't remember, two Darbonne witches, and one drunken night with Donovan before either one of them were in the circle. But what he remembered most was two years ago, when Ryder had flopped on his bed after a day in the woods. They were friends then, and barely that. A sliver of Ryder's stomach had caught the sunlight coming in through the window and he'd been looking at Liam through half-lidded eyes, waiting, wanting.

Liam hadn't understood the saying *you always want what you can't have* until that day. Until he wanted Ryder.

It felt like yesterday, that memory, those hikes through the woods, their easy, flirtatious friendship.

Nothing had changed. Everything had changed.

His phone buzzed, and he fished it out of his pocket.

Ryder: *How's that paper coming?*

Liam: *About to start it. How's work?*

Ryder: *Serving beers and fries to people shouldn't count as work.*

Liam: *As long as you're getting paid it does. Seeing Jordan?*

Ryder: *Later. We meeting everyone after?*

Liam: *I'm meeting Christy at Crescent to work on homework*

Ryder: *Ok. I'll text you when I'm omw.*

Liam had a sociology paper to finish, three chapters of botany to read, and an online math quiz due at midnight. He needed a study buddy, and if there was anyone better at juggling assignments than him, it was Christy.

He scratched under Opal's chin before he gathered his things. A slender laptop, his grimoire, botany book. He glanced from the compact dresser, crowded with candles, to his night stand. *There it is.* He grabbed his cell phone charger from the outlet next to his bed and stuffed it in his bag.

A glimmer from his nightstand amidst a bundle of lavender caught his eye. A palm-sized round mirror that was not his own was placed under the herbs. He'd seen it before, somewhere, but he couldn't remember where or when. Water beaded on the glass like dew. Liam grabbed the mirror and the water tumbled away, streaks that blurred his reflection—auburn hair sheared close on the sides. His slender mouth, furrowed brow, and strong jaw. Liam recognized himself, but he didn't.

Something was wrong with the image. It was skewed. Unfamiliar.

Liam's reflection had abalone eyes. Kelpie eyes.

He dropped it. Opal screeched from the window.

Liam: *Fuck the homework we need to talk*

Christy: *I'm already at Crescent*
Liam: *Be there in 10*

He debated leaving the mirror. It was cracked down the center, lying flat on the wood-paneled floor. Slowly, Liam grabbed the edge of it and shoved it in his bag, unwilling to give the kelpie another chance to look back at him.

"I'M GOING CRAZY," Liam said. He dropped into the seat across from Christy and shoved the mirror at her. "Actually crazy."

"Honey, we're witches. Nothing's crazy."

"A kelpie kissed me last night," he said matter-of-factly.

Christy's large, light eyes widened. A streak of teal hair was curled into a ringlet, dangling prettily out of her ponytail. "You went back to the beach?" she asked. He nodded. She glanced over her shoulder and checked to make sure no one could hear them. Her voice lowered into a whisper. "Liam, that's super dangerous. Water horses *kill* people."

He folded his arms on the table and leaned toward her. "I went for a swim, the kelpie found me... It was... I don't know how to explain it."

"You don't have to if you don't want to," Christy said. Her energy spiked, protective and clean, a burst of magic that dusted Liam's skin. Willow peeked out of Christy's purse on the table beside them. "Was Ryder with you?"

"Yeah, look, just... Go slow, okay?" He held his hand out to her. "Sorry in advance if you see anything you don't want to."

Christy glanced from his face to his hand and back again. "Seriously?"

"I don't know how else to do this." Liam chewed on his bottom lip. He didn't know how to tell her what happened, what was said and how the kelpie looked at him; the images it spun during their kiss. Having Christy dig through his memories for a moment would be worth it if she could help him figure this out. "Just—" He shook his hand at her. "Make it quick."

Christy slid her palm over his and gripped. Her magic pushed into him, tendrils of silk that wrapped around each passing thought. They latched on to a flash of the beach and squeezed. It rushed through him. The water, the kelpie's black hair and white skin, his eerie voice *the ocean sings about you* and icy breath in Liam's mouth. Ryder's bones under his hands. Hooves. Blood. It came rushing back in heightened, jumbled bits. Christy pushed deeper. Liam's memories tumbled from him, spilling messily into the open where Christy could see them. Ryder's blood in his mouth. Their magic. Ryder gripping the headboard, thighs trembling, Liam's mouth between his legs.

Liam yanked his hand away.

A sharp gasp shook Christy's upper half. She cleared her throat and pursed her lips, cheeks red and eyes pointed at the table.

"We'll pretend I didn't see that last part," Christy blurted. Liam nodded appreciatively. "Your element responded to the kiss, not you. Water is... awkwardly sensual sometimes."

He nodded.

"And the kelpie showed you..." She swallowed hard. "He showed you Ryder dying."

Liam's attention snapped to her face. "No," he blurted. "That's not what he showed me. He showed me Ryder bleeding, and a sigil carved into him, and..." Liam thought back to the images. "That's not..."

"The tea leaves, the sigil." Christy counted on each finger as she spoke. "The blood in his mouth."

"The blood in his mouth was a memory," Liam assured. "And even if it's not, it's nothing new."

Christy narrowed her eyes at him. She pulled the oversized sleeves of her frumpy beige sweater into her palms. "Necromancers have to blood-let. Water witches don't."

"If I wanted a lecture I would've texted Tyler."

"Well, you obviously aren't seeing what I did. Ryder was choking, Liam. On his own blood." Her voice shook, hardly audible over the acoustic guitar coming through the café's speakers.

Someone at the counter ordered a pumpkin scone. A chair was pulled out and pushed in. Willow's tiny paws were on his finger. Christy said his name, but he didn't respond. Liam's mind was empty but for the washed-out, flickering images behind his eyes.

Ryder gasping, the blood on his teeth, and how those two separate images made one sound.

"The kelpie's scream wasn't for me," Liam said.

Christy pulled her grimoire out in a hurry and flipped through pages. "We don't know that."

"Dry leaves mean murder," Liam said. His heart raced. He felt jilted and electrified. Anxiety pooled in his lungs.

"We *don't* know that," she snapped again.

Liam's tongue stuck to the roof of his mouth. His phone buzzed on the table, but he didn't reach for it. Willow nibbled on his thumb. Energy—the kind that belonged to a matriarch—filled the air.

"Liam..." Christy whispered. She froze, hands clutched around the edge of her grimoire, and shrank in her seat.

A warm hand wrapped over his shoulder, scented like vanilla and fig. "Liam," Thalia said, her voice as rich and commanding as it always was, "take a deep breath."

"We need to talk, Thalia," Liam said. He felt hollow, like everything he'd known had left him the instant he'd put two and two together. "It's about Ryder."

"I assumed it would be." Thalia Darbonne was slender and compact with dark, umber skin; radiant even on the gloomiest days. Power fell off her in waves. As the Darbonne matriarch, Thalia had control over one of the largest and oldest clans in the region. "Walk with me?"

Christy held her grimoire close to her chest. "I'll be here."

Thalia stroked Willow with one, long finger. "Come on, Montgomery. Let's go."

Liam swallowed the dry, jagged lump in his throat and did as he was told. He slid his phone into his pocket and left the rest of his things at the table. Thalia's hand settled between his shoulder blades. Her Crescent Coffee apron was tied over a long-sleeved paisley dress. She steered him toward the front door, stepping away briefly to grab a sweater from a hook behind the counter.

"You're all over the place," she said.

Coastal wind whipped through Port Lewis. Thalia pulled her beanie down over her ears and waited, taking slow, measured steps down the sidewalk beside him.

"There's a kelpie in Port Lewis," he said.

Thalia tilted her head, intrigued.

"I was at the beach yesterday. Me and Ryder heard it. We did a tea reading in the barn later that night and my leaves came back dry."

"Kelpie's are shifters," Thalia said. "Which form did it take?"

"Human. He looked young—our age, maybe younger."

"And you understand that kelpies bring warnings? Usually they're the first sign of a hunt, or they're doing the hunting themselves."

"And dry tea leaves mean murder," he said softly.

They turned the corner into a secluded garden settled between two buildings. Herbs grew in baskets attached to the fence, a naked tree trembled, and leaves tumbled across their shoes. Winter was on its way, breathing storms and bitter cold into Port Lewis. Thalia stopped to lean against the fence and crossed her arms over her chest.

"What aren't you saying, Liam?"

He thought of Ryder's breath on his mouth. *I won't let anyone hurt you.* "Do you practice with Jordan?"

Thalia's eyes sparked. Her power whipped around them, magic that snapped at him with hungry jaws.

"Please, just—I know it's none of my business, but I... *I do.* I practice with Ryder. And rumor has it you practice with Jordan, so—" He shrugged and tried to meet her gaze. Her dark eyes were narrowed, mouth pressed in a tight line. "You want the truth. That's it."

"Be more specific." Thalia's magic balanced on his skin like knives, ready to sink in at any moment.

Liam licked his lips and shifted from foot to foot, eyes climbing to the sky and back to her. He lifted the edge of his shirt. A dark pink scar in the shape of a planetary rune marred his hip. "Is that specific enough?"

Scars littered Thalia's arms and neck. She didn't cover them often, but never discussed them either. They were necromancy marks—the aftermath of bloodletting. Dark magic's brand. Since Thalia was the Darbonne matriarch, she was expected to practice White magic—Spirit magic.

Liam hoped that showing his scars would persuade Thalia to trust him with her own.

Thalia's nostrils flared. She said his name on a deep sigh, the way a disappointed parent would. "Ryder hasn't been practicing for long enough. What you two are doing... It's..."

"Dangerous, I know."

"No," Thalia said lowly. "You don't. Ryder isn't just inexperienced, he has two different types of magic inside him. And mixing that with you? With Water? Liam, that's... You're asking for something to go wrong." She heaved a frustrated breath. "I'm a White witch and Jordan is a necromancer. When we practice, there's balance. When you two practice, there's Fire, necromancy and Water and..." She stopped abruptly and shook her head. "That's too much in one spell. That's taking it way too far."

Liam chewed his lip. "How do you *not* take it too far?"

Thalia's tongue touched her top lip. Her magic subsided and she relaxed, shoulders slouching as her weight fell heavier against the fence. "There's no guidelines for magic like this. I can't tell you how to avoid catastrophe or what not to do, because it'll never be safe. We were sixteen when we started. Back then? Jordan almost killed me."

"I'm not worried about him killing *me*." Liam blurted. "The kelpie showed me images of Ryder's death. Of him choking on his own blood."

"You got close to it?"

"You could say that," Liam mumbled, hoping the blush dripping across the bridge of his nose didn't give him away.

"And your tea leaves said conquest was in your future. You think you're going to kill Ryder?"

"No, of course I don't think I'm going to... Fuck, Thalia. *No*," he snapped. "No, I refuse to let that happen, but something wants it to. Something is moving pieces around to make that a reality. Fate doesn't lie."

"Sometimes fate makes mistakes." Thalia pulled her sweater tighter around herself. "And usually it can be changed."

"How?"

Liam's phone buzzed.

Ryder: *where are you? I'm at Crescent. Jordan said the sigil is Mars*

Liam: *Talking to Thalia*

"Let me talk to Jordan, all right?" Thalia nudged Liam with her shoulder. "But for now, distance might be smart."

"Distance?"

"I'm only two years older than you, Liam. I know what comes with bloodletting." She arched a brow at him, a coy smile perched on her full mouth. "You want me to believe that you and Ryder don't use magic during intimacy?"

Liam's whole body flushed. The way she said *intimacy* carved a space out inside him—her voice low and teasing. He opened his mouth to respond but shut it with an audible click. He didn't have an excuse or an explanation, and he couldn't deny it.

"There's a new moon in a week. We'll plan something, all right? Stay away from the sea. Sleep in your own bed." A hint of playfulness tinged her words. "We know too many necromancers for a prophesized death to stick anyway."

He nodded. "I'd still like to *not* be the cause of it."

They walked back to Crescent Café side by side. Before Thalia opened the door, she grabbed Liam's wrist and squeezed. Her eyes snared him. "This discussion? It stays between us."

"Yeah," he said softly. "'Course."

Thalia swept inside. She hung her sweater on the hook behind the counter and flashed a grin to the two customers admiring cupcakes in the pastry case. Liam felt Ryder's energy. The bite of it hummed in his scars—magic that recognized itself in another. Ryder sat with Christy, Tyler and Donovan, his shoulders bunched, index finger tapping the table again and again.

Tyler rolled his eyes. Donovan glanced at Liam and gestured for him to join with a tilt of his chin.

"No," Ryder snapped under his breath. "It's impossible."

"You have a demon inside you," Tyler mumbled. "Nothing's impossible."

Liam took the empty seat next to Ryder.

"Did you know that there's an ancient war between the elemental Orders?" Tyler caught Liam's eye and waited.

Ryder snorted. "It's irrelevant."

Tyler flashed his palm, eyes still on Liam.

"No," Liam said. "I didn't. Why?"

"Did you know that Belial—" Tyler waved his hand at Ryder. "—happens to be the King of the Order of Fire?" He tilted his head. His upturned, dark eyes were unblinking and stone cold. "I'm sure you can guess which Order kelpies belong to."

"What does that have to do with anything?" Liam glanced at Christy. She clutched her grimoire to her chest and offered an apologetic frown. "We don't practice Demonology, a cornerstone of the Orders, and we've only ever asked for assistance from deities—" He counted on his fingers. "—what, like twice? The Orders are beyond us. We don't mess with them."

All eyes turned to Ryder. His top lip curled back in a snarl. The collar of his cloak curved around his throat and a pentacle dangled from the choker that ringed his neck. He bristled, energy lunging from him in angry bites. "I could've stayed dead," he said sarcastically. "That was literally the only other option."

"We're not saying it's your fault, Ry," Christy assured. "But…"

"But what?" Ryder's magic surged. A light above them popped and went out.

Someone startled at a table across from them. The couple at the counter yelped. They murmured to each other in hurried whispers. *It just went out. Yeah, goosebumps. I've heard rumors about the manager here. Witches? Oh, please. I'm tellin' you—they aren't shy about it.*

Thalia walked around the counter. "Must've been a bad bulb," she said. The five of them wilted under her narrowed eyes. She nodded toward the door, a subtle dismissal, and flashed a toothy smile to the gossiping customers. "It was a pie, right? We have a wonderful cranberry…"

"We should take this someplace else," Tyler said. He stood and, for the first time in front of the circle, grabbed Donovan's hand. "C'mon."

Even Donovan looked taken aback. His face flushed, and he nodded in agreement. "Maybe we can try another reading. Meet at the barn?"

"Yeah, okay," Christy said. She held out her hand and Willow scurried up her sleeve to sit on her shoulder.

Liam touched Ryder's fingertips. "C'mon," he whispered. "Let's go."

Ryder's jaw slid back and forth. He looked embarrassed and shaken and angry, but he took Liam's hand and they followed Tyler anyway.

CHRISTY FLIPPED THROUGH her grimoire. Her clawed, acrylic nail traced line after line. She tapped on the middle of one page and nodded. "Mirrors are typically used to solidify a bridge between one place and another. They're communicative tools. People use them to look further into themselves, sometimes to speak to creatures on other planes."

"Are they ever used for scrying?" Liam paced from one side of the barn to the other. He glanced at the small, round mirror next to Christy's leg. Somehow, it was wet again.

"Sometimes," she said. "But rarely. They're almost always black and they usually show a past life. This one's pretty average." She snatched the mirror and examined it, turning it around in her hand to look at every edge. "You think you saw the kelpie when you looked into it?"

"No, I saw myself, but..." He paused to glance around. Tyler and Donovan watched him from a hay bale, sitting side by side. Ryder stood with his back against the door, arms folded defensively across his chest. "It wasn't me."

"Necromancers, demons, kelpies," Tyler said on a groan. "What's next?"

Donovan's eyes swept toward Tyler. His lips tightened, but he stayed quiet.

"A fucking war, apparently," Ryder snapped. "That you think I'm a part of."

"Can we get one thing figured out before we jump to the next?" Liam asked. He rolled his eyes and pointed at the mirror in Christy's hand. "I highly doubt the Orders have anything to do with this."

"They might," Christy interjected. She placed her grimoire on the ground and read from it. "The Orders are court-based systems that divide magical practices and beings into categories. Earth, Air, Fire and Water are the four most well-known Orders. Throughout history, the Kings, Queens, and Guardians of each Order have clashed, testing their power and limitations." She glanced from Liam to Ryder and back again. "Ryder formed an attachment with Belial, the King of Fire, and since you're a Water witch, it might... I mean, it could be possible—"

"That I'm going to kill him?" Ryder said over a cruel laugh. "C'mon. I think I'd know if Belial wanted me to murder my boyfriend."

"You probably would," Christy said matter-of-factly. She swallowed and settled her timid gaze on Liam. "I'm worried it's the other way around."

Liam stopped pacing. He lifted his eyes to Ryder's face and waited for realization to slide into place. His magic thrashed, clawing to the surface. Thunder cracked outside. Rain hit the roof, slow and then fast. He inhaled a deep breath and held it until his chest ached. If there was anyone he couldn't fathom hurting, it was Ryder. "I think we misinterpreted the kelpie's scream. Me and Christy did some research and... We think... I think something is coming for you," he finally said. "And I think it's me."

It took Ryder a moment to speak. His lips parted, and he shook his head. "I don't believe that."

Tyler snorted. "That doesn't make it any less true."

"We don't know for sure," Donovan soothed.

Christy nodded. "Donovan's right. We don't know for sure, but—"

"But because I belong to the natural enemy of Liam's Order, you think he's destined to kill me? *Really?*"

"It makes sense, Ryder," Tyler said.

"Yesterday you were convinced that *I* was the murderer in the room. Funny how quickly your opinion changes, Tyler." Ryder's voice was the hiss of dark magic, the gurgle of blood and crunch of bone. "How exactly does any of this make sense? Because I'm a half-blood? Because I'm Fire and I use dark magic?"

Tyler slid off the hay bale and shrugged. "Yeah, that's exactly why. You're a necromancer, you unmake death, you're the epitome of everything natural magic is against."

He spoke plainly, as if Ryder's surprise was unwarranted. "There's a reason why darklings are solitary. They compromise elemental circles."

Liam whipped toward Tyler. His heart slammed against his ribs, anger pooling where breath should've been. "That's enough."

"It's the truth," Tyler bit out. "The Orders have been at war since they were established. You think your Water magic isn't influenced by it? You think it doesn't feel Ryder's darkness and run?"

"I know for a fact that it doesn't," Liam snapped.

Tyler waved his arm at Ryder and then at Liam. His voice rose, stirring the air into heavy gusts. "How can you possibly be sure?"

"Because his darkness is inside me!" Liam shouted.

Everything went still. The rain outside stopped. The wind whipping around Tyler died. Ryder's crackling magic quieted. Christy drew in a long, slow breath.

Liam looked at Tyler, teeth gritted and hands balled into fists. He licked his lips and rubbed a hand over his mouth, enduring the upended tension of a secret suddenly on display. He grappled for words—explanations. Anything. But there was nothing. Anger and desperation smothered his reservations. "What do you want me to say?" Liam's voice became the roar of a river, the crash and break of waves on sand. His caramel eyes turned pale, stormy gray.

Tyler's mouth pressed into a tight line.

Christy scrambled to her feet and placed herself between them, one hand stretched toward Tyler, the other toward Liam. "We'll use the mirror to scry," she blurted. "We'll use it in a—in a—" She stammered and squeaked. "—a bowl of water! That way Liam can channel through his element and try to get answers."

Tyler didn't flinch. He paid no attention to Christy. His voice was soft and worn, somewhere between worry and anger. "You could die doing that shit. Letting him syphon you? A Fire witch—a *darkling*—syphoning Water magic?" Tyler barked a laugh. "You're both asking for it, you know that?"

"C'mon, Ty, please," Christy whispered.

"We know," Ryder said and took long strides to Liam's side. "We know, Tyler. It's fucking dangerous—I'm dangerous. He's dangerous. None of this is safe." Ryder touched Liam's lower back. His fingertips crept beneath Liam's shirt, warm and sure on his skin. "If you're right about the Orders then we need to fix this, don't we? We need to figure out what the fuck is going on instead of arguing over what you approve of."

"You're risking the entire circle," Tyler gritted.

"The only one at risk here is Ryder," Liam said. The gray faded from his eyes and revealed rich brown. He heaved a sigh, relaxing into the heat radiating from Ryder's palm and the strange relief that followed an unburied secret.

Tyler's jaw moved back and forth.

"Tyler." Donovan's voice lacked its typical sweetness. He cradled his chin in his hand. Ivy nail polish tipped each finger. "Give it a rest and get some air."

Tyler's eyes tracked Liam's face. Words built in his mouth, bitten back by Donovan's insistence or better judgement. Both, maybe. He turned on his heels and left. His silhouette grew smaller and smaller as he crossed the pasture.

Donovan shot Liam a quick glance. "He doesn't mean it," he said under his breath. "He just doesn't know any better."

"Ignorance is bliss until it gets you punched in the mouth," Ryder said.

"Yeah?" Donovan arched a brow and shoved his hands in his pockets. He angled his mouth over his shoulder as he followed Tyler out the door. "I'm pretty sure he gets enough of that at home, Ry."

The barn fell into uncomfortable silence. Christy tucked pieces of multi-colored hair behind her ears and cleared her throat. She busied herself with a bowl and the mirror, with her grimoire and some candles. "We should sage the space first," she mumbled, a sad attempt at changing the subject. She sniffled and pawed at her face. "And turn off the lights, and—"

"Christy," Liam said softly. He reached for her, but she yanked away.

"I *see* it, Liam." Her voice quivered. She swatted tears off her cheeks and refused to meet his eye. "I see what's inside him and what's inside you, okay? I don't get to believe whatever bravado you both try to wear because I see the truth. I'm sad for Tyler and I'm scared for you, and this is... This is shitty for me. I always have to see things I don't want to see and know things I don't want to know. *Always*. I always have, I always will and that means I'm not allowed to pick sides."

Liam's chest fluttered. He reached for Christy's hand again and she let him take it. "I'm sorry, okay? I'm sorry you're stuck in the middle. I just... I feel like we've been fighting for fucking weeks."

"Because we have been," Ryder said.

Liam shot him a stern glance.

"We need rain," Christy said. She gave Liam's hand a squeeze and grabbed the bowl beside her grimoire. She tipped a candlestick over until wax dotted the bottom of the bowl, placed the cracked mirror in the center, and handed it to him. "Take it outside and fill it halfway. I'll sage—hey, wait, Ryder, before you go." She shook the bundle of sage at him. "Blow."

Ryder smirked and blew across the tip of the sage. Slowly, it began to smolder.

LIAM DIDN'T KNOW what to expect. He asked the sky to open and it did. He asked the ocean to guide him and it might've. He asked the water to show him, but instead, it touched him.

He recognized the floor. A soft blanket over wood paneling. Hay poked through his jeans and nipped his calf. He knew the smell of the barn, dusty and cleansed, filled with the remnants of Christy's lavender-sage and sprinkles of wet salt. But he couldn't see any of it.

Not the blanket, not the hay, not the smoke. He stared into the bowl in his lap and concentrated. Darkness looked back at him.

Bring me the sea. Bring me answers.

The mirror beneath the water was empty. No reflection looked back at him. The crack down the middle of the glass glowed ethereal silver. Liquid thread coiled from it through the water, tendrils of dreams or answers or starlight—something he didn't understand and probably never would.

"You have dark water in you, Storm Wielder." A voice vibrated within him. It was feminine—the chime of bells, the static hum that came before thunder. "Use it."

Liam tried to reach deeper. His magic slid from him, tethered around his ribs and bundled beneath his kneecaps, grounding him to the here and now. The darkness rippled and throbbed: a stone across ice, raindrops shaking restlessly in their clouds. Liam exhaled, and the Water enveloped him. His energy clashed with whatever watched and he almost choked, suddenly aware that his freedom to breathe had been seized by something older and greater and worse than him.

The kelpie's webbed hand cupped his cheek. "You're different," he said. "Like us but tainted. Changed."

Liam couldn't speak. The kelpie's thumb touched his lips and pressed down, sliding into his mouth. Liam tried to pull back, but the Water wouldn't let him. The kelpie's slippery, cold thumb hooked over his bottom teeth. Darkness pulsed. His head spun, and he closed his eyes. When he opened them, it was Ryder looking back at him.

"Use it," Ryder said, but it was also the kelpie's voice, the feminine voice from before, the voice of the ocean—all speaking at once.

"How?" Liam asked.

The kelpie pulled his hand away. He still wore Ryder's face, but this time when he opened his mouth it was Liam's voice. "You taste like power."

The kelpie disappeared. Liam's stomach lurched. His lungs burned and convulsed. He choked, spitting mouthfuls of water onto the floor beside him. He coughed and sputtered, tumbling over to catch himself on his hands as he heaved in breath after breath.

Something shuffled closer.

"Christy, don't." Tyler's voice came from somewhere behind him.

"Oh my God, Liam... Are you there, man?" Donovan asked.

Liam opened his eyes. Black, smoky tendrils floated across the floor where Ryder knelt in front of him; his onyx eyes wide and unblinking, bottom lip worried between his teeth. He curled his index finger under Liam's chin and carefully lifted his face.

"Hey, Princess," Ryder tested. "You back?"

"Don't call me that," Liam mumbled.

Christy sighed, relieved. "It's been two hours," she said. "Two hours!"

Exhaustion clung to him. He wanted to fall into Ryder's lap and sleep for days. "Sorry."

"What'd you see?" Tyler asked. He appeared next to Christy with Donovan beside him.

"Nothing at first. Then the kelpie came through and told me..." He repeated the words to himself. *You have dark water in you.* "Told me I was different." It wasn't a lie, but it wasn't the truth. Liam swallowed hard and wiped his mouth. "Said I needed to use it."

"Use what?" Ryder caught Liam's face between his palms. "Hey, focus, look at me." Liam's lashes fluttered. He blinked and leaned into Ryder's hands. "Use what?"

Liam reached into Ryder's cloak and grabbed his side, the place a fresh sigil had been carved days ago. He didn't want to say it in front of the others, to tell them more about the darkness he and Ryder shared, the transfiguration of his magic into something he no longer knew. Ryder flexed his jaw and gave a curt nod.

"Tyler, do your parents know anything about the Orders?" Ryder took Liam's hand and hauled him to his feet.

Liam let Ryder take some of his weight. His body was wrung out and boneless, still drowning in the strange sensation of being between worlds. Ryder coiled his arm around Liam's waist.

Tyler shrugged. "If I brought it up they'd ask about shit you don't want me to tell them."

"I'll talk to my mom," Donovan said. All eyes turned toward him. He shoved his jittery hands in his sweatshirt pocket. "She might know something."

"Liam…" Christy placed a hand on his arm. The kelpie flashed behind his eyes, his thumb in Liam's mouth, the silken purr of a voice he didn't know saying *dark water*. He jerked away, and Christy gasped, fingertips twitching over his skin. "I didn't… That was an accident."

"It's fine," Liam whispered. He hoped the wince that crossed his face and worry furrowing his brow was enough to keep her quiet. "Let us know what you find out, Donovan."

Donovan nodded.

"You're leaving." Tyler said it like a statement, but it was a question nonetheless.

"He needs to sleep," Ryder said. His arm tightened around Liam's waist. "We'll do a reading in the morning and let you know what the cards say, all right?"

"You do that." The distrust in Tyler's tone scraped Liam raw. "Take care of him, Ryder."

"I'll make sure he doesn't kill me." Sarcasm was a weapon in Ryder's mouth, easily aimed and expertly fired. "Thanks for your heartfelt concern, fearless leader."

Tyler snorted in response. He didn't bother waiting for them to make it through the barn doors before he snapped to Christy in a breathy whisper, "What exactly did you see?"

Chapter Three

TIME HAD ALWAYS stopped and started at the beginning and end of each day. Liam woke up, usually beside Ryder, did homework, made tea, either crawled back into bed with Ryder or followed him into the shower, and went to class or work after. They did readings in the mornings, lit incense at night, went for walks in the woods on afternoons when they had time together and spent moments alone wrapped in unapologetic intimacy.

But Liam had stopped sleeping, and now time was warped. It bent around him, mismanaged and soaked in a feeling he couldn't place. It was fear, but it wasn't. They were dreams, but they weren't. His magic was his, but it felt unwelcome in his body.

The morning after Liam tried scrying at the barn, he woke to the feeling of Ryder's fingers combing through his hair. His cheek was pillowed on Ryder's lap and the rest of him, too tall for the couch, was curled into a ball. He thought he'd been asleep for days.

"Go back to sleep," Ryder said softly. He touched Liam's cheekbone, the edge of his jaw and shell of his ear. A well-read book was open in Ryder's other hand and a slim pair of reading glasses balanced on the tip of his nose. *God*, Liam thought. *He's handsome.* "It's barely morning."

"How long have I been asleep?" Liam pressed his face into Ryder's warm belly, covered by a black tank.

"Two hours, maybe. It's four."

"Four in the morning?"

Ryder nodded.

"Why the hell are you awake?"

"I didn't wanna move you." Ryder flicked his gaze from his book to Liam. "We got here. I made tea and brought you a cup, but you were out like a light. I sat down to read, and you ended up here."

Ryder combed his fingers through Liam's hair again. Liam didn't go back to sleep. He stayed awake in Ryder's lap, watching him read, ignoring him whenever he told Liam to close his eyes.

After a few minutes of comfortable silence, Liam said, "I think we did something to my magic." Ryder's eyes snapped to his and he closed his book. "I don't know how, and I don't know what it means, but something else came through when I was scrying. A voice told me I had dark water inside me."

"Dark water?" Ryder took his glasses off.

"You should wear those more," Liam purred. "They look good on you."

One side of Ryder's mouth lifted into a smile. "Don't change the subject."

Liam sighed through his nose. "I think... I don't know what the fuck I think, but maybe syphoning my magic has done something to it. Maybe we've changed it."

"Necromancy can't change magic unless it's been completely stripped from someone. I can stimulate your magic, charge it, bend it, move it, but I can't change the natural components of it. Humans can't handle that kind of transfiguration. You'd have to be dead for it to work."

"You can leave a mark, though?"

Ryder lifted one shoulder in a shrug. His fingertips stilled on the side of Liam's head. "I don't know if I can or not."

"The kelpie said I was tainted; told me I was changed."

"There's one way to find out," Ryder said. He stroked Liam's neck with his knuckles.

"We shouldn't."

"'Course we shouldn't."

Liam's teeth sank into his bottom lip. He moved to the other side of the couch and waited, listening to Ryder's breathing, to Opal's talons shift over the edge of the bookshelf, to his magic grow needy and volatile. The idea of it—Ryder's darkness creeping inside him—was thrilling despite how often it'd happened already. He nodded and sank into the cushions, allowing Ryder to crawl over him.

"Go slow," Liam whispered.

Ryder's pupils expanded over the whites of his eyes. Steam dripped from his lips. Dark, syrupy energy wrapped around Liam's heart, clamored between his ribs, and clawed at him. Ryder's hand settled on his hip and pressed him into the couch, holding him there, still and open. He tucked his mouth against Liam's throat and said, "Don't move."

Liam held on to Ryder's magic. He let it slide around inside him and thrum in his veins. He encouraged Ryder to take, pushed until his Water was slipping into Ryder in steady streams. Liam's hips pushed against Ryder's. Desire coiled tight at the base of his spine. "I can't help it."

"Usually we're in a much different situation when we're doing this," Ryder said. He slid his hand under Liam's shirt, across his stomach and chest. Liam bent away from the couch, body and magic hungry for more of Ryder's skin, more energy, more everything. "And if you don't chill out, I'm not gonna be able to find anything."

Liam reached deeper. He closed his eyes and met Ryder's magic with his own, testing and pushing, tangling and squeezing. Ryder's breath came short. He dug his fingernails into Liam's ribcage.

"Liam, what're you...?"

There. Liam's Water snagged the edge of Ryder's darkness and pulled until it sank into him, until his Water could chew on it, taste it, savor it. Ryder gasped and lurched back. *Wait.* Magic buzzed in Liam. It filled his mouth and lungs and stomach—rich, thick darkness that twisted in him. A drop of black ink in a clear pool.

"Jesus fucking Christ, Liam," Ryder said. He crawled backward on the couch, putting distance between them. "You can syphon?"

"Is that what it is?" Liam's voice deepened into the rush of water over rocks, the sound of rain between branches. His magic urged him forward, but he stayed still. Ryder's eyes were wide and black. He ran his hand over Liam's shin. "No, d-don't—" Liam jerked his leg away. "Don't. That's... I could hurt you—this isn't natural, it's—"

"It means you can use dark magic," Ryder said.

"Why didn't we notice this before?" Liam brought his knees to his chest and hugged them, failing to calm the place inside him that wanted another taste of Ryder's necromancy. "We've been doing this for weeks, Ry. How'd we...?"

"It's impossible," Ryder said.

"Obviously not!"

"You're a goddamn Water witch, Liam—"

"Obviously fucking not!"

Opal chirped from the bookshelf. Percy hopped on the back of the couch, fur bristled and ears flat. Ryder's jaw slackened. He stared at Liam, perplexed, unhinged, a look so unfamiliar on Ryder that it was almost frightening. Something lingered with them, a force that Liam recognized but didn't—monstrous and heated and demonic. It swelled around Ryder, pulsing from him.

Belial's energy was unmistakable now that Liam was acquainted with it.

Their magic circled each other. Time turned inside out, stilling before it rushed ahead, bending until Liam's head swam. Ryder's eyelashes fluttered. His chest heaved, and he licked his lips. This was dangerous. Their magic, Belial, the unknown. If Liam stayed, he would take Ryder apart bit by bit, he would sink his teeth into every dip and curve of his body, he would carve the darkness out of him and swallow it.

Conquest.

Liam stood and toed on his shoes, grabbed his messenger bag off the counter, and fished out his car keys.

Ryder didn't move from his place on the couch. "Babe, c'mon..."

"I have class in a few hours." He was twitchy, overpowered and too tense. He didn't trust himself with Ryder. He didn't trust himself with anything. "I'll text you."

"You don't have to leave." Ryder trailed him to the front door. His energy nipped at Liam's, hot Fire and wicked darkness. Long, bony fingers gripped Liam's shoulder. "We'll figure this out, just..."

"Not right now," Liam whispered. He turned and caught Ryder by the hips. "Not like this."

"Not like what?" Ryder tilted his head. His breath stuttered from him, mouth too close to Liam's, hands scaling Liam's arms.

"With your demon watching our every move." Liam's lips dusted Ryder's. "Waiting for us to rip each other to pieces."

Ryder's jaw tightened. "We wouldn't."

"We don't know that anymore. Just..." He pressed his lips to Ryder's in a quick, firm kiss. "Not when we're like this, okay?"

Like this. Liam wished he had a better way to explain it. Overpowered. Desperate. Ready to take from each other until they were drunk on magic—unstable and uncontrollable. Ryder's energy was tantalizing. It made him insatiable.

"I trust you," Liam whispered. "But I don't trust *us.*"

I don't trust myself.

Ryder's nose bumped against his cheek. "Jordan warned me. She said I'd get addicted to you."

Liam didn't know what to say. He wanted to pin Ryder against the couch and drink his darkness. He wanted Ryder trembling beneath him, coming apart at the seams and saying his name. He wanted to take shelter in a storm. Call lightning to the sky. Feel Ryder from the inside out.

"Everyone warned us," Liam said. He kissed Ryder again and slipped out the door.

Darkness snaked through him. He rubbed his eyes and took the stairs two at a time. Opal circled above, her wings stark and prominent against the sky.

"What's happening to me?" Liam whispered. His throat burned; his chest ached.

He pulled the door of the Subaru closed and took a deep, deep breath.

LIAM DIDN'T SLEEP—not really.

After sitting through a useless hour of Calculus, he went home and took a nap to try to clear his head. His dreams were crowded with Ryder and the kelpie and the sea. He shook awake, panting and clawing at his bed, the ghost of Ryder's mouth still on him.

The candles on his altar were barely burnt. A chalice filled with water sat beside them and an assortment of crystals was spread out in a circle around it. He tried to steady his breathing, rubbed a hand across his mouth, and glanced at the clock. He'd been asleep for forty-five minutes.

Ever since he'd heard the kelpie's scream, Liam hadn't been able to rest. Sleep evaded him. His heart skittered fast and adrenaline kept spiking at inappropriate times. He hadn't slept at Ryder's. He hadn't slept at home. Candles didn't work, incense didn't work, meditation didn't work. The kelpie kept coming for him; his curious, silver eyes cutting through Liam's dreams and daydreams and nightmares.

He grabbed his phone and sent a text.

Liam: *Good sigil to use as a ward?*

Thalia: *Saturn. Why?*

Liam: *Kelpie.*

Thalia: *Has it showed up?*

Liam: *Sorta*

Thalia: *Jordan's talking to her dad about some stuff. I have a meeting and then we'll talk*

Liam: *A meeting?*

Thalia didn't respond.

Liam watched sunlight cut through tree branches on the horizon. It was late afternoon, the time right before sunset, and Ryder's magic still coated his tongue. The kelpie's gaze was all over him, watermarks that chilled him to the bone. He chewed on his thumbnail and considered a spell, something, anything, to keep that goddamn creature from finding him again.

He drew the sigil of Saturn in his grimoire, anointed it with water from his chalice, and dripped candle wax into the corners. He took his knife—a white-handled blade called a boline—and pressed it to his wrist. White witches weren't supposed to use tools for bloodletting. Not their athames.

Not their bolines or sceptars or knives, but Liam needed the potency of his blood. He needed to know if his magic was as dark as it felt.

The tip of the sickle-blade sliced his skin. Blood beaded from the wound, dark red against his beige complexion. He focused on the seam of his skin, on the rush of power that moved through him and began to surface. The blood floated from his skin. Tiny, round spheres danced in the air in front of him.

Liam turned the blood in circles. He focused on the structure of it, the way it hummed with unused power and unsure intention. He guided the drops onto the paper, following each line of the sigil until it was red.

Controlling blood, even his own, wasn't something an elemental witch should've been able to do.

You're different.

He tore the page from his grimoire and placed it against his bedroom door. Eyes closed, he focused on the sigil, his blood, the magic inside him that he couldn't tame. The blood seeped from the paper into the door and the sigil disappeared. Liam imagined a cage around his room—solid doors, unbreakable locks, strong walls. He pulled his energy from the depths of him and cast until the spell clicked into place and solidified.

Nothing that would cause me harm. He jotted another line on the paper. *Nothing that would control me. Nothing that would attempt to deceive me.* His fingers clutched the pen tightly. *Nothing uninvited.* He folded the paper neatly, set it in the smudge bowl, and tossed a lit match in with it. The paper combusted and curled inward, shrinking into a charred bundle and then into ash.

Exhaustion burrowed in Liam. He wanted to sleep for hours, days, weeks, but as appealing as the idea was, he knew it wouldn't happen. Something inside him was awake and it wasn't going to let him rest until he recognized it.

"Opal, c'mon," Liam said. He dipped his fingers into the chalice and flicked water on his bed, on his windowsill and smeared it over the door handle. Opal screeched and flew off her perch. Liam locked the door behind him when he left, messenger bag over one shoulder, his grimoire tucked under his arm, and crossed the stretch of grass between the guest house and the main property.

Opal landed on his shoulder. Despite how tired he was, Liam couldn't help the effortless bounce in his step, the strange, uninvited buzz that filled him in the wake of blood magic.

"You haven't left yet," he said softly and scratched under Opal's chin. Her talons curled into his long-sleeved shirt. "That's good for something, isn't it?"

The Montgomery estate had been in the family for three generations. It was in his aunt's care, but really, the property belonged to all of them. The library, six guest bedrooms, two master suites, eight bathrooms and an entirely too-large kitchen would stay with them for as long as there was a single Montgomery left.

The exterior could use a fresh coat of white paint and chips riddled the balcony, but otherwise the two-story mansion had held its charm over the years. Liam walked through the mud room and into the kitchen. Three small, rowdy boys argued in front of the bay window.

One shouted at him, "Hey, Liam!"

And another startled. "Oh, you've got your bird."

"Opal," Liam corrected. He smiled at the trio of twelve-year-olds. They were young witches—barely coming into their magic. Opal screeched at them and they jostled backward.

One of his cousins, the bravest of them, cleared his throat. "People are gossiping about you and Jordan's brother. The necromancer who made a deal with a fire demon? Are you two, like, you know...?"

The other two snickered and giggled. One said, "I saw him sneaking into the guest house two weeks ago."

Liam's mouth quirked into a half smile. "Maybe we are," he teased. "Why? You scared?"

"No," they all barked at once.

The one who spoke first, Elliot, tilted his head and said, "You know our mom doesn't like your *thing* with him, right? Neither does Aunt Lindsey. They talk about it all the time."

Liam folded his arms across his chest and leaned against the counter. "You wanna know what happens when you grow up?" He lifted his brows. His cousins scoffed and snorted. "You get to do whatever you want."

"Don't tell them that." Kate, a lovely, tall brunette with thick legs and a pudgy middle, walked into the kitchen. She shooed Elliot, Levi, and Thomas away. "Go...do something. Anything. Just don't make a mess of yourselves, all right? We're going to dinner in an hour."

The triplets dashed through the house.

"Liam..." Kate sighed his name. Her eyes were much like his, rich brown and almond shaped, but years cracked from them, fissures that lined her soft face. She tugged at the straps of her maxi dress. "Don't tell them about Ryder, please. They're too young."

"Too young to understand that boys kiss other boys?"

Kate flapped her hand at him. "Oh please. I look through their search history. They're *very* aware of that." Her eyebrows shot up. "And you know that's not what I'm talking about."

"His magic," Liam said.

"Yes, his *dark* magic. The magic I can still feel on you." She swept a hand through her shoulder-length hair. "Did you just come from seeing him?"

Liam smothered the flurry of magic under his skin; tempered the spike of adrenaline. It wasn't Ryder's magic she felt, but his own, and he didn't know how to explain that. "No, I haven't seen him since this morning."

Kate hummed. Her eyes tracked him, climbing from his shoes to his face. "Careful, Liam. Hey, no—don't roll your eyes at me. We're different, okay? Montgomerys have been, and always will be, Water witches. The sea lives in us."

"What happens when the sea *comes* for us, Kate? Do we always listen? Do we always do as we're told?" His tongue ring click-clacked the back of his teeth. He raked his hand over the side of his head.

She shrugged. "You'll understand when you're older."

"That worked on me when I was sixteen. It doesn't anymore."

"It's the truth. We're different. We don't respond to magic the same way others do. We never have. We never will."

The kelpie's voice bit into him. *You're different.*

"How?" Liam blurted.

"How?"

"Yes, how are we different?"

Caution crossed his aunt's face. She pursed her lips, back straight and arms loose at her sides. She glanced over her shoulder, probably to make sure the boys weren't listening. "What's going on, Liam?"

His phone buzzed in his pocket. Opal adjusted on his shoulder as he pulled it out.

Donovan: *Meet me in the woods. 15 mins.*

"What's happened?" Kate pressed. She reached for him, but he stepped back before she could touch his hand, afraid he might give himself away if she got closer. "Come to dinner with us, honey. We're meeting your mom at the brewery after she's done with Thalia. We can all talk."

Liam's head spun. His magic lashed out, defensive and cold. Thalia had a meeting. That meeting was with his mother. *The sea lives in us.* Kate was standing in front of him, her suspicion a living thing on her skin, and Liam had no idea who to trust or believe or confide in.

"The sea lives in me? No, the sea is betraying me," he whispered. The words rushed out on a ragged, tired breath.

Kate's expression softened. She opened her mouth but struggled to speak. Whatever she'd planned to say refused to come. A confession, maybe. A lapse in her judgement. Her eyes darted to his wrist. He followed her gaze to the tiny cut on his skin and the dried blood around it. He pulled his sleeve down. Kate's teeth clicked when she slammed her mouth shut.

Liam: *omw.*

"Wait, Liam—"

Liam waved his arm as he darted out the door. His jagged, dark Water snapped at her. A short gasp stopped Kate in her tracks.

"Get to the woods." Liam jostled his shoulder. "Tell him I'm coming."

Opal's feathers ruffled close to his ear and she flew into the sky.

DONOVAN SAT IN a low, curved tree, swinging his legs back and forth. Opal cleaned her feathers on the branch beside him. Lingering sunlight lit the forest. Trees were damp from a stint of afternoon rain, but the sky was cloudless dark blue: an anomaly this close to winter.

Liam watched light play on Donovan's arms. The sunset glowed on his fiery hair. He pulled the sleeves of his olive sweater into his palms, the shoulder slouching to expose a pale, freckled collarbone.

"Hey," Donovan said. His gaze stayed pinned to the treetops. "I'm meeting Tyler for dinner, so I've only got a few minutes."

"Date night?"

Donovan smirked. "Something like that."

"Look..." Liam chewed on the inside of his cheek. He leaned against the tree and stroked Opal's back. "I'm sorry you're in the middle of all this. You shouldn't have to be, and I know Tyler... He's just... I don't know, he's just really fucking hard on Ryder. It gets old."

"He's the head witch," Donovan said. "It's his job to be hard on us."

"You think he should treat Ryder the way he does? You think that's okay?"

"I didn't say that. But I know he feels awful about it most of the time. I know his parents are shitty and he's got a lot of issues. I know that he'd never hurt either of you and that he's doing his best to protect you both."

Liam toed at the grass with his boot. Whether he liked it or not, he knew Donovan was right. Tyler had his own issues to deal with—they all did. But Tyler had initiated the circle, he'd established it with Christy before Liam or Ryder or Donovan joined, and watching it turn into something he didn't recognize couldn't be easy.

None of this was easy.

"We're not here to talk about Tyler," Donovan mumbled. He slid out of the tree and adjusted his sweater, pulling it back into place over his shoulders. "I asked my mom about the Orders."

"And?"

"And she told me the war between Water and Fire has been going on since..." He gestured to the forest with a flick of his wrist. "The beginning. It's not just between demons, because demons aren't the only things that belong to the Orders."

Liam narrowed his eyes. "What else does?"

"Technically? Everything. Me. You. Opal. Alchemists. Witches. It depends on our magic, but it always aligns with at least one Order. I'm Earth, but it's... I'm complicated."

"What's complicated about you?"

"I'm not human," Donovan said.

The forest quieted. Wind stopped hushing through leaves. Creatures peeked at them from the hollows under gnarled roots and amidst tree trunks, lurking in the shadows, waiting for an explanation. Time stretched and bent. It made room for them to watch each other—Donovan, waiting for a reaction, Liam, wondering if he was still asleep. After too much silence, the trees finally whispered. *Dark Water. Predator.*

"It's complicated for you too," Donovan added.

Liam blinked. Heat rushed into his cheeks. He wobbled but stayed upright. Nothing made sense. *Nothing.* "That's a heavy implication."

"Yeah, it is. Don't worry, you aren't the same as me. I would know."

"And what exactly are you?"

"A Were."

Stories filtered through covens and clans and circles about Weres. People born with pieces of something else inside them—animals. Souls that were stitched together with old magic most witches didn't understand: Ancient, primal, wild magic, the kind that wasn't practiced out of fear.

"What kind?" Liam resisted taking a step back.

Donovan frowned. His brow softened, and he tucked his arms around himself. *Of all people.* The youngest of them, who wore knitted sweaters and painted his nails, who was small and quiet, submissive, and unable to find his magic. Donovan, who took shelter in gentleness despite his ferocious eyes. Somehow, it made sense in every single way Liam had never imagined it could.

"Don't laugh," Donovan warned. Liam cocked his head and waited. "I'm... We're cats. Leopards to be specific."

A grin cracked on Liam's face.

"*Don't* laugh," Donovan snapped. He wrinkled his nose, pawed at his face with his sleeve-covered hand, and heaved a sigh. "And no, I don't have spots and I can't turn into a leopard so don't even ask me. It's an energy thing. A spirit latches to families and gets passed down through generations. At some point the Quinn bloodline merged with leopard energy after it was redistributed into the universe and now..." He finished with a shrug.

"Does Tyler know?"

Donovan bit his bottom lip. He hesitated but shook his head.

"Christy?"

"Hard to keep things from a psychic."

Liam nodded. "So, you're a Were Leopard. The Orders are bigger than we thought they were. And you think I'm..."

"Something," Donovan offered. "I just can't figure out what. You smell weird."

"I *smell* weird?" Liam scoffed and gestured to his chest with both hands. "Seriously?"

"It's a Were thing. I can... Different energies have different—" He stopped to sigh. "It isn't actually a *smell*, it's a sense, like—shit, Liam I don't know. I just know you're different, okay? Just like I could tell Ryder was different."

"How long did you know about Ryder?" Liam's eyes narrowed.

"Since the day I met him."

"And me?"

Donovan's eyebrows furrowed apologetically. "Since I met you."

Liam's heart raced. He remembered the messy night three years ago with Donovan in his bed, drunk on tequila after a solstice party, and how Donovan had whispered *what are you* into the crook of his neck. They'd been teenagers and Liam hadn't thought a damn thing of it. He remembered every circle meeting, every summer hike into the woods, every spell they'd cast together, reading they'd done, full moon party they'd hosted, and not once had Donovan hinted at Liam's uniqueness. Liam swallowed hard. His eyes burned, and he blinked back the urge to let them cloud over, to clench his fist and call up a storm.

The forest chattered around him. *Cyclone. Sea sorcerer. Water hearted. Thief.*

"I'm sorry. I couldn't tell you. I'd out myself and I—I didn't know anything about my bloodline or my magic—I still don't. I just... I feel you changing. I *see* you changing—"

"What else did your mom say?

Donovan bristled. He glanced at the ground, the sky, at Opal.

"Donovan."

"She said that Ryder's attachment has the potential to influence your magic if you're doing rituals together. Especially if he's syphoning from you."

"And what if I'm syphoning from him?" Liam watched Donovan from under his lashes.

Donovan's clear, blue eyes widened. He shook his head and his jaw slackened. "I mean... It's a possibility that you might be able to, but—"

"I did," Liam blurted. "I have been."

"That's..."

"Dark magic. Yeah, I know."

"It's not *just* dark magic, Liam. Most witches wouldn't dream of syphoning, not because they're afraid of it, but because they physically can't do it. People aren't scared of the Wolfes because they're necromancers, they're scared of them because dark magic isn't a skill. It can't be learned."

"Who else can syphon besides necromancers?" Liam's phone buzzed in his pocket. He ignored it. "I know some psychics can, Jackals can—"

"Fae," Donovan said. "All sorts of Fae can."

Liam's phone kept buzzing. Donovan held his breath. Opal shook out her feathers and hopped onto a higher branch, peering into the coming night. Fae were insatiable and manic and ancient, they were brutal and powerful, half in this world and half in another. *That* was not possible. If there was anything Liam wasn't—he certainly wasn't Fae.

"No," Liam snapped. "Absolutely not."

"We can't count it out."

"We definitely can."

Donovan rolled his eyes. "We need to talk to the circle about this."

"Which part? You being an endangered species from the Amazon or me accidentally syphoning from my boyfriend?" Liam lifted his brows, a challenge. Donovan licked his lips and heaved a deep, unsteady sigh. "Let me try to figure this out first, all right?"

"Yeah, okay." Donovan's voice was weak and breathy. He dug his phone out of his pocket and sent a text. "I don't know how to tell Tyler," he admitted. "He'll freak out and then I'll freak out and then Christy will freak out because we're both freaking out. It'll be a mess and I'm trying to figure out how to make it less messy."

Donovan had puppy hands: far too large for his wrists, bony and long-fingered, and red from the cold. He rubbed his arms and huffed. His youth was apparent in moments like this, trapped between the people he cared about and his secrets. Liam could relate.

"Then don't tell him," Liam said.

"Are you gonna tell Ryder?"

"Yeah, when I have something *to* tell him. C'mon, you need a ride?"

"No, I biked."

Liam shrugged toward the trailhead that led to the dirt lot where he'd parked. "It's forty-two degrees. I've got a rack and tie downs; it's not a big deal."

"You sure?" Donovan walked beside him, hands stuffed in the front pockets of his jeans.

"Yeah, just don't scratch the seats." Liam flashed a teasing grin.

"Cat jokes." Donovan snorted a laugh. "Wonderful."

Chapter Four

AFTER HE DROPPED Donovan off downtown, Liam drove to the sea.

He didn't get out of the car. He looked, and he rolled down his window so he could smell, and he closed his eyes to listen. The ocean's loud roar was brutal and beautiful. It sang to the deepest parts of him, pulling eerie, familiar magic through his skin. It was dark, but it wasn't. It was his, but it wasn't. It was something he wanted to keep, but it wasn't.

Water witch, the ocean said. *Come closer.*

He almost went to the water. *Just to feel.* Almost. He thought of the conversation with Donovan, Thalia's warning, the way it felt to syphon from Ryder, and drove home instead.

Ryder: *You doing okay?*

Liam: *Yeah I think so.*

Ryder: *You'd tell me if you weren't. Right?*

Liam: *Yeah I would. I promise.*

Ryder said goodnight and Liam scrolled through the messages he refused to respond to.

Mom: *Kate said you were in rare form today? You okay?*

Mom: *Let's get lunch tomorrow. Sound good?*

Mom: *You there?*

Thalia: *New Moon is in a couple days. We'll talk then. Stay away from the sea.*

Tyler: *We need to talk.*

Christy: *Donovan said you guys talked. Is everything good?? Can I do something to help? Always here for you <3*

Liam barely slept, but when he did, it was sleep that lingered in lucidity.

He opened his eyes and peered into the darkness. Opal wasn't on her perch, but the window was cracked, letting in an evening breeze. A dish of water on his windowsill reflected the moon's white smile carved across the sky.

Energy tingled on his fingertips—a cold, warped magic that Liam recognized and didn't. It was the same feeling that surfaced in the kelpie's mirror, the same feeling that spiked after bloodletting with Ryder.

The breathy sound of a horse echoed somewhere close by: A soft whinny, the gurgle of air through wet gills, and the heavy beat of hooves. Each noise vibrated Liam's bones, humming and purring. Warmth pooled low in his abdomen and spread into his legs, his stomach, his chest.

Stillness turned the space he was once familiar with into uncharted territory. He glanced at the moon through the window and then at his door, which was no longer a door at all, but an empty, black space. The darkness twisted, and the kelpie appeared.

Liam's heart raced. He struggled to speak, but the dream wouldn't allow it.

"I've brought the sea to you," the kelpie said. He was soaking wet, bare and unbothered, opaque black feet fading into white legs and sharp-edged hips. His shoulders jutted from him, sloped and long. He stepped closer, fingers twitching restlessly at his side. The next time the kelpie spoke, it was Thalia's voice in his mouth. "It'll never be safe."

Liam was paralyzed. He couldn't lift his arms, couldn't move his legs. The kelpie crept closer, sinking onto the bed with practiced, graceful ease. His mouth touched Liam's wrist, climbed Liam's arm to his shoulder. He was strange and beautiful, awkwardly inhuman in ways that were barely noticeable.

The kelpie's mouth hovered over Liam's. He said, "I felt your heartbeat all over me," and it was Ryder's voice.

A panicky gasp ripped through Liam. He jolted out of bed—out of the dream—clutching his chest. Opal chirped at him from her perch in the window. His room was his again. It smelled of his cologne, of clean water and laundry detergent. He was afraid to close his eyes, so he got dressed instead, tamed his hair with his fingers, and slipped on his shoes.

The tilting presence of the dream hovered around him. He could only think of one place where it might not follow.

"Meet me there," he said to Opal. She ruffled her feathers and flew into the night.

He knelt to grab his bag and had to catch himself on the nightstand. His head spun. Nothing made sense. *Nothing.* He tried to steady his breathing, to blink until the impossible faded—but it didn't.

A set of fresh, wet footprints led from the edge of his bed to the front door.

RYDER OPENED THE door before Liam could knock. He was shirtless, and sweatpants hung low on his hips. Confusion mingled with worry. He ducked out of the way as Opal flew past, settling quietly on a bookshelf in the living room.

Liam couldn't bring himself to move. He stared at Ryder, wide-eyed and breathless, until Ryder hooked a finger through his belt loop and tugged. "What's wrong? I felt you from the parking lot."

"I'm losing my mind," Liam whispered. Ryder's palms framed his jaw. The dark familiarity of Ryder's apartment eased some of the tension. The smell of sage and rooibos tea, candle wax and pine. "I don't know what's happening to me. I'm having dreams that aren't dreams... I'm—I don't recognize my magic. It's like there's something foreign inside me, Ry."

"It's just the moon, Princess." Ryder's rough voice sent chills down Liam's spine. He pressed their foreheads together.

"My own element is turning against me." Liam's voice trembled. He clutched Ryder's hips and pulled him close, thankful for the warmth of his skin, for bone and muscle under Liam's hands.

"No, it's not," Ryder said. His lips brushed Liam's around each word. "Magic just speaks a different language than us. Sometimes it takes a while to figure out what the fuck it wants."

Ryder's fingers fell away from Liam's cheek. A teal fern swayed over the edge of the counter. Opal sat on a bookshelf and chirped at Percy who dozed on the couch. Their familiars were calm. A candle sparked to life on the coffee table. Liam's nerves subsided. The strangeness from his studio—the kelpie, the footsteps, the dream—disappeared in Ryder's shadow.

"Let me make you some tea," Ryder said. He stepped toward the kitchen, but Liam caught his wrist.

"I don't want tea," Liam said. He traced the veins in Ryder's wrist with his thumb. Shadows chased candlelight along the walls and across the floor. Desire ached in him. He wanted to forget. He wanted to be known—to be seen. And if there was anyone who knew him, who would see him, it was Ryder.

Ryder's eyes flicked around Liam's face. He rested his arms over Liam's shoulders and raked his fingers through the shorn hair on the sides of his head. Magic throbbed between them. Ryder's magic. Liam's magic. The parts of each other they'd stolen and kept—darkness that clung to Liam's ribcage, Water that dripped from Ryder's heart—clamored through blood to get to their skin.

It was the middle of a charged, haunted night, and Liam wanted to be wanted.

He kissed Ryder hard, a deep kiss that radiated in him. They stumbled down the hall, pausing once when Liam pressed Ryder against the wall. He tilted his head, opening his mouth wide for longer, deeper kisses. Ryder moaned into his mouth, a gust of steam that made Liam wince, and sucked Liam's bottom lip between his teeth.

"Careful," Liam whispered. He watched Ryder's pupils shake, expanding and retreating again and again.

"I know," Ryder said. Liam pinned Ryder's wrists above his head. His fingertips played along the lines in Ryder's palms, feeling futures and pasts. Ryder's eyes slipped shut and his head lolled back, giving Liam room to mouth at his throat. His pulse jumped on Liam's tongue. A whimper fluttered from him and he whispered, "We don't belong to our magic, you know. It doesn't matter if you're dark or not. You're still you."

Liam rolled his hips against Ryder's. No, their magic came from within, a living, tangible essence. Controllable on occasion; shared and splintered. But Liam didn't know if he had the fortitude to be what he was becoming, to hold on to darkness and not let it sweep him away.

Ryder snapped his fingers as they stumbled into the bedroom and a cluster of candles on the altar lit. An incense stick sparked. Liam felt along the soft skin of Ryder's belly, trailed his thumb over his hip, and slid his hand down the front of his sweats.

"What if we're part of this war?" Liam pressed the question against Ryder's ear. He touched Ryder slowly, rubbing him in gentle, teasing circles.

"We're not." Ryder's breath was shaky on Liam's cheek. "Stop thinking about it."

They tossed their clothes away and Liam took shelter in Ryder's bare skin. He opened his mouth over Ryder's collarbone, the crescent scars on his chest, the keys of his ribcage and barely-there curve of his waist. Candlelight dripped over the bed, deepening the shadows beneath Ryder's sharp features.

Liam would never get used to this. To Ryder, squirming and whimpering with his fingers tangled in Liam's hair. To the taste of him, the smell of him, the sound of his voice shredding over Liam's name. Liam bit the soft skin of his inner thigh, trailed his lips to the center of him and kissed him there.

Ryder was soft in his hands, hips canting eagerly against Liam's mouth. "Don't tease," he whined.

"That sounded a lot like *please*," Liam said. He bit Ryder's thigh, trailed his mouth to the place where his thigh met his hip and sucked a mark there. "But I might not've heard you right."

"Go to hell," he said over a soft, breathless laugh.

Liam curled his arms under Ryder's thighs and pulled him closer. Liam's breath and lips touched him but didn't move.

"Please," Ryder yelped. "God, fuck you. *Please*."

Ryder's breath came short. Liam took him apart with slow strokes of his tongue and bent lower to lick into him. Ryder's moan was sharp. He writhed on the bed, his back arched, fingers tight in Liam's hair and twisted in the sheets. The candles sparked again, their flames growing and swaying. Liam loved this—Ryder's body under his hands, Ryder's hips jumping when Liam's tongue ring flicked against his clit, the low curse that slid from his lips before he pulled Liam up into another deep, messy kiss. He fit his legs around Liam's hips and pushed, flipping him onto his back.

"Easy," Liam whispered. He gripped Ryder's narrow waist, eyelashes fluttering as Ryder sank down on him. Ryder's stomach rolled, thighs tense and back arched, riding Liam slow but hard. Even though his eyes were Llewellyn green, there was no denying Ryder's necromancy. It spilled from him, a gust of steam that billowed from his lips; power that rushed into Liam and held on.

Ryder watched him, mouth parted and cheeks flushed. Their stuttering breath filled the room, accompanied by the pop of a candle wick, the shush of car tires on rainy streets and soft, shaken moans. Liam pulled Ryder's hips into another slow grind and closed his eyes.

Pleasure cracked inside him. Liam's heart kicked. He felt the sweep of Ryder's hand over his chest, the wrap of Ryder's fingers around his throat. He craned into it, encouraging Ryder to squeeze, to hold him down. Liam met Ryder's heated gaze. His hips jerked and he gasped against Liam's mouth, shaking and breathless.

Liam had seen this before—Ryder's trembling mouth, the way he gasped, how his fingernails dug into the sides of Liam's neck. He'd seen it when the kelpie kissed him and when Christy sifted through his memories.

"Sorry," Ryder whispered.

Liam blinked and ran his hands over Ryder's ribs. "For what?"

"I always go first."

Liam rolled Ryder onto his back, curling one arm under Ryder's knee. "Don't ever apologize for that," Liam rasped. His hips snapped—deep, hard thrusts that wrung sharper moans and shorter gasps from them both. Soon Liam was coming too, his teeth in Ryder's shoulder, quivering and overwhelmed.

His Water magic pulsed. It was frenzied and frantic, desperate to be used.

"Hey." Ryder panted. His palm settled on Liam's cheek. "You still with me?"

"I'm always with you." Liam leaned down to kiss him and tasted Fire on his tongue, darkness on his breath.

Ryder was hazy and gentled. He wrapped around Liam as they lay on their sides. "See," he said pointedly, "we can have sex without you accidentally murdering me."

"Yeah, because we didn't use magic." Liam ran his palm over Ryder's buzzed head. "Not much, at least."

"I can't help some of it," Ryder murmured. A sheepish smile tugged at his lips and Liam loved it, the shape of his mouth, the cliff of his cheekbones, the glint of mischief that never faded from his eyes. "Now will you talk to me? What happened?"

"The kelpie was in my studio, I think. Or... Something. Fuck, I don't know. I had a dream, woke up, and there were wet footprints on the floor."

"What'd you dream of?"

"The sea," Liam said. "You."

Ryder stole a kiss. He wrapped his arm over Liam's shoulder; his hand cradled the back of Liam's head. They exchanged breath, noses almost touching. "We could do a binding? Seal off your doorway with a sigil?"

"I already did," he whispered. "Nothing should be able to get through unless it's called."

"And you're sure you didn't call the kelpie?" Ryder's eyes bored into him. His honesty was unwavering and true, raw trust that Liam never questioned.

But Ryder's honesty didn't give Liam any answers. He wanted to say yes, of course he was sure. But something in him twisted at the thought, a place so distant and otherworldly that Liam barely recognized it. He shook his head and swallowed, inching closer to Ryder's warm body. "I'm not sure of anything except this," he said and thumbed at Ryder's jaw. "And our circle."

"Did Donovan get anything out of his mom?"

Liam's chest tightened. "Nothing concrete. The Orders are more than we thought they were." *We're more than we thought we were.* "Demonology isn't the biggest issue we're facing, I guess."

"It wasn't an *issue* to begin with." Ryder's gripped Liam's side. "Belial hasn't changed anything. He's just...there. Watching."

"You've changed," Liam said. "You died and came back, and whatever came back with you woke something up. Something in me, something in us. I can't... I can't focus on anything. I can't sleep. I can't escape it."

"Focus on me," Ryder said. He steadied his breathing and dug his nails into Liam's skin. "Reach for me."

"Ry—"

"I trust you."

"I don't trust myself."

Ryder's eyes softened. He wrapped his arm around Liam's middle, sealing their torsos together. "C'mon," he whispered. "Try."

Liam's magic hummed in his fingertips. He kept a tight grip on it—the magic he barely understood—and tried not to move as it dripped into Ryder. He went slowly, his energy cool and fluid, curling through Ryder's vertebrae. Ryder's lips parted, his pupils shook, black expanding and retracting. The sharp barbs of Liam's magic hooked into Ryder's darkness and dragged it closer.

"S-slow," Ryder stuttered. Liam pulled until throbbing, aching pulses of Ryder's energy flowed into him. "Like that..."

Ryder's lashes fluttered. He opened his mouth to try to catch his breath, heartbeat echoing through Liam, rippling the air around them. Shivers ran down Ryder's arms.

The trust and submission that came with syphoning created eroticism that Liam couldn't get enough of. He watched heat fill Ryder's cheeks, watched his body twitch, his chest heave, felt his fingernails dig in. He focused on Ryder's wet lips, his lidded eyes and shaky gasp. His magic pushed deeper, and Ryder's eyes squeezed shut, body curling closer.

Liam asked, "What does it feel like?"

"I can't explain it," Ryder whispered. His magic sparked, burning in Liam's core. "Keep going."

Liam's magic momentarily retreated, and Ryder made a wounded noise—a clipped, breathy whimper that splintered Liam's reservations. Ryder's eyes turned black. He rushed into Liam, his magic strong and hot. Liam gripped Ryder's cheek and allowed it: The pass of their energies, the tangling of their magic.

"Careful," Liam blurted. He slid his hand around the back of Ryder's head.

Ryder stared at Liam. They slithered through each other, climbing over bones, sifting through blood and secrets. Ryder syphoned from Liam and Liam syphoned from him—darkness and Water and Fire and something unknown all colliding in effortless bursts.

"You're afraid," Ryder said, voice low and haunting.

They were bare and spent, walking the line between dangerous and not. Of course he was afraid. Afraid of himself. Afraid of Belial. Afraid of the kelpie. Afraid of what he might turn into.

"Not of you," Liam said.

Their foreheads pressed together. Liam closed his eyes. The give and take of their magic subsided and slowed with their heart rates.

"Feel better?" Ryder's fingertips trailed Liam's spine.

Magic stirred contentedly under his skin. "I don't know."

"Look at me."

Liam opened his eyes. Ryder didn't startle, but he went still, gaze hard and unwavering, pinned to Liam's face. He narrowed his eyes and leaned back. Caution came and went. His lips parted, he reached out, setting his fingertips beneath Liam's right eye.

"What is it?" Liam held his breath.

Ryder shook his head. "Your eyes..." His fingers touched Liam's eyelashes. "They're different. Like opal, maybe. Or labradorite or..."

Abalone.

His heart dropped into his stomach. Everything Donovan had said in the woods reconstructed itself. *I see you changing.* Liam scrambled out of bed and almost tripped to get to the bathroom. *Fae. All sorts of Fae can.* He flicked on the lights and stared at his reflection, at tan olive skin and dark hair, at his trembling mouth and wide, abalone eyes—kelpie eyes.

It was impossible. *Impossible.*

Ryder's magic appeared before he did, a wave of heat that sizzled on Liam's skin. The lights in the bathroom flickered. "Tell me what's wrong," Ryder said. He stepped behind Liam, one hand on Liam's back, the other clenched in a white-knuckled fist. "What's happening?"

Explanations came to a screeching halt in his mouth. He stared at himself, unrecognizable and unfamiliar, and set his hands on the sink. "I need to get to the ocean."

"That seems like the absolute *worst* idea," Ryder said.

"I think..." Liam stared at his reflection. He remembered being tossed by the waves and the kelpie kissing him, he remembered the kelpie in the mirror and in the bowl and in his bedroom. Liam met Ryder's eye in the mirror. Ryder's gaze hardened. His mouth thinned into a line and he shook his head. "Kelpies are Fae, aren't they?"

"Yes—" Ryder pulled on Liam's shoulder, turning him away from the mirror. "—they are. Why does that matter?"

He tried to blink away the opalescence from his eyes, but it stayed strong. "Something was trying to send a message. Premonitions of you dying and me becoming this."

"Becoming what?"

Liam stared at his bare feet, at Ryder's toes twitching on the tile. Liam pulled memories from circle meetings and family gatherings. He looked back on the details—things he would've missed. Thalia's clever question: *Which form did it take?* Donovan's nostrils flaring every time Liam returned from the ocean. His mother's altar. Kate's caution and ease. The helpless, dangerous pleasure that hummed in Liam's bones when he syphoned. How the fissure in that tiny, mysterious mirror split his reflection down the middle.

Ryder grabbed Liam's jaw with his thumb and index finger. "Babe," he said impatiently and yanked Liam's face toward him. "Becoming what?"

A long-forgotten memory lit behind his eyes. Lights wrapped around a tree. A Yule feast spread over the table in the dining hall at the Montgomery estate. Cinnamon wafting in the air from mashed sweet potatoes, celery chopped and scattered over the stuffing platter, a glass of champagne pressed into his hand. "Set intention, honey," Lindsey said. It was the year before last, and Liam could smell cabernet on his mother's breath. She'd leaned in close and her festive lipstick had left a red mark on his cheek. "You're twenty. The Water will come for you sooner than you think."

Liam remembered the round mirror she dug out of her purse, how she held it for him as he thumbed her lipstick away. He remembered thinking she'd had too much to drink.

Ryder heaved a sigh. He cradled Liam's cheeks in his hands, eyes wide and worried. "You need to sleep, Liam."

"I can't," he said. He let his head go heavy in Ryder's palms. Thoughts kept circling. Memories. Whispers. Realizations. Liam understood it, but he didn't. He felt it all over him; sudden, jagged knowing that cut through every doubt and excuse in the back of his mind—*I can't be. How? There's no way*—all silenced in the wake of cold, brutal acceptance. "If I ask you to stay here, will you?"

"No," Ryder snapped.

It was worth a try. Liam sighed. "Fine. We need to get dressed."

"I'm not taking you to the beach."

"You're taking me home," he said.

The blood drained from Ryder's face. He tensed and his throat bobbed as he swallowed, shoulders hunching toward his ears, hands going still on Liam's face. Ryder tilted his head, regarding Liam with a practiced glare that Liam knew well. Movements like that—the way Ryder's jaw flexed, his eyes narrowing, how he took measured, even breaths—were the subtle things Liam understood. Bits of Ryder that bloomed out of familiarity.

And God, how Liam loved every single one of those movements. The twitch of Ryder's brow and curl of his top lip. The way he sharpened when he was nervous, all his angular features tensing at once. How stillness was a place on him, carved in bone and breath.

"Home? Like to Kate's house?" Ryder asked.

Liam slid his hands from Ryder's hips to his ribs. Ryder's fingers trailed his jaw, coming to rest on Liam's throat. "Yeah. I have a feeling my mom's there too."

A line formed between Ryder's brows, confusion and worry and skepticism all battling on his face.

Liam smoothed his thumb between Ryder's brows and kissed him. "Trust me, okay?"

Ryder watched him carefully. His eyes cleared, the black pooling inward like water toward a drain. He nodded and pinched Liam's chin. "Always."

LIAM SAID THE word to himself a thousand times as they drove. *Kelpie. Kelpie. Kelpie.* He drummed his thumb on his knee and watched Port Lewis pass by the window. Movie posters glowed outside the theater, people wandered from one bar to another, mist blanketed the streets.

Ryder's long fingers curled over the gear shifter. "You gonna tell your mom everything?"

"What's your definition of everything?"

"The Orders, being kissed by a water horse, losing sleep, practicing..." He paused to chew on his lip. "Practicing blood magic with a necromancer."

"My aunt already knows about the magic," Liam said. "She felt darkness on me this morning. I bet she already told my mom about it."

"Then what are we doing here?"

Elder trees stood tall around the Montgomery estate, a half moon of wide, dark trunks and leafy branches. Ryder put the car in park and grabbed a smooth, round stone out of the cup holder. The labradorite caught moonlight coming in through the windshield, turning the gray, polished surface green and navy. His pale fingers looked strange and alien wrapped around it, too bony, too perfect.

"Getting answers," Liam said.

"What makes you think they have them?"

He plucked the stone from Ryder's hand and dropped it back in the cup holder. "Because..." He slid the mirror out of his pocket. "I'm pretty sure this is my mom's."

"You didn't think to share this information sooner?" Ryder glanced from the mirror to Liam.

"It's been on her altar for ages, right next to her chalice by the window. When I found it, I knew I'd seen it somewhere, but I couldn't figure out where, but then I remembered... It makes sense now, this thing, Thalia, my eyes, the kelpie, I don't know how I didn't realize it sooner."

"Realize what?"

Liam tossed the word around his mouth and swallowed it. "How long did it take before you knew you were different? When your parents told you or when you felt it for the first time?"

Ryder's brows knitted. He inhaled a sharp breath and tilted his head against the seat. "I always knew. I just didn't really believe it until I started having dreams, until my magic started waking up."

"Exactly."

"What're you saying, Liam?"

"Something in me is waking up," he whispered. Liam swallowed hard, watching Ryder's fingers trace the ridge of his knuckles. "And I'm scared, because I think I know what it is."

Ryder watched him expectantly. Liam imagined a moment like this would be more than it was. The build-up; suddenness that turned into ratcheting breath, the question that somehow became a clear, obvious answer. The one he should've guessed days ago, before he syphoned, before the scrying, before his tea leaves spelled out a future he didn't understand.

Liam should've known what he was the moment he heard the kelpie's scream, and somehow, in some lost part of him, maybe he did.

The porch light illuminated the large pillars outside the entryway. Liam glanced through the windshield toward the front door and saw his mother's silhouette, her arms crossed, eyes lingering on them from the door.

"C'mon," Liam said. He stepped out of the car and ignored Ryder's protest.

The car beeped and locked. Moonlight cut through the darkness, bruised by storm clouds gathering overhead.

"*Tell* me," Ryder hissed. He grabbed Liam's wrist and stumbled to keep up with him. His fingernails dug in. "What do you think it is?"

Liam twisted his hand around until he could properly lace his fingers with Ryder's. He swallowed hard, the taste of the word still foreign and strange in his mouth. He wondered if saying it would change them. Ryder was a necromancer. Donovan was a were-leopard. Liam being what he was—what he thought he might be—wouldn't be enough to drive a wedge between them...

Would it?

"Liam." Ryder's voice was stern and haunting, layered with growls and cries and shrieks. He squeezed Liam's hand and rounded on him, forcing them to pause before the front door. Ryder's eyes were pitch black. He looked scared, almost.

One deep breath later, Liam said, "I think *I'm* a kelpie."

Ryder's hand didn't loosen in Liam's grip, but he went still. His eyes narrowed, lips pressed in a thin line.

"This isn't how we wanted you to find out." Lindsey leaned against the doorframe. She appeared like a wraith, silent and cold, watching them with dark, dark eyes. "But your lifestyle choices have..." She tracked her gaze across Ryder. "Complicated things."

Liam and his mother were both tall, dark-haired, and tan-skinned. They shared deep-set eyes and a sloped, dainty nose. Her jaw flexed, the line of it as prominent and strong as his. A scar cut across Lindsey's left cheek, curved toward the edge of her eye and the corner of her mouth. She crossed her arms over her chest and gestured inside with a wave.

"I'm right?" Liam hoped she might laugh, but she didn't.

Lindsey stayed quiet. Her breath halted, caught in her throat like a rabbit in a trap. He watched her battle with an answer, mouth squirming to keep the truth at bay.

"*Mom*," Liam snapped.

"Yes," Lindsey said. "You're right."

Ryder's hand still didn't loosen in his grip.

For some reason, Liam thought his mom might laugh. *Just kidding.* He thought she'd take him by the arm and offer him tea. *Oh, honey, it's nothing like that.* But she watched him instead, unmoving, unblinking, unfamiliar. Liam's heart slammed against his ribs. He felt it in his throat and his wrists and in the soles of his feet.

Black smoke blanketed the ground beneath Ryder's boots. His magic filled the air. Darkness seeped into Liam's skin—powerful, volatile energy that made the wind go still. He slid closer to Liam. Heat radiated from his palm into Liam's trembling hand.

"Careful, necromancer," Lindsey said. She hadn't moved an inch. "We're trying to avoid a war. Not start one."

"What war?" Liam knew the answer, but he closed his eyes and sighed anyway. "You're kidding, right?"

"Come inside."

Liam stood firm.

Lindsey rolled her eyes. They flashed—dark brown, then silver, and back to brown—before her gaze settled on him. "You're so young, honey. It's hard to explain."

"Don't be condescending," Liam snapped. His teeth clicked and he closed his eyes, enduring the hot wave of Ryder's magic and the static of a storm brewing. "Christy was right? The Orders have something to do with this?"

"They have everything to do with this."

Ryder's teeth gritted. "Explain."

"Inside," Lindsey said gently and gestured through the door with a flick of her wrist.

Liam watched his mother closely. She sighed and nodded, waiting. He wanted answers. He *needed* answers. His fingers tightened in Ryder's grasp and tugged. "Put it away, Ry."

"You're joking," Ryder growled.

"It's fine, c'mon." Liam tugged. Ryder didn't move at first. His magic snapped at the air, sharp-toothed and looking for a fight. The black smoke snaked away and faded; the color of his eyes expanded and retracted, black, green, black-green, until they finally settled on green. Ryder's magic lingered just beneath the surface, poised and ready to strike: A tightly coiled rattlesnake. "No one here is gonna hurt you, you know that. It's my *mom*."

Liam hoped Lindsey might add a bit of reassurance, but her silence was deafening.

Liam tugged again, and Ryder followed, trailing Liam through the door and into the Montgomery house. Even though this was his home—familiar and real and unchanged—Liam was grateful for Ryder at his back, his hand gripping Liam's tight, his magic defensive and protective.

Lindsey closed the front door and walked past them toward the kitchen. Vaulted ceilings boasted a grand staircase that hugged the left and right walls with ornate filigree banisters. Thick strings of blue candle wax clung to bronze candelabras that jutted from the walls, and thick metal frames held generational photographs of Montgomery ghosts. The floor was polished beige tile, reflecting the light from a giant, crystal chandelier. The ocean snaked through the house. Seashells hid in plain sight, wrapped around banisters or carved into baseboards. Door handles were etched with crashing waves.

They followed Lindsey into the kitchen and stood next to the island while she put a kettle on the stove. Kate was next to the back door, arms folded over her chest, her white nightgown stark in the shadows.

"Hello, Ryder," Kate said softly. "It's good to see you."

"Sure it is," Ryder said. He stood close to Liam, unwilling to put distance between them.

Liam cleared his throat. "Why did you meet with Thalia today, Mom?"

Lindsey flicked one set of the kitchen lights on. She took her time, steeping a batch of green tea, setting four mugs in a line on the counter, and heaved a sigh. "Thalia is the Darbonne matriarch. She's aware of the agreement our ancestors made in the 1700s, and she needed to clarify the terms."

"What agreement?"

"A contract with Leviathan, the Queen of Water."

"A demon?" Ryder asked. He snorted and leaned on the island, his hand burning hot in Liam's.

Lindsey's eyes flicked to Ryder. "Yes, *darkling*," she hissed. "The Montgomerys belong in her Order but don't belong *to* her. Unlike the attachment you've formed with Belial, we don't have strings."

"It's more complicated than that," Kate interjected. Her gaze settled on Lindsey, eyes narrowed and mouth tight. She took one of the mugs and held it between her palms, close to her lips. "We cut our strings by making a sacrifice."

"What strings?" Liam blurted. "What agreement? What *are* we?"

"We're kelpies, sweetheart. Like you said." Lindsey placed two steaming mugs on the island in front of them. "But a long time ago, one of the Montgomery men made a deal with Leviathan. He asked her for a life on land—a life without the need to return to the ocean. Leviathan asked what the Montgomery family would give in return. They negotiated a deal: every Montgomery who chose to live in human form would give a sacrifice."

Ryder's fingers went slack in Liam's hand.

Liam turned his eyes toward the steaming mug and stared at it, watching heat coil from the surface of the water, listening to the silence unspool into a strange, tangible essence around them. The idea wasn't unwelcome at first— a sacrifice, a bargain—until Liam remembered the images the kelpie spun. The premonition. The instructions.

"A blood sacrifice," Liam said. "Right?"

Kate's lips parted. She looked at the ground, at Lindsey, at the ground again. "Yes," she said quickly. "A life for a life."

"And you two have done this?"

"Obviously," Ryder said under his breath. His hand almost slipped from Liam's, but Liam grabbed it and held on. "Or else they'd be hooved and have gills. You all would."

Lindsey scoffed. "We aren't always equine."

"No, but the kelpie I saw didn't look exactly human either. Why are we different?" Liam asked.

"We've been on land for long enough to mask the thalassic aspects of our bloodline. Fae magic is malleable." Lindsey glanced from Liam to Ryder. "We evolved to blend in."

"And what happens if I don't give Leviathan a sacrifice?" Liam followed his mother's eyes and stared at Ryder, the unspoken truth ringing clear in the quiet kitchen.

"The ocean will take you," Kate said.

"Looks like you're out of luck." Ryder swallowed hard. "Good thing my family knows how to unmake death."

"To cheat a demon isn't wise. To cheat the Queen of Water? A war declaration," Lindsey said.

"So that's it?" Liam blurted. He took a step back and swallowed around the lump in his throat. "Ryder gets an attachment, a kelpie shows up in Port Lewis, I do dark magic, and suddenly I'm supposed to murder someone? *My boyfriend?*"

"A kelpie hasn't stepped foot on these shores in decades *because* we've kept up our end of the bargain. Your dark magic is what brought it here. Playing with things we've kept dormant, things we make sacrifices to keep at bay—that is what created this situation. The Order of Fire lives in him and the Order of Water lives in you, and when you two—" Lindsey wrinkled her nose and lifted her chin. "—syphoned from each other, you got Leviathan's attention..." She stared at Ryder, eyes flashing silver again. "Thalia thinks a ritual on the New Moon will fix what you two have started."

"What kind of ritual?" Liam asked.

"The kind that strips his magic from you and your magic from him." Lindsey nodded back and forth between them. "And after that, you'll go your separate ways."

Ryder looked like he'd been physically struck. He bristled, mouth tense and eyes wide. "What? No... I'm not—I—"

"That won't solve anything!" Desperation clouded Liam's voice.

Kate shushed him and pointed toward the ceiling, gesturing to the second floor where his cousins slept. "It'll keep Ryder alive," she whispered. "The magic you've taken from each other will be given back, you'll make the sacrifice, Ryder will stay with the Wolfes and everyone will go on with their lives."

"That's not an option," Liam said.

"You're right. It's an ultimatum," Lindsey assured.

A storm stirred outside the bay windows. Trees rattled and shook. The old house creaked, cracks and crevices letting chilly wind whisper through the halls and corridors. Liam suddenly did not know this place. He did not know his aunt or his mother, his own magic or his bloodline. He was a stranger in a memorized place.

"You don't get to make that choice for me," Ryder said. "I'm not leaving my circle."

"There's no other way." Kate sipped her tea and turned her gaze toward the window. Rain streaked the glass, blurring the shape of trees on the outskirts of the property. "Magic comes with a price. You know that better than any of us, Ryder."

"It's what we're willing to pay that matters," Ryder snapped.

"Yes, it is. And your life is Liam's toll. Leviathan wants your blood, darkling. She wants you dead," Lindsey said.

Kate let out a sharp breath. "Lindsey. Be gentle."

"There's no room for gentleness," Lindsey said. She clutched her mug with trembling hands. "I will not lose my son over a fling with a half-blooded necromancer. If it were up to me—"

"It's not up to you." Liam tugged on Ryder's hand until they were walking toward the front door, almost tripping over themselves to get to the car.

He didn't look back when his mother called his name, he didn't bother putting his seatbelt on or turning the headlights on. As soon as Ryder closed the passenger door, Liam stepped on the gas and drove away from the house, away his family, away from secrets and truth and discoveries he wasn't ready to make. Away from a price he wasn't willing to pay.

They drove through Port Lewis in silence. When Liam's phone buzzed, he ignored it. When Ryder received a text, he didn't look. The quartz pendulum swinging from the rearview mirror was the only thing that made a sound, jingling on its chain as the car swerved down the windy road that cut through the woods and led to the sea.

The ocean does not need to make a weapon out of love. It is, in its own right, born a weapon already.

Liam reached for Ryder. He smoothed his palm over Ryder's thigh and gripped. "My mom is just scared, okay? She's a control freak and when she doesn't know what to do, or when she doesn't understand something, she..."

"We shouldn't be here. The beach isn't safe right now." Ryder's head rested on the seat, turned away from him. He pawed at his eyes and fixed his gaze out of the window. Liam tasted Ryder's apprehension. It circled him like a vulture.

"Ry, look at me."

Ryder didn't.

"Ryder," Liam said. He parked the car in the gravel lot overlooking the ocean. Lightning splintered the darkness far out over the water. He curled his fingers around Ryder's chin and tugged.

"This is my fault," Ryder whispered. He rubbed tears off his cheek with the heel of his palm. "You told me to slow down. You wanted to stop. I'm the one who did this—not you, not your mom, not Kate. It was me."

"It was us." Liam leaned over the center console. He thumbed at Ryder's wet cheek and whispered, "Baby, c'mon."

Steam leaked from Ryder's lips. He snorted and yanked away. "Don't *baby* me. You know it's true. I don't need your damn coddling; I need to figure out how to fix this."

"We'll talk to the circle."

"Because they'll be a great help."

"They might be the only help we have," Liam said.

Ryder shook his head. "Tyler wants me gone as much as your mother does."

"You know that's not true. He's just –"

A flurry of white feathers hit Ryder's window. Opal's talons scraped the glass. She let out a string of desperate, loud shrieks. Ryder startled, cursing under his breath, and his eyes immediately turned black. Opal kept screeching and chirping, her wings flapping against the car as if she was trying to clamor her way inside.

"Open your door," Liam blurted.

But Opal was gone a second later. She flew into the night, darting through the black sky like a misplaced star. Liam's heart pounded in his throat. It was Opal's fear or his own that filled him—the steady, chilling instinct that they were being watched.

Liam closed his eyes when he heard it. He chewed on his lip, let his hand fall away from Ryder's face, and listened to the sound of hooves outside the car.

Chapter Five

THE KELPIE'S BREATH fogged the air. His hooves made hollow, loud sounds on the gravel. The water horse called to them: a winded huff, a barely there whinny, a shredded, gravelly noise that gurgled and bubbled.

Liam opened his door. Ryder scrambled for his wrist and squeezed hard.

"Absolutely fucking not," Ryder whispered.

"Stay here."

"Liam—"

Liam pulled his arm away and stepped out of the car. The kelpie regarded him with a tilt of his head. His long, black hide was damp. Gills fluttered on his throat, below strange, pointed ears. His soaking-wet mane was littered with seaweed and sand and shells. Abalone eyes sat too far apart on his equine face. They appeared too human for his animal form.

The words rushed from him before Liam thought better of it. "I refuse."

The kelpie's tail flicked, sending water splattering on the ground. He stood taller than any horse Liam had ever seen. It was odd, remembering the kelpie who kissed him in the ocean, and knowing this creature and that boy were one in the same. The kelpie flared his nostrils. His attention snapped past Liam and he stomped in place.

The passenger door closed. Ryder's magic caused the air to tighten, the trees to chatter, the ocean to sing.

Darkling. Sea Sorcerer. Thieves.

"Get in the car, Ryder," Liam said.

Ryder kept his distance. He didn't speak or move, but dark magic snaked from him.

The kelpie took a step, another. His giant body morphed and dripped, edges softening like a blurred photograph. His hooves became bare, black feet. He stepped from himself as if he'd stepped from a shadow—suddenly one thing, and a second later, something else.

"Powerful little witch," the kelpie said. His powder white body was completely bare, lean and angular. His black feet faded into gray calves and porcelain thighs. Black marred his palms like soot stains. He was awkward and alluring; beautiful like a dead language. "No wonder he stays on land for you."

"Leviathan sent you, right?" Liam stepped between the kelpie and Ryder.

The kelpie craned to see around Liam's shoulder. He inhaled a deep, long breath. "Does he taste like he smells? Like anger," the kelpie purred and swooned, his rich voice slipping across Liam's skin, "and vitality and honey and—"

"Yes," Liam hissed. He blocked the kelpie's view. "Now answer me."

"I admire your candor." The kelpie lifted his hand and touched Liam's cheek. "I can almost taste him on you. Desperation." He leaned in and took another deep inhale. "Love, even."

Ryder made a displeased noise. Liam stretched his fingers out behind him, trying to keep Ryder at bay. The kelpie's lips touched Liam's jaw. He was cold and wet, scented like brine and rot and fish.

"I came to you many times, Liam Montgomery. Did I not?"

Liam's eyes clouded. Gray blanketed his pupils, but beneath them, the shine of violet and aurous blues glinted. He heard Ryder take a breath, the ocean roar in the distance, and his own heartbeat drum in his ears.

"Uninvited," Liam said.

The kelpie's eyes narrowed. A coy smile lifted the edges of his pale mouth. "It seems lies come as easy as truth to you. You are more like us than I thought."

"I never asked for this."

"When you stole his magic, when you tasted his blood, when you let him crawl inside you? That, Liam Montgomery, is when you asked." The kelpie's fingers were too long, with extra knuckles and more bone. They traced the line of Liam's jeans, barely grazing his skin. "The ocean will not wait. You will give him to her. Or I will give *you* to her."

"And what happens if you give me to her?"

"Liam," Ryder snapped.

Liam held his hand out again, willing him to stay quiet.

The kelpie cocked his head. His hand stilled on Liam's waist. "You would sacrifice yourself for something that isn't yours?"

"He *is* mine," Liam said. His voice fought and ruptured. All the Water in him seeped to the surface, bleeding into the center of him where darkness throbbed and squirmed. His magic lashed out, a thorny whip of dark energy and sharp ice.

The kelpie opened his mouth and the surprised sound that came from him was the shush of the sea and the scream of a horse and the yelp of a wounded boy. His eyes hardened and he bared his teeth, fingernails digging cruelly into Liam's hip. "You are Water, you are *kelpie*," he seethed. "You have an obligation; a birthright. And you will fulfill it."

Opal's screech cut through the air above Liam's head. She circled, flapping her wings and chirping restlessly in the sky. Car tires crunched gravel. A pair of headlights shone in Liam's eyes and turned the kelpie's skin near-translucent. Violet veins webbed the inside of his arms, stained his throat and fanned beneath his eyes. He was otherworldly, menacing and beautiful, and Liam wondered if he would ever look like him.

"Opal must've brought them," Ryder said. Black smoke snaked from beneath his feet. "We should go, Liam. Like, right now."

The kelpie didn't bother looking at the Jeep. He disregarded Christy's footsteps and Tyler's soft gasp. Donovan slid from the backseat. The wind howled and kicked. Liam took a step back. Ryder's fingers curled over his shoulder.

Christy glanced from Liam to the kelpie and back again. She shifted her weight from foot to foot, perched in the gravel on heeled boots and in frayed high-waist jeans. Tyler put his arm in front of her when she tried to step toward them.

"This is... He's..." Concentration furrowed Christy's brow.

"Come with me," the kelpie said. His voice was lower, gravelly and distinct.

Liam stood his ground. He watched the kelpie's nostrils flare, his opalescent eyes blink, and he listened to thunder sound over the sea. What would he become if he went? What would the ocean turn him into—all its mysteries and violence and magic. Would Liam become more Fae, darker, vicious, hungrier for power? Was that what he was supposed to be? Or would he stay and fight and risk losing the person he'd already almost lost once before? He didn't have time to decide, because Ryder squeezed his shoulder and stepped in front of him.

"Ryder, no," Christy squeaked.

"Don't," Tyler said, a desperate plea.

Liam grabbed for Ryder's arm, but he pulled away. "Ry—no, you can't—"

"I can," Ryder said. He glanced over his shoulder and met Liam's eye. "Call Jordan, okay? There won't be much time. It has to be right after, or..."

The kelpie purred. He slinked into Ryder's space and gripped his cheek with one, webbed hand. He clucked his tongue like a parent would to a child. "You are brave, necromancer."

Christy surged against Tyler's arm and shouted, "Fae magic can't be undone!"

Panic bloomed in Liam's gut. Ryder's short gasp was trampled by another burst of thunder. The kelpie's body slid against Ryder, eating up the space between them. It made sense and it didn't. Everything they'd done: the syphoning, the dark magic, when they tethered over their reading weeks ago. It all made sense in a way it hadn't before.

Fae magic could not be undone. The New Moon ritual would not have worked. Thalia had lied to his mother, and Liam did not know why. Their magic could not be separated. If the kelpie killed Ryder tonight, they would not be able to bring him back.

Liam's world narrowed down to Ryder's tense shoulders, his ratcheting breath, and the kelpie's smooth, white skin. He opened the passenger door of his car and reached for his bag, digging around blindly until his fingers hit cold, sleek metal.

"Too brave," the kelpie said.

Ryder's gulp was audible. His magic pulsed, hot and dark, thrashing around in the kelpie's grip. Ryder's body was still, but his energy fought to squirm loose. Steam lifted from Ryder's skin. The air vibrated. Waves crashed on the shore, trees chattered and whispered, and the air dispersed, leaving them suspended in the slow, awful place before a prophecy comes true.

"It's a sacrifice she wants?" Liam asked.

Christy cried out. She almost climbed over Tyler to get past him, but he didn't budge. "Liam, don't!"

Liam grabbed Ryder's shoulder, hauled him back, and drove a black-handled blade into the kelpie's stomach. The kelpie convulsed. His eyes widened and his mouth parted, shock and terror turning his expression boyish and innocent. He clutched Liam's wrist with a webbed hand. Liam twisted the blade—he would never forget the sound the kelpie made, a breathy, horrible whimper. Liam closed his eyes. The kelpie's energy rushed around them. He sagged on the blade and his hand trembled around Liam's wrist. The storm paused. Lightning stopped mid-strike across the sky. Mist hovered in place. Wind died. Even the ocean, volatile and mighty and unrestrained, went quiet.

"Liam..." Tyler took a step toward him. "What the fuck did you do?"

Liam glanced at the kelpie. Blood leaked from between his thin, white lips and stained his teeth. His fingers slipped from around Liam's wrist and he toppled to the ground, a heap of pale, wet limbs in a puddle of dark, dark blood.

Ryder quietly said, "I'll fix it."

"You can't." Liam leaned against the car and looked out over the dead, waiting sea. "Fae magic can't be undone."

"And?" Tyler blurted.

Christy squirmed away from Tyler and darted toward Liam. She turned him this way and that, looking for abnormalities—gills, fins, and hooves. "How is this possible?"

"How is *what* possible?" Tyler's voice lifted into a shout.

"I'm Fae," Liam said. He shook his head at Christy and rolled his eyes, trying and failing to brush her away. "It's complicated, all right? We're kelpies. Me, my mom, my aunt, my cousins. The Montgomerys are water horses and apparently we have some deal with—"

"Her?" Ryder said.

Queen. The forest whispered. *Storm. Beast. General.*

A woman stood in the water. Her legs went on for days, long and lean and the color of pennies. Her body was a composition of lines and edges, smoothed in some places and rigid in others. Her shoulders were too wide. Her hair, sopping wet and black as the night sky above them, clung to her breasts and ribs and stomach. The silhouette of her, the shape of her, the height of her, was enough to make Liam consider bowing.

Ryder, who wouldn't bow for anything or anyone, straightened his back and fished a match out of his pocket. He struck it and grabbed the flame, dancing a bundle of fire between his palms. "Hope you're ready for this, since, you know, you just murdered one of her servants."

The wind parted. The storm raged again. Lightning flashed, illuminating the kelpie's body and the two cars.

"Sacrificed one of her servants," Liam corrected. He watched her move, this Queen of Water, how each step was calculated, how the mist made room for her.

Christy stayed close to Liam. Tyler inched his way toward them and Donovan followed, standing next to the back bumper of the Subaru. It didn't necessarily make Liam feel at ease knowing his circle was still by his side, but after what had happened with Ryder, it was a start.

Leviathan stepped off the sand and onto the bank. Her hair whipped like smoke, forming an intricate design atop her head. Braids mingled with polished, black curls, and above her brow sat a jagged, sharp crown adorned with gems and bones. Her shoulders became the jagged, silver points of a sleeved dress. Liam thought it might be made of skin, dolphin or shark or orca. Her hands were clasped in front of her, covered in ornate, metal gloves that turned her fingers into knives.

She was deadly and gorgeous, and Liam was afraid.

"What a strange little circle." Leviathan's voice was rich and warm, fond in a way Liam didn't expect. She tilted her head, resting her gaze on each of them individually. "A necromancer, a psychic, a leopard, a water horse and an elemental witch. How do you ever get anything done?"

Liam heard Donovan's breath stutter. Christy whispered, "It's okay."

Leviathan mock-gasped. Dark blue stained her mouth and bled into her skin. Dimples formed as her grin stretched, sharpening her unnaturally high cheekbones. Her clear, white eyes rested on Liam. "Secrets don't make friends."

"You wanted a sacrifice. I gave you one," Liam said, keeping his tone as even as he could.

"That you did, little fish. Come here. Let me see you." Leviathan held her hand out to him. Reluctantly, Liam took it. She pulled until he was close enough to smell. Her hands, big and cold, framed his neck. She loomed over him, a force of nature that he wasn't prepared to face. "You slaughtered your own to protect a son of Belial. That is treason."

Liam held his breath. "I didn't ask to be in your Order."

"No, I suppose you didn't." Leviathan's nose touched his cheek. She leaned down and pressed her lips against his ear. "Love is a wretched thing, Liam. It turns even the boldest of us into wasted potential."

Ryder's magic cracked like a whip. He jolted forward, but Tyler grabbed him by his shoulders and stopped him in place.

Leviathan's attention snapped toward him. She took Liam's chin between her fingers and turned his head, forcing him to look at Ryder. Their cheeks pressed together, hers cold and wet, his flushed and dry. "Such power," she purred. Her voice was every song the sea had ever sung to him. It rang deep in his bones. "Is that what you wanted? To taste him. To feel him." Her laugh vibrated from her chest and into his shoulder.

"No," Liam gritted.

"You can lie to yourself and you can lie to him. But you cannot lie to me." Leviathan's metal fingernails dug into his jaw.

Ryder's eyes were pitch black. Flames burned in his palms and steam rose from his skin. He didn't look away from Liam. Even when Leviathan pinned her ferocious eyes on him. Even when her clawed hand drew beads of blood on his cheek. Ryder refused to look away from Liam, and Liam refused to look away from him.

"His magic has nothing to do with it," Liam said. He tried to jerk his face away, but Leviathan held him in place. "I loved him before I knew about it."

Leviathan hummed. "What a pity."

"Let him go," Christy said. She took a hesitant step and Donovan grabbed her by the back of her jeans. "Please," she squeaked. "Please, just let him go."

"Oh, how darling. The psychic is the only one to speak for you?" Leviathan let Liam go and straightened, standing tall above them. "I see your heart, girl. How lonely it must be to watch your circle mates fall in love—" Leviathan quirked her brow at Donovan. "—and lust."

Christy's cheeks flared red and her mouth shook. "My loneliness is irrelevant." She swallowed painfully. "It doesn't matter. It's never mattered."

Leviathan moved in fluid pulses. She snaked toward Christy and settled one long, sharp finger beneath her chin. "Lying is a demon's job. It doesn't suit you."

Liam met Christy's eye and her gaze softened. She held her breath, easing away from Leviathan's metal fingernail, and asked, "What do you want?"

"Your secrets interest me—how desperate you are to keep them from each other. But it isn't you and your loneliness—" Leviathan mock pouted. "—or your Were, or even your leader..." Her eyes traced Tyler slowly. "And all his beautiful anger that I want."

"Then who?" Liam said.

"You." Leviathan turned to face him. She jutted her finger at Ryder. "And him."

"I'm right here, bitch," Ryder snapped.

Leviathan's laugh boomed like thunder. It was the crash of waves, the roar of a waterfall. She grinned, angled her mouth toward Ryder, and blew like she would at a candle. The flames in Ryder's hands went out.

"I see you, half-blood," Leviathan assured.

Ryder's magic was frenzied in the air, powerful enough to turn Liam's stomach. Ryder gritted his teeth and inhaled a deep breath, empty hands forming white-knuckled fists. "You wanted me dead, right? Do it yourself."

Liam's heart kicked in his chest. He almost tripped to get in front of Ryder, placing himself between the man he loved and a demon Queen. "I'll give you anything else. *Anything*."

Leviathan tilted her head. Her ghostly eyes ran from Liam's shoes to his face. "You have held up your end of the bargain. I will honor that."

Relief spiked through him.

"But—" Leviathan held up one finger. "—I want eyes in this circle. Make me an offer in four weeks." Rain began to fall, but it didn't dampen her skin or clothes or hair. "It's only fair."

Liam took a step back. "All right. Four weeks."

Christy geared up to say something, but Tyler hushed her.

Leviathan looked from Liam to Ryder, Ryder to Christy, Tyler then Donovan. She stepped off the bank and walked to the water. Her long dress left streaks in the sand. The waves arched, clearing a path for her. Time ruptured, as if all the magic around them, theirs and the forest's and the night's, paused. The sea closed around Leviathan and she was gone.

No one made a sound. Rain carried the kelpie's blood toward the sand. Tyler's familiar, a red fox named Castle, scampered from the woods and took shelter behind Tyler's legs. Ryder's fingertips touched Liam's waist.

It wasn't over—this, them—their unceremonious introduction to the Orders.

It was the beginning of something.

"Burn the body," Liam said softly.

Ryder did as he was told. Christy stayed quiet. Tyler and Donovan didn't say a word. A few yards away, the ocean sang, and Liam remembered the kelpie's voice, how haunting and true it'd been. *Water is only patient when it needs to be.*

The kelpie's body disintegrated. Silence carried their secrets like ships unto uncharted waters, and Liam didn't know if they would find their way back. Christy stared at Liam. He felt her caution pelt him like the rain. Tyler's silence lay heavy with questions and accusations. Donovan kept to himself, restless and uncomfortable in his skin. Liam was just as restless and just as uncomfortable.

They stood around a puddle of blood and ash by the back bumper of Liam's Subaru. Christy stared at the ground, arms crossed tightly over her chest. Donovan shoved his hands in his pockets and looked at the sky. Tyler cleared his throat and said, "We need to talk about this."

His Fae blood was awake. Dark magic moved swiftly through his veins. An unfamiliar, primal part of him reached for the sea, but his heart reached for Ryder.

"Not tonight," Liam said.

"When then?" Tyler's eyes flashed to Liam. His seriousness was palpable, a stern, cold vibration that leaked from Tyler's pores and filled the air. "You killed someone. This is... We can't just brush this off. There are consequences. There *has to be* consequences."

"And I'm sure I'll face them."

"*We'll* face them. Your actions affect us all, don't you get that?"

"I get it," Liam seethed. "But I didn't ask for any of this and I didn't have a goddamn choice. You think I wanted this?" He wiped his hand on his jeans and left a red mark behind. "To be what I am? To do what I did?"

"We've all had to do things, Tyler," Ryder said softly. "You know that."

Tyler shook his head. "No, I don't. You wanna know why? Because unlike you two I stay away from dark magic and out of the Orders. Circles are sacred, and you've turned this one into a—"

"Circle mates come through for each other," Ryder interrupted. "That's the whole point."

"Circle mates keep each other safe." Tyler glanced from the blood at their feet to Liam. "And you're doing a shit job of it."

"Tyler," Donovan scolded.

"Don't," Tyler bit back. He ran his fingers through short, black hair, a frustrated motion, and gestured with a wave to Ryder and Liam, and then to Donovan. He squeezed his eyes shut and gave up, dismissing them with a hard swipe through the air. "This wasn't how it was supposed to be. It wasn't... Just don't."

"Tyler, c'mon..." Liam took a step, but it was too late.

Tyler hopped into the Jeep and slammed the door. Donovan offered an apologetic glance and got in on the passenger's side. Liam looked to Christy, hopeful that she'd stay, that she'd give him the benefit of the doubt, but when he stepped toward her, she startled. Her wide eyes were glued to his bloody hand. She hesitated then shook her head. A pained, conflicted grimace curled her trembling mouth, a prelude to tears and sniffles.

"This is dangerous," Christy whispered. She clutched her hands together in front of her and took a step back. "I just... I'll text you. Let me try to calm him down."

Liam didn't attempt to get closer to her. He nodded. Christy nodded back, and she slipped into the Jeep and they drove away. It wasn't over. Liam didn't know if it ever would be. Deals with demons. Murder. Blood magic. A circle in shambles. What had they done to land themselves here?

He slid into the driver's seat. Ryder sat quietly beside him, his feet on the dash, a tiny amethyst cluster balanced in his palm.

The ocean kept singing. Liam kept listening.

"You okay?" Ryder tested.

Liam shook his head and rested the tips of his bloodied fingers on the bottom of the steering wheel. "Can I stay with you tonight?"

Ryder reached over and cradled Liam's jaw. He pulled until Liam turned, his eerie, abalone eyes uncovered and glinting in the dim moonlight. Everything inside him felt undone—his magic, his energy, his blood, his memories. But this—Ryder's hand on his face, his gentle gaze and warm breath—was enough to remind Liam that he was still who he had always been.

"Sure, Princess," Ryder said and leaned over the center console to steal a kiss.

Chapter Six

THE RAIN FOLLOWED them to Ryder's apartment. They shrugged their wet coats off and hung them over the bedroom door. Percy meowed at them from the kitchen counter while Ryder put the kettle on the stove, and Opal pecked on the window until Liam let her inside.

Everything was quiet. Ryder's breathing. Liam's footsteps.

Ryder handed him a mug. "Jasmine with honey," he said softly.

Liam willed the spoon in his mug to stir. It turned in circles on its own. "Thank you."

His phone buzzed on the counter. The screen showed message after unanswered message, but he didn't reach for it. The tea was hot on his lips, comforting and sweet, but it didn't settle his magic. Water and darkness pulsed restlessly inside him alongside questions and worries and what if's. He didn't know what to say to his mother. He didn't know how to tell Thalia—he didn't know if he could *trust* Thalia. He didn't know what was going to happen to their circle, or if Christy's fear was of him or what he'd done, or if his circle mates would ever look at him the same after what he did tonight. If he would ever feel at home in his body again.

Liam had gone to the ocean days ago in search of answers and found more questions. More secrets. More power. More risk. More danger.

"Liam." Ryder's voice pulled his attention. He set his mug on the counter and wrapped his hands over Liam's knuckles, curled around the sides of the mug. The spoon stopped turning. Hot tea splashed onto his fingers. "You're shaking."

Liam let out a small, wounded breath. Ryder eased the mug out of his hands. "C'mon." Ryder guided him down the hall and into the bedroom. "I'll start the shower."

Unruly magic sparked in Liam's chest. He closed his eyes and leaned against the doorframe, listening to the water run, to Ryder move around the bathroom. Familiar fingers tugged at the bottom of his shirt. Liam pulled it over his head and dropped it to the floor. Ryder flicked open the button on his jeans and pushed them down.

"Look at me," Ryder said.

Liam opened his eyes. Ryder peered back at him, his black eyes ruthless and haunting. His fine-boned features were softened by the barely there candlelight scattered throughout the room. The bathroom was dark, clouded with steam and littered with clothes. But Ryder was there with him, terrible and beautiful and unmistakable, and Liam was more in love than he thought was possible. It was startling and brutal and real, this love, this life.

"You're still you." Ryder's fingertips grazed Liam's jaw.

"I murdered someone tonight, Ry," Liam whispered. "What does that make me?"

Ryder's magic dripped across his bare skin, slow, dark tendrils that sank into Liam. It pushed between his ribs, coiled around his heart, and squeezed. Ryder pressed into every dip and curve of Liam's body. His teeth grazed the shell of Liam's ear. "Let me be clear." Ryder took Liam's hand and slid it between his legs. "I'm not a White witch and I won't validate your goddamn regret because you did something that needed to be done. We challenged a demon tonight. You saved my life tonight. And if you hadn't killed him, I would've."

"That doesn't answer my question, Ryder," Liam snapped. He rubbed Ryder hard and slow, fingers slipping through warm, wet heat.

Ryder's breath came short. He clutched the side of Liam's neck with one hand and dug his fingernails into Liam's ribs with the other. Ryder's mouth hovered over his lips, onyx eyes staring back at him. "It makes us dangerous."

Liam caught Ryder's bottom lip between his teeth and bit. His head spun, his heart rioted, and the truth lit in him like a flame. Yes, they were dangerous. They were untamed and dark and wicked, and Liam wasn't sorry. He moaned when Ryder licked into his mouth, swallowed the steam that leaked from Ryder's lips and pushed him into the shower.

Ryder laced his pale fingers through Liam's hair and pulled him into a deeper kiss. He shoved Ryder against the shower wall and memorized the sound of Ryder's rough whimper, the groan that echoed from his mouth into Liam's, and the shaken, desperate gasp he couldn't keep at bay. Ryder's tongue rubbed against Liam's before he broke away to breathe.

Liam pulled Ryder's thigh over his hip and gripped his waist with both hands, pulling him into a hard, slow grind. His cock slid against Ryder's clit, and Liam watched Ryder's lashes flutter, his lips part, and his back arch.

"Let it out," Ryder said. His fingernails dug into the back of Liam's skull and tugged him into another breathless kiss. His jaw worked, lips pressing and pulling, teeth nipping Liam's bottom lip. His magic rushed into Liam without warning. It tangled between his vertebrae, pulled on him and tempted him.

The bathroom was full of shadows, barely illuminated by light that came in from the open door. Liam felt the darkness in him shiver—his Fae energy itching for something to bite into. He squeezed Ryder's hips; his magic sank into Ryder's necromancy and pulled it closer. Ryder's gasp was sharp. He kept Liam close, their lips touching, bodies humming with shared power. Ryder syphoned from Liam, and Liam syphoned from him. It was unrestrained. Impossibly intimate. Dark and raw and addictive.

"Fuck," Ryder whispered. He reached between them and wrapped his fingers around Liam's cock. "You taste like chaos."

The water started to run cold. Liam pawed Ryder's hands away and reached back to turn the shower off. Their magic sparked around them, between them, inside them. It made Liam's head spin and his hands shake; it turned his eyes silver and made him want. He pulled Ryder out of the shower and accepted the hard clash of their mouths, the bruising kiss that came with teeth clicking and ragged breath. Liam grabbed Ryder's face. He pulled until Ryder opened his mouth wider, until every kiss was wetter and hotter, distracting them from their slippery feet on the tile. Ryder winced when his back hit the vanity.

"Turn around," Liam said, voice breathy and winded. He didn't wait for Ryder to comply but grabbed his waist and turned him.

Ryder's hands landed on the counter next to the sink. He caught Liam's eye in the mirror and panted hard. Liam had to stop to look at him. The flush of Ryder's cheeks and chest, his kiss-bitten lips and shaking thighs, God, his everything. Liam kicked Ryder's legs apart and watched the muscles tense under Ryder's skin. He set his mouth between Ryder's flexed shoulder blades, ran his palm down the slope of his arched spine, and left bruises on his waist where he dug his fingers in. Ryder's eyes fluttered when Liam finally pressed inside him—he spread his legs wider, arched his back more, let his head roll back.

Liam didn't think about his lineage. He didn't think about Leviathan, or what was to come, or what they'd started. This—gripping Ryder's waist like a lifeline, his slack jaw and half-lidded eyes watching Liam in the mirror—was all Liam wanted.

Ryder rocked back against him. "Harder," he sobbed and reached for one of Liam's hands.

Liam laced his fingers through Ryder's over the edge of the counter. He ground in deeper, his hips snapped harder, he tucked his mouth against Ryder's neck and set his teeth around Ryder's loud, fast pulse. Heat gathered at the base of Liam's spine. He felt Ryder pulsing—his magic, his body— and tasted his heartbeat. Ryder's eyes stayed on Liam in the mirror; his raspy moans echoed in the small, humid space, growing steeper and steeper, until his mouth trembled and his eyes slipped shut and he squeezed Liam's hand.

Ryder's body went rigid and he cried out, turning his head to muffle the sound against his arm. Liam watched. He saw Ryder's brow furrow, how tension drained from his face and was replaced by raw, effortless pleasure. Shadows gathered beneath Ryder's cheekbones, down his throat, under his cliff-edged collarbones. Every part of him coiled as tightly as possible, and released. Even his breath. Even his magic.

The mirror was fogged, but Liam caught the flash of color in Ryder's eyes—his black fading back to green. Liam's hips stuttered, he pushed in deep, and bit down on Ryder's shoulder, enduring a slow, blinding orgasm that lingered in each heavy breath.

They didn't move for a few minutes. Ryder's legs shook. Liam closed his eyes and rested his forehead on Ryder's nape. Their heartbeats filled the empty space like war drums.

When Liam finally did turn the shower back on, Ryder's knees buckled, and Liam looped an arm around his waist to keep him steady. It wasn't only the sex—it was the syphoning, the ritualism, the intensity—that made him weak. They eased under the water. Ryder's arms snaked over his shoulders and Liam pulled him close, taking shelter in the aftermath of vicious magic, and the physical display of a love he couldn't define.

"I don't care what we are," Ryder said. He scrubbed soapy hands over Liam's chest and shoulders. "I don't care what people think of us."

"There's some lines we can't cross," Liam said.

Ryder's nose bumped against his. "Not when it comes to you. I'll never let you die, remember? I meant it when I said it."

Liam's lips dusted Ryder's mouth. He didn't bother responding.

Love is a weapon.

They crawled into bed. Ryder pulled Liam to him and they pressed close beneath the sheets, bodies warm and sated, magic buzzing contentedly beneath their skin. Ryder's breath was warm on his chin, his palm soft on Liam's cheek.

"I love you, Ry. You know that, right?" Liam whispered.

The candles burned low. Incense curled through the air. In four weeks, a full moon would bring the Queen of Water back to Port Lewis. But for now, Liam was here, bare in Ryder's bed, with the promise of immortality whispered between slow kisses. Sometimes he forgot how young they were, but moments like these, promises like that, reminded him that they were new and capable and feared.

Ryder's mouth quirked into a smile. His thumb drifted over Liam's cheek. "Yeah, I love you too."

It was the kind of quiet that came before a beginning—something awful, something beautiful.

But Liam didn't care, because Ryder's fingers were tracing the sigil of Mars low on his back, and he was drifting into a dreamless, peaceful sleep.

HONEY

DAYLIGHT SLIPPED THROUGH the blinds in the living room.

Percy was asleep on the couch. Opal ruffled her feathers, sitting quietly atop a bookshelf next to a vibrant caladium. It was the morning after, and the kelpie's death still lingered in Ryder's mouth. He tasted it—chaos and antiquity and sweetness. He'd wanted to tear its throat out. Drink its blood. Take its power. But Liam had pushed a blade through its stomach instead and landed them in an impossible situation.

The tea kettle whistled. Ryder moved it off the burner quickly and craned over the counter, glancing down the hall. Liam was finally getting some sleep after God knows how long; Ryder didn't want to be the one who ruined it. Thankfully, Liam's soft breath was all the response he got.

"Mint," he whispered. The cupboard was stuffed with an assortment of teas, but of course, he couldn't find the one he wanted. "C'mon, where the hell...?"

Paws pitter-pattered the floor. Percy hopped onto the counter and swatted at a box stuffed between the sugar jar and the toaster.

Ryder heaved a deep sigh. "Thanks." Percy sat on his haunches and peered up at him, swishing his tail contentedly. "It's been a long night."

It was early enough in the morning to hear the stillness. Wind swept under the crack in the window and water streaked the glass, left over from a rain shower hours before. Port Lewis was barely awake, stretching awkwardly into a new day. He wondered if the sleepy little town wore stains from all the blood spilled in its streets and forests and on its beaches. He wondered if murder wasn't considered murder if it was called sacrifice instead.

Ryder rested the steaming mug against his mouth. He stood in front of the window, peeking through the blinds. Mist clung to trees surrounding the apartment complex. Sunlight illuminated the backside of thick clouds. Ryder remembered Liam inside him. His bruising grip. His silver eyes, his desperate magic.

Opal chirped from the bookcase. Liam's energy appeared before he did, new and sweet, curling gently around Ryder's bones. His breath hit Ryder's neck, arms wrapped around his middle, lips soft on Ryder's ear.

"How long have you been up?" Liam asked.

"A little while. You get enough sleep?"

"Yeah." Liam craned over Ryder's shoulder and hummed. "Tea smells good."

"I'll turn the kettle back on."

Ryder tried to walk to the kitchen, but Liam kept hold of him, face buried in his neck. He took a deep breath, the kind of sigh that usually came before an apology.

"Don't, all right? We'll figure this out. We always do," Ryder whispered. He angled his chin over his shoulder and caught Liam's eye.

"Donovan texted me last night and told me the same thing." Liam eased away, letting Ryder slip out of his arms. "But I don't know how we figure something like this out, Ry. We... I..."

Ryder crossed the apartment and put the kettle on. His back was to Liam, but apprehension still hovered around them. The kelpie's blood was still on their hands. Last night wouldn't let them be.

"Should we text them?" Liam leaned against the couch, arms crossed over his chest.

Ryder shook his head. "Do you remember how things were before all this shit? Before our magic went haywire?"

"Yeah, but—"

"I miss those days." He dunked a mint tea bag in a mug of steaming water. "I miss casting stupid spells with you and doing readings and not worrying about this bullshit. I miss... I mean, I don't miss pining after you like a fucking schoolgirl, but I miss how it was before we..."

"Went dark?"

"No, before we felt bad about being who we are," Ryder said. He handed Liam the mug and glanced from him to the floor. The apartment was still quiet. "The darkness doesn't matter. We do—how we react to it, what we do with it—and I'm not ashamed of that."

Liam brushed Ryder's knuckles with his fingertips. "Remember when we meditated over the ley line last summer? I fell asleep with my head on your stomach, you played with my hair, and we practiced astral projecting? I wanted to replay that day over and over."

"I couldn't astral project for the life of me," Ryder said, lips split into a grin. He hadn't been able to concentrate. Every breath Liam took stole his attention, every sweep of his lashes, every movement he made. "Remember those honey cookies? The ones Thalia made for the summer solstice?"

"Yeah," Liam said over a laugh. "We ate *all* of them. Christy was so pissed."

"I still have some of that wildflower honey the cookies were made with." He didn't know if Liam would take the bait, but he had to try. He placed his free hand on Liam's cheek and slid into his space, breath on Liam's mouth, eyes locked with his. "Let's turn off our phones. We'll stay in, practice, be alone for a while. Anyone worth a damn knows where we are; they'll knock on the door if they need us."

"What're we gonna do with the honey?" Liam's voice was low and playful.

Relief pooled in Ryder's gut. He wanted time—just a day—to forget about the Queen of Water and the dead kelpie and their dangerous magic. "I have boxed cupcake mix, lavender in the spice rack and heavy cream."

Liam bit back another laugh. "You want to stay in and make cupcakes? Is that what I'm hearing?"

"Yeah, that's what you're hearing," he murmured, lips close to Liam's mouth. "You good with that?"

He leaned into Ryder's hand on his cheek, turning until his lips dragged over his palm. "Tyler works till five. Phones stay off until then. Deal?"

"Deal."

Liam's mouth tasted like mint tea and toothpaste. Ryder savored a slow kiss, following the part of Liam's lips, the stroke of his tongue, and chased him when Liam eased away. They stood in the kitchen and watched each other. Liam's copper eyes were soft, lulled by the morning light coming in through the window. He pinched Ryder's chin, pressed his thumb to Ryder's bottom lip, and smirked.

"I'm gonna take a shower," Liam said. He stepped out of Ryder's space and sipped his tea. "You wanna smoke when I'm out?"

"Not if it's indica. I'll fall asleep on you."

"I've got sativa," he assured and walked down the hall toward the bedroom. "You got papers?"

"Yeah," Ryder shouted after him. "Where's it at?"

The shower started. "In my bag!"

Ryder dug through Liam's messenger bag until he found the blue prescription bottle and the tiny silver grinder. He glanced at the label, *Sour Diesel*, before tapping finely ground greens in a line across the middle of a thin square paper. He'd never been that great at rolling joints, but he was good enough. His fingers were slender and nimble, and he'd smoked since he was thirteen. This shit was second nature now. Once he finished rolling, he licked the edge of the paper, set the joint on the counter, and dug through the cupboards.

The cupcake mix was the easy kind that only needed water and oil. Ryder pulled out a lemon, dried lavender, and the hand-labeled jar of gold honey. He preheated the oven and whisked the ingredients until the batter was creamy, and then started filling the cups on a cupcake tin.

Liam's hair was still damp when he walked into the kitchen, bare chested and coconut scented. Sweatpants hung low on his hips. Water clung to his eyelashes. Ryder hated him for being so beautiful. No matter what he did, no matter how powerful he was, Ryder's vulnerability would always lie at Liam's feet. Even like this. Especially like this.

"What?" Liam crossed his strong arms over his chest and tilted his head. One side of his mouth lifted.

Ryder snorted. "Does looking like that ever get old?"

"*What?*"

"C'mon, I've been your best friend for two years. You've hooked up with every hot witch in Port Lewis, and you don't even have to work to get their attention." Ryder slid the cupcake tin into the oven then leaned against the counter, watching Liam's smile stretch into a grin. He gestured to Liam with a sweep of his arm. "You could be in a goddamn magazine."

Liam tipped his head back and laughed. He leaned off the counter and slipped his hand over Ryder's stomach. "Were you jealous?" Warm brown eyes snared Ryder in a playful gaze. "I bet you were."

"Fuck off, of course I was," Ryder said. He snatched the joint off the counter and put it between his lips. Liam pawed at him when he stepped away, hands settling on his hips, mouth light and teasing on the nape of his neck.

They stumbled toward the couch. Ryder focused on the twisted tip of the joint, brought his Fire to the surface and directed it. The paper lit, and Ryder inhaled, pulling smoke into his mouth and lungs. Port Lewis woke outside the apartment. Tires shushed through puddles. Birds sang. But all Ryder heard was Liam's soft breath on his ear, his low voice, and the crackle of burning paper.

"You distracted me every time," Liam said. He plopped down beside Ryder and reached for the joint, but Ryder held it away from him. "Remember that one time we hooked up with the Johansson twins?"

Ryder choked on a surprised laugh. He took another drag and curled his hand around Liam's jaw, leaning in until their lips grazed. Slowly, he blew the smoke into Liam's mouth. "Yeah, I remember. I'd been trying to hook up with *you* the whole night, but you kept dodging me."

"I didn't even like Mindy," Liam said. He tugged until Ryder's thighs slid over his lap. "But you were so fucking distracting. I knew I'd cave if I didn't find entertainment."

"Entertainment? That's all she was?" He handed Liam the joint and watched him take a drag. The way his lips rounded. How he hissed when he inhaled. "Me and Max had a good time."

Ryder remembered that party. It was the summer after he'd met Liam. They'd been friends for a few months and

Ryder hadn't been shy with his glances or his flirting. The Johansson twins had been visiting from their coven in Portland, and when Mindy followed Liam, Ryder pulled Max into the bathroom next to the bedroom they'd disappeared in.

"I know you did, I had to listen to you two," Liam said.

That might've been on purpose. Ryder rested his palms on Liam's chest and grinned. He remembered Max's uncertainty, how Ryder had to claw at his shoulders and whisper filthy things into his ear to get him to act the way he wanted. To make noise. To fuck hard against the wall where Liam could hear them.

Ryder's lips touched Liam's. He kept his eyes half-closed, watching from under his lashes. Liam exhaled tangy smoke and Ryder inhaled. They smoked until the joint was almost gone, shotgunning back and forth. His head was light. Warmth seeped to the top of his skin.

"Did you think about me?" Liam reached around him and dropped the roach on the coffee table. His hand smoothed over Ryder's lower back, curved over his ass, and pulled him closer.

"I always thought about you," Ryder whispered.

It was the truth. Ryder had fallen in love with Liam slowly, but he'd wanted him from the moment they met. Hands clasped. Introductions said to each other in friendly voices. Eyes dancing over cheekbones and jawlines and bodies. Ryder had thought about Liam when he fucked other people, when he touched himself, when he dreamed and daydreamed.

Liam's eyes were tinged red. He tilted his head back against the couch and traced the line of Ryder's sweatpants with his thumb. "You didn't ever feel compelled, right? Like, you never... It wasn't..."

"Oh, c'mon, Tinkerbell, you think that's why I liked you? Because you compelled me to?" Ryder's laughter bubbled from him in airy giggles and ugly snorts. He framed Liam's neck in his hands and pressed a kiss to his temple.

"Do *not* call me that," Liam snapped, but the fury in his voice ruptured when he laughed. "I don't know, all right? I don't know what I'm capable of or what I might've done to people. Fae magic isn't... It's not..."

He pressed against Liam, biting back a gasp when Liam's hand slipped up the front of his shirt. "It's powerful and old, and it hits like cocaine. Does it bother you?"

"What?"

"That I'm addicted to you?" Ryder stared at him, fixed on Liam's undulating pupils and slack mouth. He arched his back when Liam's thumb found his nipple. "That I'd do unspeakable things for the chance to take a bath in your blood?"

"It's way too early to talk about bathing in each other's blood, Ryder."

Ryder's laugh was softer this time. He didn't bother saying anything else. He was high and relaxed and in Liam's lap, and the only thing he wanted to do right then was kiss him. Their lips met, pressing and pulling, the slow, careful kissing that Ryder wanted to live in. Liam's tongue stud clicked on Ryder's teeth. Ryder pulled back to kiss the corner of his mouth, to breathe with him, and cracked his eyes open to catch the flutter of Liam's lashes when they kissed again.

It'd been a while since they'd had the chance to do this. To make out and not worry and get a little lost in each other.

Liam's hands were under his shirt, warm on his skin, traveling from hips to ribs, ribs to lower back, tailbone to shoulder blades. They kissed tenderly. Ryder smiled against

Liam's lips. Liam dropped his hands to Ryder's thighs and dug his fingers in. It'd been days of anxious unknown. Weeks spent syphoning energy and cutting skin and being rough with each other.

This gentleness was a relief.

They tasted like weed and tea. Liam moaned into his mouth, and Ryder curled his arm around the back of his head, holding him close. Ryder's hips flexed. He dragged his tongue over Liam's bottom lip and kissed him until his heartbeat drummed faster and his breath came shorter, and until the timer on the oven sounded. *Beep. Beep. Beep.*

"Cupcakes'll burn," Ryder mumbled, craning to look over the back of the couch.

"Seriously?" Liam's teeth scraped his neck. "It's fine. I like burnt cupcakes."

"Nobody likes burnt cupcakes." He slid off Liam's lap despite the annoyed whine he got in return and walked into the kitchen. Oven mitt. Ryder glanced around. *Where the hell is the—*? He snatched the mitt off the top of the spice rack and pulled out the cupcake tin. "They smell good. You gonna help me make the frosting, princess?"

Liam huffed.

"How much honey should we add? I put a few tablespoons in the batter already."

"A few *table*spoons?" Liam sniffed the air and smirked, eyebrows lifted high. "That's a lot of Thalia's honey."

"It's been a few months, hasn't it? We got it in July. She said it would lose its potency after a while," Ryder said. Thalia's wildflower honey was collected from her personal beehives, and Thalia's beehives were housed by bees that only collected from flowers in the Darbonne garden. Magical flowers meant magical honey. "The euphoria only lasts a couple hours."

"We *just* smoked."

"So? It's not like it's meth, Liam. Chill out."

Liam sighed.

Ryder scooped a tablespoon of thick gold honey into a mixing bowl and added heavy cream and sugar. The hand mixer whirred. Liam watched. Soon enough, fluffy clouds of whipped cream were left behind.

"It's quiet," Liam said. "I'm turning on music. Preference?"

"Nothing from your gym playlist."

"Wow, harsh," Liam teased.

While Ryder dolloped whipped cream atop the cupcakes, Liam connected his phone to the speaker on the coffee table and searched for something to listen to. He started one song. Switched. Started another. Switched. Finally, he settled on an EDM station and left it alone.

The last time they'd had any of Thalia's honey it'd been the dead of summer, and Ryder had been irrevocably in love with Liam.

Now it was the dead of autumn, and Ryder was in the same place he'd been, but differently. Because now Liam loved him back. He'd loved him all along, Ryder thought. Somehow. In some way. But now, here, after they'd pulled each other's darkness to the surface, Ryder knew it.

Liam hummed at the cupcakes. He glanced from Ryder to the honey, deliberating, then dipped his fingers into the jar. Everything happened slowly. Maybe it was the weed, or their magic, or being in the aftermath of something truly awful—maybe it was none of those things—but everything blurred. Liam pressed his sticky fingers to Ryder's mouth, and he couldn't focus on anything except the way silver flecked the edges of Liam's eyes, how his lips were still kiss-swollen, and his cheeks burned red.

Ryder's lips parted. He felt Liam's fingers drag over his tongue, tasted the sudden bloom of thick sweetness, and sucked. Liam pulled his fingers free, gathered whipped cream off the edge of the bowl, and spread it on Ryder's neck.

"Be easy with me," Ryder said. He craned to give Liam more room and tried not to gasp when he licked the whipped cream away. "Last night was intense."

"Define easy," Liam said. He sank his teeth into Ryder's neck.

"Just..." He closed his eyes, unsure if he knew how to ask for what he wanted. Instead of answering, he placed his hands on Liam's stomach, gently traced his hipbones, followed his ribs to his chest, played along his collarbones, then pushed his jaw away.

Liam met his eye. Curiosity sparked behind his lashes, but it looked more like concern than Ryder liked. He masked his embarrassment with a quick flick of his brow and nodded toward the cupcakes.

"Breakfast?" Ryder teased.

They put two cupcakes on a plate but forgot to grab forks. Liam didn't press him for an explanation, even when they climbed into bed and ate the cupcakes with their hands. He just watched Ryder as carefully as he always did. Sunlight beamed in through the window and bounced off the mirror on the altar, sending stripes across Liam's olive skin.

The honey wasn't as potent as it used to be, but it got the job done. Ryder's head spun. He chewed on his bottom lip and licked frosting off Liam's chin. His bones vibrated. Magic pulsed and fluttered, filling the room.

Everything that had happened last night and everything that was going to happen after today faded.

"We should do a reading," Liam blurted.

Ryder's lips were on Liam's fingers again, licking frosting away. "I can't concentrate on anything right now."

"So? We can still do a reading." He stretched and pawed at the nightstand, grabbed the maroon pouch and upended it. Cards spilled onto the bed between them. Liam pulled his hand away from Ryder's mouth and gestured to the cards. "You first."

He couldn't focus on anything. Nothing. *Nada*. All he could think about was the way Liam's skin tasted. How handsome and wild he was. *Get it together*. Ryder swallowed and reached for a card. He flipped it over.

The Two of Cups.

"Connection," Liam said softly. "Unity."

Ryder briefly met his eye before his gaze fluttered away, bashfulness squirming inside him where confidence usually lived. "Your turn."

Liam flipped over a card.

The Six of Pentacles.

Fuck. Ryder let out a breath. "Domination. Strings getting tangled where they shouldn't."

"Makes sense," Liam said. He plucked the card from the pile and gave it a once-over. "I may have single-handedly destroyed our circle last night, and I might have to let a demon into my head because of it, and I'm not even remotely close to what I thought I was. That's a big fucking knot if I've ever seen one."

"And what did you think you were?" Ryder gathered the cards and slid them back into the pouch. When Liam didn't give him the Six of Pentacles, he snatched it and placed it with the rest of the deck.

"An elemental witch." Liam shrugged, shoulders loose and hands restless in his lap. "Human."

"And what does being a kelpie change?" Ryder slid off the bed and stood in front of the altar. It was a mess, he thought. Books stacked everywhere. A thin layer of ash dusted the wood. His athame gleamed beside charred palo santo. He snapped his fingers and the tip of an incense stick ignited. "You're still you."

"That question I asked you before, about being compelled, it was a serious question," Liam said. His voice softened and he wilted on the bed, looking a little too lost, a little too raw. "What if you... What if wanting you from afar all this time made you—"

"Don't," Ryder snapped. His teeth clicked and his magic flared, and Liam went silent. Darkness thrummed in his veins.

Usually, Ryder would deflect. He would shut down the conversation, play it off, tease his way out of it, but Thalia's honey disintegrated his guard. He couldn't escape the way it felt. He couldn't hide from the hurt. Liam hadn't meant to, Ryder didn't think he would ever mean to, but he'd shot an arrow through Ryder with those words.

Made you.

"No one makes me do anything." Ryder turned. He found Liam's slack jaw, his embarrassed blush and bloodshot eyes. "I didn't fall in love with you the first time you smiled at me, Liam."

"I know, I just—"

"It was the second time."

Liam's lips clamped shut. He met Ryder's eye and stayed there, quiet, waiting.

"Did I have a stupid fucking crush on you? Yeah, I did, everyone knew it. But I didn't love you until later. And when I did? When I realized it? Trust me, it wasn't heart-eyes and butterflies." Ryder crawled back onto the bed. The space between him and Liam felt cavernous. "I remember knowing how you take your tea. Being happy to fall asleep in your bed because I'd wake up and see you in a light no one else did. Wanting you so fucking bad and knowing I couldn't have you."

He watched Liam's throat flex around a painful swallow.

"Fae magic is ancient. Powerful." Ryder slipped closer. His skin reached for Liam's. His magic curled around the Water in Liam and squeezed. "But I'm a necromancer," he rasped, voice haunting and low. "And I would've felt you inside me."

"I'm sorry," Liam whispered.

"Don't apologize. Just tell me you understand," Ryder said. He bracketed Liam's hips with his knees and straddled him, arms over his shoulders, torsos pressed together. "Tell me you know how I feel about you is true, and that you don't have to question it."

"I get it," he said. His hand swept up the back of Ryder's shirt. "I'm just scared, Ry. I don't know what's real and what's not."

"This is real," Ryder assured him. He gripped Liam's face, fingers curled over his jaw. "I'm real. You're real. What we have is real. Right?"

"Yeah," he said. He pulled on Ryder's hips, touched him reverently, following his bones with his fingertips. "Yes, yeah, you're right."

Liam's nose bumped his cheek. His palm pressed between Ryder's shoulders, drawing him closer. They kissed softly at first then Liam's breath stuttered from him and he bit Ryder's lip, dug his fingernails into his skin. Liam gave him the same rough, familiar touch he loved—his nails left red marks on Ryder's back, his teeth harsh and sharp in his neck.

But it was half past noon and last night had left Ryder drained and sore.

"Be…" Ryder's voice quaked. He gripped the back of Liam's head and closed his eyes, savoring the way Liam's thumbs dug into the hollow of his hips. "Be easy, okay? Be gentle."

Liam quirked his head to the side. "*You're* asking *me* to be gentle?"

"Fuck you, yes, I am. Last night was a lot. Don't give me shit for this."

"I'm not—I wouldn't, ever, but why didn't you say something?" His hold on Ryder immediately softened, as did his eyes and the lines of his mouth when he frowned. "I could've slowed down or not… I don't know, not…"

"Slammed me against a wall?" He leaned in close. Dragged his lips over Liam's cheek to the shell of his ear. "Fucked me on the counter? I loved it." He felt Liam's magic stir. "But my hips didn't. So, stop overthinking every little thing and just…" Ryder wouldn't say it if someone paid him to. *Make love.* He'd rather choke. "Go slow today, all right?"

Liam's arms looped around his waist. He didn't grip as hard. But he still moved like he always did, fluidly, purposefully. He kissed Ryder deeply, palms light on his lower back, breath warm in his mouth, magic buzzing between them. Smoke curled through the room from patchouli incense. Sunlight hit Ryder's skin once his shirt was tossed away.

Time dripped like the honey Ryder had sucked from Liam's fingers. It slowed—everything did. Their bodies. Touches. The way they kissed. Ryder's heartbeat was the loudest and fastest thing in the room.

Ryder pushed until Liam's back hit the bed. He crawled down Liam's body, lips feathering his collarbones, his sternum, his belly button. Liam tasted like the sea. Ryder left hickeys on his thighs, dragged his mouth across the length of his cock and listened to him gasp. Ryder watched his jaw slacken and his eyes close. He watched Liam's knuckles go white as he gripped the sheets, felt his hips jump when he swallowed around his cock.

Intimacy wasn't new for them, but this was. Liam's hand on his jaw, pulling him up into a kiss. The way he slid his hand between Ryder's legs and whispered, "Can I kiss you here?"

They were swept up in each other. Ryder's eyes stayed green. Liam's stayed brown. They didn't syphon or bleed.

Liam held Ryder's hips in place, breath hot, his tongue following the path his lips took to Ryder's clit, lower, inside him, to his thighs, his center. Ryder tangled his fingers in Liam's hair and arched his back, gasping in deep breaths. His magic was lulled by the honey, but his body was awake and overwhelmed, trembling and heated.

The room was hazy with smoke and sex and lavender. Ryder tasted himself and the ocean when Liam kissed him. He gripped the sheets above his head, stretched across the bed with his legs wrapped around Liam's waist. Liam teased him, sliding his cock against Ryder's clit before he pushed into him. Ryder kept his eyes open, watching Liam breathe, watching him bite his lip, and flushed when he realized Liam was unashamedly looking back at him. Eye contact was something else like this. Visceral. Stripped.

They moved together. Ryder felt every stutter of Liam's hips, every flex of his stomach when he pressed Ryder down and ground into him. Pleasure built in him with every movement, every breath, every touch.

Ryder rolled his hips, pushing himself closer, forcing Liam deeper. His voice was raw and graceless. Raspy whimpers and soft moans careened over the music playing in the living room. Liam's thumb circled Ryder's clit and he jerked, gasping in another ragged breath. He clutched the sheets tighter, the magic in him spiked, and he came with Liam's name tumbling over his lips.

They didn't move for a while. Liam caught his breath, and Ryder relaxed into the bed, body still humming. He noticed the scars on Liam's hips and chest. Liam touched a rune close to Ryder's pelvis. The sweat on their bodies dried. Liam set his hands on either side of Ryder's shoulders. Their noses bumped. Lashes swept over cheekbones. Everything was still and quiet and honest.

"You okay?" Liam's gaze met his. He kissed Ryder's cheek, his temple, the corner of his mouth.

Ryder didn't know what it was. He didn't know if he was afraid or too high or if his vulnerability was too sudden to accept. He remembered the look in Liam's eye, how he threw himself in front of Ryder—*I'll give you anything else.*

He nodded and pulled Liam into another kiss. They were tangled. Ryder's arms were around his neck, Liam's thigh tucked between Ryder's knees, pressed together in the middle of Ryder's messy bed. They kissed until Liam had to catch his breath, until the incense stopped burning and the sun was chased away by a stint of rain.

They didn't get dressed. Ryder made more tea and Liam found old gel pens—the glittery kind—in the nightstand drawer. They showered together, drank mint tea, and stayed close. Liam traced the scars on Ryder's body in red and orange. Ryder added stars to love bites on Liam's thighs and called them constellations.

The bedroom was their sanctuary. After the weed and the honey wore off, Ryder slid closer to Liam. They laid on their sides, facing each other. Liam drew a heart on the curve of Ryder's palm where his heartline melted into his wrist.

Ryder rested his free hand on Liam's neck. "I love you, Liam Montgomery. But if you ever try to die for me again, I'll..."

Liam finished coloring in the heart. He let out a long sigh and swept his gaze to Ryder's face. "You'll what, darkling?"

Ryder would not cry. His mouth quivered and his throat closed and his eyes burned. But he would not cry. "I'll kill you," he bit out, voice shredded and too soft. "And then I'll bring you back and fight with you and—"

Liam kissed Ryder before he could keep going. He kissed him hard and he pulled him close, and Ryder's heart reached through blood and bone to find him.

The sun was low in the sky.

Ryder held onto Liam. He kissed him deeply, roughly, and he kept this—today, them—tucked behind his heart, cloaked in darkness and magic. A place he could go back to, a memory he would always have, a reminder that viciousness lived with gentleness. That their love was more than dark magic and blood rituals and sacrifice.

"I love you, Ryder Wolfe. But I've already killed for you." Liam pressed the words into the tiny space between their lips. "And I'd die for you, same as you'd die for me. That isn't changing."

Ryder flared his nostrils. He swept his thumb over Liam's cheek and tried not to flinch when Liam reached over him to grab the phone off the nightstand. Before Liam could look at the screen, Ryder kissed him again. He bit Liam's lip, and he dragged his tongue across Liam's teeth, and he kissed him until they were breathless.

Because the day was ending.

Liam kissed him until the phone turned on. He rolled him onto his back and kissed him like they might not get the chance to again.

The phone buzzed.

Night had arrived.

"What'd he say?" Ryder asked.

Liam glanced at the screen, then at Ryder, and turned the phone to face him.

Tyler: *Meet at the barn at 7. We need to talk.*

"You ready?" Liam asked.

Ryder didn't know if he was or not. He didn't know what was coming or what they might have to do or where they went after today. But Liam was beside him, watching him, waiting.

And if Liam was there, Ryder could be brave.

About the Author

Brooklyn Ray is a tea connoisseur and an occult junkie. She writes queer speculative fiction layered with magic, rituals, and found families.

Twitter: @brookieraywrite

Website: www.brooklyn--ray.tumblr.com

Also Available from NineStar Press

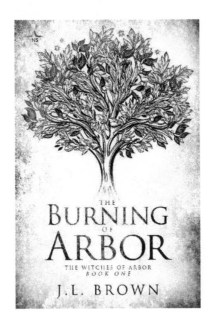

Connect with NineStar Press

Website: NineStarPress.com

Facebook: NineStarPress

Facebook Reader Group: NineStarNiche

Twitter: @ninestarpress

Tumblr: NineStarPress